BRAVO BURNING

BRAVO

BURNING

DONALD TATE

CHARLES SCRIBNER'S SONS / *New York*

Library of Congress Cataloging-in-Publication Data
Tate, Donald.
Bravo burning.
1. Vietnamese Conflict, 1961–1975—Fiction.
I. Title.
PS3570.A77B7   1986   813'.54   85-29481
ISBN 0-684-18605-5

Published simultaneously in Canada
by Collier Macmillan Canada, Inc.

1 3 5 7 9 11 13 15 17 19   F/C   20 18 16 14 12 10 8 6 4 2

Printed in the United States of America.

For Fran and Bonnie

Contents

Contents

BRAVO BURNING

1

Bad Company

Before it's too late, Mr. President. Sir. Before the bullshit swallows us all. Let me make one thing finally, iridescently clear: I didn't seek the honor. Glory wasn't on my mind, not for a Saigon minute. Heroic fantasies were for guys like good old Harry. Or Banzai Sheridan. Or mad-dog Red Dog. But they wanted me there, you see, wanted a lot of us. They—the all-wise, the radiantly sure—plunging ahead, brilliantly charting the course, directing the destiny, boldly ordering us into the future as if they really *knew* things. It seemed they were in some awful jam. Down in this land called Viet something, Nam something.

The truth is, I had hardly heard of the place. I was already moving in another world. I had a wife—an epic adventure, a bloody revolution in herself. I had an occupation, a pretty promising occupation if one was going to live the straight and rooted life. For a while there, for a golden glimpse, my American Dream future stretched before me like shining track, and who could doubt that I was on the splendid choo-choo to success. Or so it seemed. So it all seemed back in those strange and delirious times.

Mr. President, that was right before they—you, sir—bumped

me off the sunny track, started jerking lives around. One day I looked up and here came the authoritative source and noted brown-noser from battalion headquarters, Staff Sergeant Benson, hustling past the barracks and on across our company's dusty road. We were Bravo Company, also known as Bad Company because our superiors commanded us to run around forever bellowing "We bad! We bad!" in the hope that somebody, maybe even Bad Company, would begin to believe it.

Benson—Bravo's clerk before oozing his way up to battalion —had detoured toward our ragged, weary chow line, and you could tell from the soulful gleaming in his eyes (*rat's eyes in a coalbin*) that he was really on fire to tell us something lousy. It was this swarthy little character's style to tell us mainly the bad stuff, and for this we called him Bad News. And though met by an unusually heavy barrage of four-letter pleasantries, he strode on so darkly, twitchingly doom laden that I could feel it coming off him. I could feel it all coming. Or so it seemed, so it all seemed that early summer afternoon way back in '67.

Now he stood before us, eyes darting, squirmy, full of nervous news, popping, popping a rolled-up paper against his skinny thigh, all puffed up with his secret but uttering not a word.

As the chow line closed around him, Benson smiled his deeply sincere little rat's-ass smile and talked at the bottom of his voice with great authority.

"Now youse people, don't let out a worda this"—he raised a finger, shushing us—"but the wonderful plan is that youse out-standing Americans, all youse lucky fucknoses right here, are flying over posthaste and on the double to kick ass and win this whatchamafuck war, this Vietnam Conflict, is what the wonder-ful fucking plan is."

Bad News, who always seemed to be rushing to a place of greater importance than where he was, grinned like a ferret with its throat cut, wriggled out from under the debris of our faces, and scurried on down the road.

I looked over at Harry. Harry, of course, was pleased.

4

REWIND

Harry. Good old Harry. Red hair, a freckled grin you couldn't beat off with an entrenchment tool. One-time audacious quarterback. The look of a man always about to call the big play, the one that would win no matter what the odds or the opposition. When really revved up, and when not sleeping, full of awesome nerve, irrepressible Harry. Ready to take on anything, cheerfully. Harry Hammarth wasn't married. He said he wanted to travel first. He wanted to travel to the Vietnam War, wanted to take on the Vietnam War.

His and John Kennedy's War. A couple of beers blew his cover, the freckles caught fire . . . the paying of any price, the bearing of any burden, the opposing of any foe. . . . That was what the country was all about if it was about anything that mattered. Harry's great drama, Harry's great story. He had been a young journalist-on-the-rise covering Washington, but his paper hadn't seen fit to let him cover the big one. Harry told them he would go to Vietnam for green bananas. He would pay them to please let him go. He longed to listen to the lullabies of the poet Ho Chi Minh. "Perhaps in a year or so," his managing editor said. "Right now, you're needed here." But Harry needed himself elsewhere. Goodby, it's been swell, but boring. And so he walked out the door and down the street. The recruiting sergeant was pleased. Harry asked for nothing fancy. He asked for and got, to the utter disbelief of his workmates, straightleg dumbnuts infantry, guaranteed grunt. "The only way to go," he said. Like his dumbnuts father before him.

Harry wasn't quite born on the Fourth of July, and his father wasn't quite the complete hero. He had left Harry with stories of great battles, a mantel adorned with war medals (he was one of the most decorated infantrymen of World War II—the biggie, he called it), and a bedroom decorated with empty bottles, when he passed on from scientific drinking.

"A half pint every hour for three or four weeks won't hurt

you—that's the way scientists drink," Harry told me his old man, the eminent booze authority, counseled him before his liver threw up the white flag.

Harry's limit was three beers. What he really had an appetite for—maybe his father left him that, too—was this passion to test his own limits in extreme circumstances. We talked a lot about our football days: manly sport, me a runner, him a passer, a bomb thrower. Harry needed more than sport. He chased adventure the way hot young men chase hot young women, but mere promiscuous physical adventuring wasn't really enough. He later got deeply involved with—had a serious affair with— words, which were never enough either. A bad verb rarely killed.

Harry the Hammer sought it out, rode toward it irresistibly at full gallop—the meaning of being alive and having balls. And though he would grin and say, "What bullshit," I think he even needed to feel noble. He really seemed willing to pay the price. To bear the bloody burden. And he thought he had found the place.

2

Holding On

Now another sergeant leaned out the chow-hall door, requesting our presence in his magnificent palace of eating. Grumbling, gabbling soldiers shuffled forward. I saw the Louisiana sun steamrolling over the tops of the barracks. "Not as warm as Vietnam," Harry enthused, and I felt something with cold feet march down my spine. From down in Bravo's area came the sound of many boots running, young men chanting:

> "Hey, Bo Diddley, Bo Diddley, have you heard?
> Ho Chi Minh is a little red shitbird."

And something happening inside my head. We went into the low-ceilinged, boot-stomping, soldier-shouting mess, and it was getting worse. We were going down the chow line, the clamoring, yammering shit-on-a-shingle line. There was Turnip Greens Turner, Bad Company's jowly, mouthy mess sergeant, muttering his ancient kitchen obscenities. There stood his fine cooks, tall white hats tilted idiotically, looking fat and furious and red-faced, splattering out this milky brown substance—splat—eye-balling me as though waiting for something, some grunt of gratitude, perhaps. And all the time, Harry kept up his inspirational chatter about Vietnam. Everybody talking, talking about Vietnam, Vietnam. Moving down the line to the glorious globs of mashed potatoes—splat, Vietnam. Down to the cabbage—splat, Vietnam. Down to the beans—splat, Vietnam. Vietnam this and Vietnam that.

"The South China Sea," Harry sang joyously. "Vietnam by the South China Sea. What a faraway-sounding sound. What a mysterious-sounding sound. What a—Mike, did you know that out of the last four thousand years, the Vietnamese have been fighting three thousand seven hundred and ninety-one of them?"

"I didn't know that," I said—I think I said.

It didn't bother Harry. Good old Harry. But in the chow line—boots scraping against the sand-gritty floor, trays slamming, hard voices yelling, fans blowing hot air in my face—it bothered me. Because in my head, things weren't going well. I kept thinking about my wife, leaving my wife, and things suddenly went really rotten.

"Excuse me," I said, I think I said, deserting my tray between the beans and the Jell-O.

"Hey, you," bawled a white-hat, waving his gravy spoon, "drag your butt back here!"

But I kept going through the tables, head swelling, floating off like a balloon in a high wind, jerking the rest of me along, and made it outside, sailing toward the road. There were trees along the road. Great green trees arching over the road. And I saw them coming, gleaming in lockstep, silvery polished helmets all aglitter, shadows of the trees tumbling over them.

The big drum went by, booming in the slanting sun. The tuba oom-pahed past, dazzling my eyes. All the shadows marching past, so clean faced, so stern jawed, shiny heels and toes kicking dust. Kicking out from under the trees, dust rising, helmets blazing, baton jerking, moving so loud and mighty, mighty loud —*boom, bam,* hot damn, here we go to Vietnam.

Leaning off the curb, I started to go after them. I wanted to ask them something very badly. My mouth was open, but nothing came out, and I held on. Something held me.

"Take it easy, tiger." It was Harry behind me, his freckled hand grabbing my arm, his red hair burning brighter than the June sun. Or so it seemed. So it all seemed that summer evening a hundred years ago in the shadows under the trees.

"Sure," I heard my voice, the almost cool outside voice mumbling to Harry. "No sweat."

So I held on. And they went on down the road.

REWIND

Roland. He had been into the violent sport of reading, hanging around libraries. Baby-faced, dimple-dappled Californian (voted fourth cutest boy in his high school class), who dropped out of college and Roman Catholicism to embark on an expedition into the deeper seas of his eternal psyche. At some point, he had washed overboard. Briefly, wallowed wide-eyed in Zen and California sin. Managed to half-drown in the mystic depths of psychedelia, bumping into all sorts of dark and druggy demons down there. Came bobbing up to light candles against the war, only to be swept crashing against the olive-drab rock of the U.S. Army. Draft bait. They hooked him, rudely whacked off his blond locks and "all that was beginning to come together in the inchoate pieces of my being." He sometimes talked like that.

Roland Donahoo was basically one of the nicest, most gentle-eyed fellows you would ever want to meet. To the last, he trusted that logic (After all, if they needed six copies of everything, was not some process of logic at work somewhere in those catacombs of paper?), even justice would prevail in the military system of the land that freed the slaves, and that he would be allowed to slide through his service as a clerk-typist in some far-rear area, perhaps as far rear as California even. He expressed

9

bewilderment when he was designated 11-Bravo Infantry. He was truly stunned when an automatic rifle was placed in his soft hands. Donahoo, Roland J., saith the system, remanded to the custody of the Vietnam War, there to engage in mortal combat the enemies of freedom. Like it or not, baby face. The system was in a hurry.

3

The Samurai

When we walked in, Bad News Benson aimed his finger at his head and pretended to shoot himself. Battalion headquarters, packing to go to war, did not seem delighted to see us. Nevertheless, Roland and I asked to speak to our battalion commander.

"The colonel is temporarily not here at present," fretted Bad News, skittering behind stacks of paper. "The XO's handling your can of garbage."

We maneuvered through the chaotic room and sat down outside the office of the executive officer, Major Bradley Sheridan. Moments later, a large figure with a wide mustache, upswooping into tight points, poked his head out and aimed his finger. I stood up.

"Him," said the major. This officer seemed in a hurry, a bit agitated, occasionally cross-eyed.

Roland went in, the conversation came out. It was not encouraging. When Roland sought to convey his doubts, his qualms, his objections over going to Indochina, this officer replied that it was not a bad thing to adrenalize-up before the battle. One didn't, after all, want to go waltzing off to war too loosey-goosey in the head. Did one?

When Roland tried to explain that he was neither eating much nor sleeping well and was at a spiritual low ebb, he was assured that things would change markedly for the better once the troops began deriving the benefits of Vietnam's healthy tropical climate, the tasty battlefield grub, and the stimulating combat environment.

"I would like to apply for conscientious objector status, sir," Roland said.

"Well, it's too late for that," replied the major. "When did this attack of conscience seize you, Donahoo?"

"I have been thinking about it for a long time, sir. I tried to come earlier, but the first sergeant said I would have to wait."

"Wait for what?"

"Just wait, sir."

"Well, it's too late now, kid, far too late. You've waited too long."

"But Sergeant Smoker said—"

"Listen, it doesn't matter. It's too late for backing out. In my eyes, you are on your way to becoming one hell of a splendid soldier, Donahoo. Just keep up the good work."

"I am not a splendid soldier, Major. I have been defining myself in relation to the army, trying to give the experience of the military a fair trial, sir. But I am not a soldier."

"You're experiencing a little buck fever is all, lad. Many experience it."

"Sir, I don't mean this disrespectfully, but I cannot become a paid killer and do what we are doing to human beings across the earth."

"You don't know anything about what we're doing across the earth, kiddo."

"I know enough, sir. Also, I am tired of being treated like a moron, sir."

"Like a moron?" the major said soothingly. "I didn't know."

"It's just that I'm tired of people pushing me around and calling me shithead and fucknose, sir."

"I never dreamed that was happening."

"Tired of being put down and humiliated. I am an aware, thinking human being who is sick-tired of this whole military scene, sir."

"Surely," replied the major with feeling, "you are not yet sick-tired. You may be sick-tired in six months, but as of today you are a little discombobulated is all. Believe me when I say I am abjectly sorry, Private Donahoo, that you have been addressed harshly by our rude, crude sergeants. Sorry that you have been compelled to clean the unsightly latrines or carry the inconvenient pack and rifle long distances during your experience of the army. Yes, these insults to your individual person must cease. I myself will caution our coarse NCOs to watch their foul tongues, to be more mellow in their approaches to you henceforth."

"Thank you, sir."

"Of course, some of them could still have the old fuddy-duddy notion that turning you into a disciplined fighting—excuse the harsh term—*man* could be of value to you where we're going. And we are *all* going, Donahoo. Now is there anything else I can do to lighten your heavy load, kid?"

"I don't want to fight anyone, sir."

"Yes, but you *will* fight."

"Sir, I have nothing against those people."

"Once you get to know them you will. They are not as nice as you."

"Major, I come here advising you that that is not my scene."

"Yes, and I sit here advising you that back-out time is over. This battalion, this brigade, this division is shipping out under very urgent orders, my boy, and we are leading the parade. We have pulled in every clerk and jerk and gold-bricking flake and fighting flower child we could lay our hands on to muster this unit up to strength. Not that I am placing you in any of those categories, Donahoo. But there will be no more farting around."

"I do not think it is a crime to object to becoming a slave of the military machine," persisted Roland. "Most of the people I know feel that way."

"The people you know," groaned Sheridan, "were all born yesterday and shortly thereafter became rock stars and leaders of men. But this is one old guy who's getting a little sick-tired of hearing all this deep kiddie agony, all these in-depth kiddie solutions on how to run the universe. I find you kiddies against the war with the same penetrating insights that make you for free dope and aimless fucking."

"If that's what you think of us, sir, no wonder it is difficult to communicate with you," Roland said gravely but politely.

"Me, difficult?" the major reacted in mock shock. "Once again, accept my apologies. "The edge in my voice is from a simple lack of sleep from trying to prepare our watery-eyed milklappers to go fight killers with iron balls who sleep in trees and tunnels and eat lizards for breakfast. But we'll keep at you. And I'm betting that before it's over, young Roland Donahoo, you'll be one heck of a gung-ho humper. So there, we've thrashed it out. Anything else? I want you lads to have your say."

"There is much else, sir," Roland said softly. "I do not wish to be any gung-ho humper. I see no reason why, just because I am a certain age, I must go, against my deepest instincts, to that scene of mindless destruction."

"Yes, yes, anything else?"

"Nor do I see why I should surrender control over my own destiny and fight in an immoral war, sir."

"Immoral? Who says? We're going out there to save people from communism, kid. In case you haven't heard, communists can be bad assholes. They're the immorals, not us."

"I cannot accept that reasoning, Major. There are deep philo-sophical differences between us, sir."

"Look, tiger, if after your tour of Vietnam you still think it's immoral, I'll find you the right war in a great place at a swell time. No blood, plenty of good cheap dope, and the inspiring rock music. Deal? Fair's fair."

"I have given up rock music, Major, and that is hardly fair."

"Groundpounder, I am noting all your very interesting observations. If I was of your mind-set, I would view my Vietnam experience as a unique learning opportunity. You will encounter a condition called *combat*. Wilder than dope, more exciting than strange pussy. A once-in-a-lifetimer, kid. And I pledge to you this golden opportunity to broaden your horizons shall not be denied you."

There was a sound like the palm of a hand slapping wood and, moments later, chairs scraping and the major chuckling, "Come back anytime, Roland. These little tête-à-têtes with our tigers are always interesting. You understand, kid, we're a bit pushed for time. Otherwise, we could just go on and on."

Roland emerged looking paler than usual. He glanced over at me, shook his head, and trudged toward the door. "This stupid stuff," he was saying, "this stupid stuff."

"Bad news?" cackled Bad News.

Bad News was going, too, so I wasn't sure why he was all that enthused about our misery. Unless he thought he was some kind of hero-in-waiting. Or was just insane.

A minute passed, and then the XO sang out for me to come in. As I entered the disheveled little room, he was banging on a stuck desk drawer with his fist. He looked up and then gave the drawer one more knock before waving me to the straight-back chair beside his desk.

I smelled gin.

"Well," said the major, doodling in the margin of my 201 file with his right hand while flicking ashes off his cigar with the other. "Well. Hmm. So your head is a balloon or a rocket or something about to fire off to the moon. But why come to me? I'm not in the space program."

I stared at the ends of Sheridan's mustache, upswooping, which flapped like little brown wings when he talked. He was balding somewhat, and his big body had crept into paunch. He was originally from New England somewhere—or was it old

England? He smiled oddly, and he was not at all times the commander of his eyes or his face. When he became emotional, his forehead, thinly spiderwebbed with scar tissue, reddened like a network of tiny blood-running trench lines. There was another road on this battle map, nearly hidden, twisting out from under the mustache. The major chain-smoked cigars, and there was a bottle of gin in the stuck drawer at his right hand. The underedge of his mustache being wet, I got the impression he had just partaken of a belt.

"So let's get right down to cases, young Michael Ripp." The cockeyed major spoke in that same gratingly polite tone that had shredded Roland. "You don't want to go to that tropical paradise, Vietnam. Have I guessed right?"

"That's right."

"Ah, yes. Do you realize I cannot even pack my personal gear I am so busy listening to the lamentings of our lion-hearted pussycats who want to go meowing off home before they have even tasted the battle?"

"Well, Major—"

"Maybe you just need a shot of testosterone. Many do these days."

He was flipping through my file now, nodding and mumbling commentary.

"Hmm, married man. Twenty-three years old. Says here you were working in—am I reading this right—the underwear business? Sexy. Never mind, kid. Don't let me bug you. I get all kinds in here. Ah, scored high on your basic infantry tests. Finished first in PT. Damn good. We'll do the old push-ups sometime. Not a bad shot either, it says here. Now we're cooking. Though you'll find the scores tend to sag a bit when the target is shooting back. Look, soldier, it encourages me that you are a strong young fellow, material we can work with. Not one of these guys who sobs that we are committing crimes against humanity the first time he's asked to police up a cigarette butt. You're not another one of those are you? Please, say you're not."

He kept going, the strange smile seizing his face now and again. He would seem to fill up, then subside, and I got the feeling I was about the last 201 file in my executive officer's day.

"Major, about my wife—"

"Ripp, I've heard them all. I should be a writer of sad songs. 'And then I wrote'—but I see I bore you. Dogface, whatever your problem is, a year from now you'll laugh at it. So why don't you just trot on back to the barracks like a good doggie and clean your weapon or something. We've got a lot to do, and there's not much time."

He blew smoke from his cigar, slapped the flat of his hand on the desk top, and stood up.

"Major," I said, sitting, "I can't go to Vietnam."

"I really don't want to hear that sequence of words anymore today."

But he sat back down, and I started in again.

"I tell you," he interrupted, grimacing, bent over a little sideways as though someone had thrust a knife in his ribs, "all our draft-age, long-haired lads are becoming Jesus Christ all of a sudden. Throw a little war at them and they start pissing Jesus—"

"It's about my wife, Major—"

"—except when they get in front of the old TV cameras. Then they get all ballsy-wallsy. Lads who wouldn't know VC from VD get all ballsy-wallsy. We'll see how ballsy-wallsy they are in Vietnam. Right, Roland?"

"I am Ripp, Major."

He leaned back heavily in his chair, his paunch rolling upward.

I leaned forward. "Major Sheridan, I am requesting a deferment from overseas duty."

"So you are," he replied wearily, "so you all are. And on what precise grounds are you doing that? That you are a balloon?"

"My wife is having a baby—is *going* to have a baby—is the grounds."

He gazed at me, his eyes having a hard time lining up. "Does the doc expect trouble?"

"All I know is, she says she won't have it without me."

"Aw hell, kid, that is just hysterical female guff. What I'm asking is, does the doc see serious complications in this pregnancy?"

"Going to Vietnam is a serious complication."

"Wait now, hold up a minute." He raised his hand. "Let us not slide deeper into the accumulating manure here. Let us get the old regs out. Let us just read the old reg on that. Sure, right here: 'Pregnancy deferment will be authorized only if the pregnancy or delivery is expected to have major or serious complications.'

"So"—he chewed his cigar, shrugging—"that's about it. As much as I would like to help you, my hands are tied."

Looking almost sympathetic, he closed the old regs. How neat to have one's life charted by the old regs, I thought. One was so ranked, so ordered, so knowing-right-where-one-was when one lived by the old regs.

"Hey, soldier, don't look so down. I'm sure you and the missus will cope beautifully. It works out. Listen, I, too, had to leave home and hearth once for a sexy place called Korea."

Sheridan pointed to a picture on the wall. There he was, the ruddy-faced young lieutenant hunkered down with other grunts in a snowy trench. He was scarless, mustacheless, clean-cut, crew-cut. He was still crew-cut, although there wasn't that much left to cut.

"Heartbreak Ridge," he said, voice lowering to near reverence. Talking about the old days now. *His* old days. "They were good men. Damn good men. But you know the saying, 'For the Samurai . . . to die in battle is to die at the moment of perfection.'"

No, I didn't. "Excuse me, Major—"

"God, what a bash," he went on softly. "Nothing like it before or since for this old horse. Got a little banged up, left the army after that one. Went out to make the big bucks, live the thrilling civilian life. As you can see, I'm back in. We've got a *live* one going, kid."

He reached down and grabbed the roll of flesh at his side. "Combat is no place for thirty-seven-year-old tubs of lard, but I'm trimming down fast. You won't know me in a couple of months. . . . There are clerks and warriors, kid, and I'm no damned clerk, no **damn staff** weenie."

"Major, about my wife. . . ."

But the major didn't hear. He seemed to have marched off into bugle-land somewhere. When he came back, he looked at me vaguely. "Well, this time we're going to handle their case, the way we didn't in Korea. We're going to finish it. No more half-ass wars. You know what a communist is, don't you, Ripp?"

I had heard of them. In my brief time in the army, I had heard many times that they were godless pricks who needed a good ass-kicking. It had a ring to it.

"I don't know that much about it, Major."

"Just want to stick your head up your ass, huh, kid? Where's the adventurer in you?"

"You should meet my wife."

He leaned forward, eyes beginning to glow. "*Out there*, Ripp, you will find out something very valuable to you as a man. Doesn't that intrigue you at all?"

"What will I find very valuable to me as a man?"

"Think of it, you could spend your entire life being a little homebody, futzing around in fascinating underwear. So, dog-face, we're giving you this golden chance."

"What golden chance?"

"The chance to leave the world of the fat-asses and join the ranks of men. To find out whether deep down you are a hero or a zero. And you should be thanking us, kid. You should be groveling in gratitude."

"Thanks a lot, Major."

"We're getting into some deep water here, you understand. But am I starting to connect, kid? Am I penetrating your mist?"

"Well, Major, I'd like to see you explain that to my wife."

Sheridan sighed and slumped back in his chair. He sat there flipping the lid of his Zippo back and forth with his thumb.

"Ripp," he said, voice now flat, the glow all gone, "we've got marching orders and we've had to slap this outfit together with eighty percent hard-core titty-babies. We've got people fresh out of basic like you, and kids who can't shoot a can of shaving cream straight, going into battle against veterans of twenty-five years' experience fighting in the Indochina jungles. Dwell on that for a moment, troop. It could keep you alive over there."

"I would like to dwell on my wife and baby for a moment, Major."

"When's that baby due anyway?"

"I'm not exactly sure."

"How's that?" He gave his mustache a quick twist.

"She just told me about it last night."

"When did the doc tell her?"

"Well, she hasn't seen the doc yet, but—"

"Then how"—he twisted harder—"oh, how, oh, how is she so sure she's with child?"

"Are you married, Major?"

"Not currently."

"Well, they know. *She* knows. She's late in her . . . and all."

"She knows, huh? How many times have I heard that before?"

"She definitely feels she's pregnant, Major. *Definitely.*"

The flame was burning in his Zippo, and for a moment I thought he was going to light up his mustache instead of his cigar.

"Private Ripp, you just stun my ass. Just daze me out. You come skulking in here—you take up my time—I talk to you as a man—me, a field soldier, wasting my time on this—now look, there is a *war* on, and you are going to that war if I have to prod your behind with my bayonet every step of the way."

"What was that you said about Samurai, Major—'The moment of perfection'—what was that? I want to tell it to my wife."

"You know—" Sheridan grimaced. "Aw, to hell with it. I'm tired of hearing it and tired of saying it. Just remove your yellow buttski from this office. And don't worry about Samurai. They wouldn't piss on the likes of you."

"What about my wife and baby, Major?"

"Fuck off, soldier! I draw the line here. Here the line is drawn. No more of this wackygibber. I will not debate women and babies with you. Forget women. Forget pussy. I am noting your world-shaking tragedy right here in the proper blank of the proper form. Oh, it reads well, Ripp. But that's it. No more dicking around with words."

His cigar smoked, his mustache flapped, but his mouth remained furiously, contortedly merry as he scratched a blue streak across the paper.

"There"—he dropped the pen—"all official. Hand-holding time is over. Now just back on out of here."

"But what do I say to my wife?"

"What do you say to your country, soldier?"

"My country's not pregnant."

"Don't be funny. Out. *Get out*, I say."

"I'm serious, Major. You don't know my wife."

"I'm beginning to know *you*, Ripp. Now, for the last time, stick on your beanie and hop right out of here before I stockade your ass. Move, troopie. On the double. Don't you hear good? That's a direct fucking order! Roll your yellow wagon out of here! You are dis-missed! I SAID, DIS-MISSED!" reiterated the not-currently-married major.

REWIND

My wife. The first time I ever saw her it was *pow!* Hello, forever. Right then, leading the band down Cherry Street back home. "Here she comes, boys, Miss Electric Fanny!" some high school hard-on had cackled. I heard the drum thumping . . . and then, around the corner: female sunburst on a gray afternoon. Long legs in white boots. Hips swaying, golden hair flying, breasts and buttocks bouncing, all-American young woman and nutcracking machine ablaze in fire-engine-red sequins. Charlotte, strutting past, a bumping, thumping blur, zapping us with flesh, jarring the street, shaking the rain out of the sky. Wowwheeee! Some mighty fine steppin', the boys all agreed.

The wiser boys agreed it was something more than just bountiful tits and ass, what she had. She was some kind of moving, breathing, sexual mine field, elemental explosions going off all around her. Break your heart, little man, step on your gonads, blow you away.

She would come walking, electric-stepping into a place, most any place helpless guys gathered, and you could time it. Pretty soon, heads would begin to turn, eyeballs would roll, dart, glow. It was as though Char was just oozing it, trailing it out behind her, hormonal fog. Before long, all the young studs, all the healthy primates would start to stirring, wandering around a little crazily. It wasn't just her walk. Even the simple innocent act of sitting down, that feathery, twisty slow-motion dusting of the chair with her Aphrodite ass, the ritual fire of the crossing of the legs, of just sitting there thighs smoking, waggling her foot (*her* eyes darting a little), could bring the studs milling around her so restlessly (some panting intellectual leaning over to peek down her blouse), so tongue-hangingly stupidly eagerly that sometimes it got funny even to disturbed me. There were times, when she was discovering her talent, that she would randomly pick a guy, coyly aim herself at him, and with a whisper and a little girl giggle bet me she could have him sniffing helplessly in her tracks within minutes. They came like ravenous dogs in a meat house. And more than once they got meat.

That was early on. Down the road, it got less hilarious and more stimulating, like a case of temporary insanity that kept getting extended. Was that true love? I wondered. . . . What women did to you? You could spend your waking existence trotting after her in a sweating, scowling, slavering obsessed funk, clubbing off the swarming foe, virtually every Homo erectus alive. Or you could master the art of remaining cool in the face of the horny pack. I had once driven my fist through a car windshield for seventeen stitches mastering that art. There was my war.

Even here, beside the camp, sunning herself by the backyard peach tree, or hanging out the sexy wash, or just walking down the street, whatever it was that emanated from Char seemed to have lit up a regiment. (*Forget my wife? Easier to cut my dong off, Major, and forget that.*)

So she had that power, really hellacious female force, but she never seemed the happiest of young ladies. Back home in Larchmont, Louisiana, she had once been a religious person. The day I first touched her—we were 18—she had sat down across from me at a table in the town library, all fetching and desirable and come-hithering from head to toe. She opened a book. She began to read, moving her lips, with great concentration. The Holy Bible, the very first page of the Holy Bible.

Green-eyed, hot-mouthed, bosom-heaving honey, sitting so neat and smelling so sweet, reading about Creation. I don't know what happened to religion. She sang radiantly in the church choir for a while, and I don't know what happened to the singing either. She dropped things and moved on. When she was sad (she was often sad), she wrote poems about the wind and the rain. In the full bloom of her poetry period came that feverish night during our junior year in college: We started majoring in living together. Just ran away and did it, committed marriage. But so much was going on about then, too much—Vietnam was going on. And one day she didn't write poems anymore.

What ever did I see in that girl, my aunt had asked me once. What tried-and-true, rock-of-ages qualities did I admire most? All of them, Auntie: smoke, heat, chemistry, fire and mystery, ethereal vibrations, wild Eros music, brain-mesmerizing female magic stuff. She had it all, and she sure had me. Gaze into her eyes once, Auntie. She could have been Jacqueline the Ripperess, running around fucking the fire, and it would have mattered not. It was hard to tell what my wife would become, but dangerous to the puny mind of man is what she was.

4

Nothing Ever Better

They sang the old song, the night marchers, scuffling along the road in the shadows beyond the fence:

"Oh, if I die in a combat zone . . ."

And inside the house, Char marched barefooted past open suitcases, her things scattered all around, declaring that anybody dumb enough to go to a combat zone deserved whatever he got in a combat zone.

"Don't go!" she fairly screamed. "They can't throw you in a cage and carry you over there."

"Just pack my boots and ship 'em home . . ."

Her face was red, her hair wasn't combed, she looked a bit messed up. She went round and round in nervous little circles, and she paced back and forth. She sat suddenly down, and she stood suddenly up. She was crying and trying not to cry.

"What about our baby? I'm not having it without you."

"Sure you will, honey."

"You heard me, Mike. No little army jackass is popping out of me."

"Great. I needed something to think about nights over there."

"What do you think *I'll* be thinking about nights over *here*?"

"It's what you'll be *doing* I'm worried about."

It was our last sweet night in the cramped upstairs of the once-white old house by the camp. The house was the last one on a dead-end street that ran into the camp fence, and there was a great fat oak in the front that leaned over the house and rubbed up against it. Beyond the fence, troops came and went noisily, bobbing along the road into the lights and shadows of the sprawling Louisiana camp that never slept in these days of the great Vietnam buildup.

The marchers grew quieter. I lay on the old brass bed by the window, there was a shade torn in the middle, and a ripped curtain with faded roses. I listened to the tree scraping against the screen, to Char moving across the warped, creaking floor, moving not too steadily. She had been smoking some grass, drinking a smidgen of wine. She drank a cup of coffee. And then four more cups of coffee.

She bent over in the funny little slant-ceilinged room, picked up the guitar that she never played anymore, looked around for some place to put it, then just dropped it, bump-thwanging to the floor.

My wife wore her too-tight yellow shorts and her too-small yellow halter, neither of which, when she bent over, adequately contained her. Long, long sun-bombed hair flowed around her shoulders as she moved around the room, rolling those hips. She did not look pregnant.

All evening the performance had gone on. It was not yet as memorable as the one three days before, after the pig-headed army doctor (the second and senior pig-headed army doctor; the first and junior she had dismissed as unfit to command a stethoscope) had spelled it out to her one last time: Yes, she was indeed impregnated. But no, he would not write a statement swearing that her pregnancy was in desperate trouble. Nonsense. What he *would* swear to was that she was wonderfully gifted for the birthing process. With that structural arrangement, those hips, why she could fire forth whole regiments of beautiful bouncing baby grunts for her Uncle Sam if she but so desired.

My wife did not so desire. What my wife desired was to blow up the American Army.

It had really started at the university. We would walk down the hill to a place called the Bitter Inn. A sign in the window said "Sweets & Lunch." Nobody ever knew why. The Bitter Inn was only open in the evenings, and we drank beer there out of big steins and sang German drinking songs under the white lattice-work ceiling. We drew our pints from barrels set up behind the long tables and drank till our bladders squeaked, trying to feel something. It was only 3.2 beer, but we were full of music and noise and not much sense. That was college night life and the way to protest then. At closing time, the Bitter Gang would clear out and go singing defiantly up the hill toward campus, daring stuff. Pot was still a something you cooked in for many of us way down there in the South. That was about the time our President, who had been avowing that American boys would never be sent to fight the wars of Asian boys, changed his mind. Things started changing, getting wilder, and it seemed that everybody was avowing everything. Before long, the Bitter Inn became a radically different kind of place, though they never changed the sign.

And then one day, my wife committed her first revolutionary act; began demanding to be taken seriously for her cerebral processes. Even as I learned to become a good soldier, she came under the influence of coffeehouse activists near the camp. They included a few of the old Bitter Gang, and greater gurus who had floated in from that far and distant land, California. They set Charlotte on fire. She said she now saw The Great Society for what it was beneath its shining surface. She said she now saw the Vietnam War for what it was beneath its shining surface. She said she now saw the South for what it was beneath its shining surface. She said she was now finished with dreary old Larchmont, wasn't going back to that Southern swamp to have the baby. She was finished with her father the pig, finished with the ghastly remains of my family. We debated it fiercely, but she insisted she was going to run with her peace people until I came back from killing and maiming. "Because they are doing exciting things and I want to be a part of it, and that's where our baby should be born, among people who are changing the world."

Before all that, before the army grabbed me, there had been another phase that could have made some difference. This— our domestic phase—lasted eight months. It might have lasted a lot longer. How can I say it wouldn't have? Soon after marrying, I had dropped out of college, accepted a job with my uncle, and my wife and I found ourselves in the world of upwardly aimed, corporately striving, conspicuously consuming young Larchmont marrieds.

Not all *that* conspicuous, but I put on real neckties and daily drove to and from the real working world—and most of the time, Char even put on clothes that covered her. I insisted on that. We bought respectable furniture. We bought little gadgets, big machines. We moved into a house on a newly civilized street in Larchmont.

"Why do they murder all the trees?" Char wanted to know— and began writing a tree poem. She didn't finish it; something else came up. For the first time, we started talking babies. Char became obsessed. She wanted to have a baby, *now*. She attacked me before breakfast, mauling me in the bed sheets. She insisted that I come home for lunch and a quickie, and I would stagger back to work, lunchless, still dripping, pants spotted, eyes glazed, limp with loving. And then after dinner—God, instead of television, there we went again, bones crunching together, thigh upon thigh, straining together maniacally. When we weren't doing it, I was fantasizing doing it—wonderfully creative stuff, no question of burnout. I was as much a captive to

my wife's spectacular flesh as she was to the idea of having Little
Baby. Only Little Baby didn't come.

Still, things went nicely enough. It was more than golden
sex. Char seemed strangely content. She smiled a lot. She didn't
flirt. She didn't seem bored. I could see her growing—not her
belly, her attitudes. She was getting ready. She *knew* she was
destined to be Mother. And in business (my Uncle Ned's business: underwear factories), I had climbed aboard the sure-fire
express-to-success as assistant to my uncle, with nothing but
smooth track stretching ahead. And then the army bumped us
off the track. Things weren't so smooth anymore. Things weren't
working right anymore. We weren't so creative anymore.

"Come on to bed, honey."

"What for? I'm sick of doing that. There's more to life than
that."

"I've got to be up and out of here by five."

"So what?"

"So come on to bed."

"Is that all you think of? I'm really tired of that. Didn't I tell
you I'm tired of that?"

She came on finally and sat down hard on the bed. Down it
sagged. One of the legs was broken. A brick supported the bed.
The bed slanted. She raked her hand through her hair and began
to cry. She cried pounding her fists on the bed and she cried
kicking. She kicked the pillows off the bed and she tried to kick
me. She cried loudly and then she cried softly. She cried
whimpering and hiccuping and started blaming everything on
rotten pot. She called me rotten pot and said I had never loved
her, only it, the region where her thighs flowed together, said
I cared nothing about the dignity of her womanhood.

"I'm sorry," I said, reaching across, brushing her breasts,
snapping off the light. "I love everything about you."

"Don't do that."

"What?" I asked, getting a pain in my head.

29

"Beg."

She sat there like a statue in the dark. I pretended to go to sleep. The moon came slanting in the window. I watched her breathing. I started caressing my statue's shoulder, nuzzling her shining hair. I grew bolder and slipped off the halter, floated my hand over the shimmering tips of my statue's shadowy marble breasts. Then pulling my statue down deeper into the bed, trying to work off her shorts, getting them down with difficulty, inch by inch they were so tight, finally tugging and jerking at them as they stuck on stone hips, hearing something rip.

Jerking them on down. Looking down moon-silvery legs, at the light playing over her bellybutton, the glow of her moving thighs. I heard the old house popping its bones, the big tree stirring. Pigeons tucked up under the eaves made pleasant little noises as her hips began slowly to rise and dance with the moon.

She pressed against me suddenly, and I felt her shiver, and then there was this strange little voice.

"I'm sorry," said the tiny muffled voice, like a child's down in a closet, ". . . sorry. . . ."

"Promise me you'll handle it, honey," I whispered, holding her. "Promise me."

"So sorry," whispered the little voice.

"It's only a year. Really promise me, Char. Mean it."

"I promise. I mean it. Only just say it to me."

"You're so beautiful, honey. I love you."

"Say it again. Just *say* it."

I said it.

Her hands relaxed and her body came curving around me, and all at once she was crying softly that what we had could never die, because we were one person, inseparable, the absolute same essence, that nothing could ever part us. She whispered that she would love me forever, and after forever. Char could be sweet, so sweet.

"Forever," I whispered back, kissing her damp eyes, her lips.

"You won't do this with them?" she moaned.

"Who?"

"Those girls over there."

"Those monkeys? No way."

"Promise me?"

"I promise."

"Really promise me. *Really*."

"I do promise, I do. And you won't do this with any guys over here, will you?"

"Never."

"Don't just say it. Mean it, Char."

"Nobody *ever* but you anymore. It's *nothing* without you."

The old brass bed was rocking. Her face was tilted back, eyes glittering, lips parted, and she arched up out of that golden tangle of hair and thrust those moon-gleaming breasts up at me, nipples shining like silver bullets. "Kiss them, Mike. Kiss them. Take a little bite. Take a big, *big* bite."

And then the lovely legs parting wide and spurring me forward, forward, and onward and onward, and she was doing exquisite little things with her hands, and onward and onward, her mighty steed, and she was whispering, "Say it again, Mike. *Say* it."

"I love you, honey. I love you."

"And I love you."

We said it again and again. I was on my knees, gazing down at her, the moon shadows bathing my goddess, and then we were burning, burning, all crushed together in sweet forever burning, and far down the road the troops whooped hoarsely, and she moaned so softly, and the pigeons murmured, and the old tree was scratching, scratching against the screen, and I felt her heart beating wildly against my chest—there was nothing ever better than this—and oh, Jesus, how I loved her.

5

War Crime

Very early that morning, we sat at the kitchen table sipping coffee and looking out the window toward the rows of dull yellow barracks in the grayness of the camp.

There wasn't much left to say. And we weren't saying it. Char smoked a cigarette, then just stared out the window and fiddled with her cup, tapping it against a crack in the saucer. Once I reached for her hand and started to give her a little pep talk. She shook her head slowly back and forth and tapped her cup against the crack in the saucer. She lit up again, and sat there tapping and smoking, taking it in and breathing it out.

Outside, a jeep horn started honking. A soldier from my outfit was down there, late and in a hurry. The horn blew again, and I let go of her hand and picked up my duffel bag. With Char behind me, we went bumping and creaking down the dark, narrow inside steps. *Goodbye, old house.*

"You understand," I whispered to her at the bottom, "that we love each other and that's all that matters. The only damn thing."

There were large tears in her eyes, big green, liquid, sleepy eyes gazing up at me.

"Nothing can beat what we have," I swore softly, squeezing her shoulder.

She nodded but didn't say anything.

The horn squawked again as we stepped out onto the porch. It had been very still, but now a little breeze hit us. Char pulled her robe tightly around her in the chill. The old blue one, her sentimental robe, the first present I had ever given her, buttonless now and fastened at the top with a safety pin. Her hair spilled around the robe. I looked down at her feet, bare on the dirty porch planks. Such pretty feet. I looked at her hands. I looked at her breasts and hips swelling under the robe. Looking hard to remember.

I kissed her wet cheeks. *The professor. He had loved her cheekbones, the exquisite high cheekbones, but that was another bad story. . . .* I held her and kissed her for the last time, wanting to devour her. The horn blasted again and I had to let go. We whispered things, and then I threw the bag up on my shoulder and went down the three stone steps and out under the sighing old tree toward the jeep. *Goodbye, old tree.*

Ahead, glowing faintly, the sun edged up over the rooftops. Trucks were roaring somewhere. I felt dazed. The jeep was already rolling when I climbed in. We jerked forward. Going down the little street, staring back at her, I kept thinking, *Why is this happening?*

I waved to her, then waved again as we neared the corner. She lifted her hand, seemed frozen there on the porch as sunlight fell across the house. Pigeons fluttered atop the house darkly. She was very small now in the blue robe and getting smaller. But there was the golden glow of her hair with the sun hitting it. She really had wonderful hair. I focused on that. I would remember that. Then we turned the corner and I couldn't see her anymore.

"Just a crime," the driver was muttering. "Just a fucking *crime* to have to go off and leave something like that so all alone."

6

Old Lightning Blue

We flew from Louisiana to California, part of the great flux of American humanity toward God's Big East. Our battalion, wearing the patch with the slashing blue bolt of lightning on the shoulder, was among the forward elements of the Second Brigade of the famous Big Blue Division, sentimentally known as Old Lightning Blue. ("Born in battle, forged in the fires of three wars, and never found wanting. Ready to strike anywhere, anytime. . . .") We were to be airlifted to Vietnam, and the bulk of the division would follow by ship. At a base near San Francisco, we gathered for the big jump. It was military mass movement, the atmosphere of cattle cars, bawling and groaning, chaotic but getting there. We were herded into old WW II barracks with cracked windows and leaking urinals where we waited for the word. With bureaucratic swiftness, the word did not come.

There was time to kill, but time was killing me. I was sitting on the sunny steps of my barracks, brooding about Charlotte, when I saw Bravo's first sergeant trooping toward me. The stripe wearer. He seemed to be saying something at me. Yes, he was, at me.

34

"*Yeww* there, Ripp. When I address *yeww* I want to see military bearing. I want to see some bounce in your dead butt. *Yeww* damn people give me a case of the ass. *Yeww* damn people haven't learned nothing in all the time I been teaching you."

I hated it that he should have to take time out from his busy schedule to cheer me up. But there was no detail too nitty for Sergeant Ernest Smoker, the lovable loose cannon and short-fused stick of military megalomania whom we knew as The Smoker. Earlier, he had considered my request to call my wife with his usual charm and empathy: "Permission fucking denied."

Now I made another effort, forcing a smile, pointing out that we weren't doing anything anyway, that there was a phone nearby, and that common sense dictated that it wouldn't hurt the mighty war effort if I made this one last little call.

"Soldier, the point is: *We*, the fucking army, decides these decisions, not *yeww*, the individual dipshit enlisted swine. And we have decided that by no means are you leaving my sight to make no calls to Sweetie."

"Be serious, Sergeant. There's a phone right over—"

"Orders have been issued. You will fucking obey them."

"The order is that *you* will tell *me* when I can talk to *my* wife?"

"You got it, numbnuts. Because you troops, especially thumb-sucking jerkoffs like *yeww*, are restricted to this area until your crying ass gets safely shipped to Vietnam where it belongs."

The Smoker was a burly fellow, with sloping shoulders that seemed to grow out of his ears. A seamed, mash-nosed, narrow-eyed, almost-perpetually-pissed-off demeanor that gave him the look, even sitting on the can, of an enraged wild pig. Breath so bad that you bumped into it like a wall. He also tended to sali-vate more than most people. To avoid a spittle shower, it was best to keep just sideways of him, as I was doing now, like a boxer circling. This caused him to complain contemptuously that us new guys couldn't even look him in the eye.

"I'm warning you, Ripp, I run a tight shop, and any turdbird what messes on my company is in great danger of ranking high on my shit list."

He gave me a malevolent look and plunged off, as though seeking someone else to hook into. I sat back down. He talked to all of us like that—or worse. Maybe everybody was on his list. Some said he had the old sergeant blues; others said he had a little worse than that.

Ernest Smoker ranted about the sorry changes occurring in his army. He didn't care for this generation of American manhood ("What manhood?"). He didn't like the new blacks with the fat hair and all the handjiving and bopping and shucking and dapping and lip-flapping and mean-eyed stares. It wasn't military. He didn't like the college-kid privates confusing up the ranks with unmilitary questions, some flower babies asking him *why,* and others telling him why and presuming to explain all about life *now* to him. He didn't like me. He couldn't stand the sight of Roland. He bristled at Harry ("What the hell's so funny today, freckle-nuts?"). And he wasn't fond of another member of our squad, Sam Ching, because of Ching-Ching's half-Chinese ancestry and resemblance to the rice-snappers who had stitched those thick, white welts across his grizzly-bear gut fifteen years before.

It didn't matter much to The Smoker that we weren't going to do battle with the Chinese or North Koreans. "A slant is a slant and nothing but a slant in his lying, thieving, yellow slant heart, and that includes these rotten, stinking Veet slants, and killing slants is my life's business, and you can bet that business is going to be nothing but booming when Old Smoke gets there. Because I don't like them, see, not the way they look or fight or smell or shit or screw. If they ain't worth screwing, hell, they ain't worth nothing."

So said The Smoker. In contemplation of his coming business, he had spent free weekends back at camp curled up under his sheet with bottles of Jack Daniels, emerging only to piss and cuss. He would come tromping out of his room in shorts and clogs, walking pigeon-toed, slinging them out like bricks in front of him. Suddenly, he would halt, eyes fixed downward, and stomp on some speck or insect that had dared to invade his barracks. Shaking voluptuously on his belly were tattoos of girls, dancing naked in the scars of his old war. After eradicating the foe, The Smoker would lurch on latrineward. Minutes later, he would stomp back to resume his musing behind a locked door, where some said he talked in strange tongues.

Once he was heard growling over and over for hours, "You're on my list, goddamnit. Ya hear me, goddamnit? You're on my list . . . you're on my list. . . ." But no one knew who the new one was on his list because so many were on his list, infecting his army. The only one able to communicate with him at such times was old red-eyed Turnip Greens Turner, a fellow lifer and juicer. Along with The Smoker, other lifer-juicers in our outfit tended to fiercely distrust the new men flooding the ranks as probable dopeheads and gutless lice—unreliables, to be carefully watched.

I went inside and flopped on my bunk. Dice went whackety-whack against a wall somewhere in the barracks. Harry, the good journalist, snoozed on the bunk to my left, an army newspaper across his face. "G.I. Morale Up," the paper said, and I wondered what it was like when it was down.

A few bunks to the right, a poker game had sprung up.

"Well, just looky here everybody, three more little ol' bullets. Ain't 'at just somethin' else? Ain't 'at just too much?" chortled a soldier with squinty eyes and a pockmarked face named Canny Peacock.

Other soldiers sat around cleaning weapons and sharpening knives and bitching and wondering, a whole lot of scary talk about where we were going. To keep us sharp, The Smoker had been falling us in and falling us out—stomping in bellowing, "Awright, awright. This is it, dirtbags, this is it. *Yeww* people've had the good life too long, just *teww* long. Move, move, MOVE!"

Outside, Captain Billy Wilson, the rookie commander of Bad Company, would conduct quick little inspections, speaking softly, commenting how darn pleased he was with our obvious élan, our glittering sharpness, our readiness to serve and take the big trip, while beside him The Smoker looked ready to puke.

We were not that sharp. Sprawled in the middle of a tangle of gear clogging the aisle was a thin, yellowish body with a transistor radio to his ear.

"Hey, Ching-Ching. Turn 'at shitty noise down!" yelled a poker player called Red Dog Peacock, who was Canny's cousin —and a very poor poker player.

"Old Ching-Ching's practicin' playin' dead," tittered Canny.

Ching-Ching rolled over and opened his eyes. "Chrize, man, I can't hardly hear it as it is. Jeez Chrize, I sure wish I was somewhere else, and I didn't even like it there."

Ching-Ching, the little half-Chinese from San Francisco, was always wishing. While wandering around looking for a good, free religious retreat to live in for a while, he woke up to find himself in this man's army. Now he picked himself up off the floor, stuffed his radio into one of the big pockets of his baggy fatigues, started fiddling with his taped-together glasses, straggled over to watch the poker, sat down on a duffel bag, fished a partially smoked joint out of his breast pocket, and lit up.

One of the players, a dumpy, round, forever-smiling fellow named Too-Fat Schwartz, was discussing the case of the revered leader of our battalion, Colonel Gurgles. Schwartz had been one of the colonel's favorites ever since the day when he had failed to address his colonel properly. Schwartz had also failed to salute his colonel with the correct hand. At the time, Schwartz had been wearing pitch-black glasses and was so outrageously obese, his belly poked through the nearly bursting buttonholes of his fatigue blouse. Too-Fat-to-Fart Schwartz, as we dubbed him, was not so fat now, but was still outrageous. I never quite understood where Too-Fat came from—New Jersey or Pennsylvania or some place—but he liked to describe himself as a survivor. His best trick was to call out to our colonel, no matter how far away he was, "Good morning, *sirrr*" or "Good evening, *sirrr*" in a loud, nasal voice.

"So Gurgles told the major his only fear of Vietnam was that we would—catch this—get stuck somewhere *out* of the action, that we would suffer the horrible fate of losing our fighting identity."

Too-Fat laughed. We all laughed at the leader of our battalion.

"Our fighting identity. Gee, I sure couldn't live without that," sighed Ching-Ching.

"You ever see him goose-stepping around like he's General Rommel or somebody?" asked Too-Fat. "He's crazy."

"Man, they're all crazy practically," said Ching-Ching. "Except Sergeant Smoker. He's groovy. He keeps telling me how tough it was in the old army."

"It's always tougher in the *old army*," said Too-Fat. "The first guy who joined the army back in 1775 told the second guy how much tougher it was in the *old army*."

"Raise you fightin' men four bits," said Canny, tossing quarters onto the blanket.

"And I thought you had something," Too-Fat said, smiling.

"Why not make it four bits more?" said Canny.

"I'll be happy to see that," said Too-Fat. "How about you, Red Dog?"

"Now watch where you're steppin', cousin," cautioned Canny. "You know how you stepped in it last time."

The Peacocks were from around Lickskillet, Georgia, where even the dogs were patriotic, and Red Dog didn't see anything funny about that. Red Dog's real name was Purly, and he had "Made in Georgia" tattooed on his butt. Purly Theopolous Peacock. And he didn't see anything funny about that.

"You watch where *you're* steppin', jackoff," grunted Red Dog, tossing out a lot of nickels and dimes.

"That's only ninety-five cents," said Canny.

"Hell, you say. Deal them cards."

"Ol' Dog really knows how to step in it," giggled Canny. "This is no shit. Just 'fore we left home, ol' Dog's dick was kindly running loose. He found his *true* love. And when her ol' man found them sittin' in this joint havin' a good time, he came over, said 'Howdy do,' and hit Dog on the head with a beer bottle. When Dog came to, he was in basic training, heh, heh."

"That's ninety-five percent pure d boo sheet, deal them cards."

"Oh, well, down and dirty," said Canny, preparing to deal, then swelling up and starting to giggle again.

"What it was, see, how Dog stepped in it this time was, he and this town gal had shacked up a little and Dog thought he wanted to live forever and ever with her. But she kept hollerin', 'I don't have no shoes to wear.' One day, Dog up and nailed one hundred thirty pair of her shoes around the walls, all around the walls. There were forty pair of them panty hose hanging around in the bathroom. Dog was strangling in panty hose."

"Boo sheet. Just deal them cards."

"But she was a good gal," said Canny. "Fine lady. First time they met, at this dance, she came up and stuck her tongue in his ear and said, 'Want to fuck?' "

"Better'n any gal *you* ever had," snorted Red Dog. "You can betcha booties on that."

"It was his *true* love," giggled Canny. "Only she would only let him do it from the rear. She kept tellin' him to squeal like a pig if it feels good—oink, oink. But the good part was, she laid a germ on him. I done tol' him to get hisself a country girl. Not mess with no town girl. Town girls are loaded up with the clap. Dog's pecker nearly fell off. Couldn't even pee. How's it feel now, Dog? Need some hep to pee?"

"No hep from you, crazy fucker."

"Oink, oink."

"Deal them cards."

"Fold," said Too-Fat, dropping his cards.

"Now talk about crazy," said Canny, dealing. "Major Sheridan, 'at ol' boy's got the craziest eyes I ever seen. Like he's been busted upside the head once't too many times, like ol' Dog here. They kindly float around inside his head like little dead minnows."

"Dog's?"

"Naw, 'at major's."

"I hear his skull's half iron," said Too-Fat.

"Well, I guess it would be wise of me to bet four bits more," said Canny. "So up to you there, Dog."

Red Dog worked a big chew of tobacco around in his jaw as he pondered.

"Naw, Sheridan, he ain't half as wacko as ol' Gurgles." Canny shook his head. "When Gurgles goes on how he's gone win this war in a week usin' our fine behinds as his secret weapon, well 'at be gettin' me a wee bit upset. You bettin' or not, Dog?"

"Think I'll call," snuffled Red Dog, who had a bad cold and a worse temper.

"Please, don't be steppin' in it again, dear cousin." Canny winked. "You know I got to be sittin' here with three big fat bullets. You got to know that."

"Boo sheet. I got to call your wise ass."

"Please, don't, dear cousin," said the squinty-eyed cousin, winking and smiling slyly. "You owe it to yourself to back down."

"I may not make it, but I'll be caught tryin'," said Red Dog, his face growing redder, his bulging jaw working faster. "Ain't no way you can draw no three aces three times runnin'. Ain't no way."

"Why come I can't? I'm warnin' you. Ain't I warnin' him, troops? Be careful. Well, come on old granddad, don't just sit there. Do it or climb off the pot."

"Call your bluffin' ass," said Red Dog, slapping down three queens on the blanket. "Let's play poker."

"Way to go," Canny smiled over his cards, holding them teasingly close to his face. "Oink, oink. Way to go."

"Just show them cards, peckernose." Red Dog chewed harder, a brown foam on his lips. "Let's see them big bullets."

"Yes, sir, you can always count on old Abdul the Bull here to step in a big mushy pile of it, heh, heh."

"You gone shoot the shit or play poker? Let's see them cards."

"I warned him. A big, fat pile of it, heh, heh."

"If I don't see some cards 'fore I spit," growled Red Dog, puckering up, "somebody else gone get stepped on."

Canny acceded to Red Dog's wishes and placed his cards on the blanket lightly, one at a time, tapping each with his fingertips. "Well, 'at's one, heh, heh. And 'at looks to be two. Is that not two? And here, right here—read 'em and weep—is big three. Three big bullets, good buddy. Right here, big as a caterpillar's tits. Like I told you. Didn't I tell him? Looks like old Abdul the Bull done sank down in it once again, heh, heh. A real sizeable pile of it, oink, oink."

Red Dog spat tobacco juice just past Canny's large nose, a blob of it spattering the butt can on the post behind him, a piece of it catching Too-Fat on the shoulder, and a string of it landing on a tall soldier named Skinny Lenny Wilkens, who was leaning over to watch. There was a lot of cussing and yelling, and the poker game meandered on in this fashion.

Ching-Ching, removing himself from the line of fire, shifted over by me. He stared at his new map of Vietnam with some puzzlement.

"Chrize," he mumbled, "there it is, Mike. I always wanted to go to Asia, you know, as a tourist or something like that. But Chrize, I'm no good to myself dead, man. Alive, man, I'm cool. I'm neat. What do I need with this Vietnam place?"

Ching-Ching looked at Harry snoring under the paper and sighed. "I don't like to say this, but he's the one who should be practicing playing dead."

It seemed a most strange wedding of men in our ace outfit. Red Dog had joined up the day after Canny had been inducted.

42

Canny said Dog was in trouble with the law. Dog said he had gotten the itch to go kill commies after watching an old war movie. Harry's itch ran deeper.

Ching-Ching thought of Harry as a mystery man, that a woman might be after him, or that he might be in need of chemical help.

"I mean, I'm certainly in favor of going around and bearing everybody's burdens and all like that, but to *volunteer* to come to this poor, dilapidated place. Could it be he's hooked on some new, untested, mind-snapping chemistry or something of that variety?"

"Not Harry."

"Hey, this stuff is okay," said Ching-Ching, exhaling. "It's all right. Need some?"

"Pot is for petunias," I said.

"You guys . . . I couldn't live like that." Ching-Ching shook his head. "My personal Vietnam strategy is to keep a sorta low high going the whole time, you know, a candle in the window, kind of glowing through the entire experience, you dig, Mike? Chrize, yes, that's all there is to it practically."

Ching-Ching was usually fine. Once he got going, he talked kind of hyper-hyper. Sometimes he snipped his words. Sometimes he didn't finish sentences. Sometimes his eyes glazed over, trailed off into elsewhere. This didn't matter except like the time he envisioned the barrel of his rifle as a heavenly joint which he tried to smoke with a groovy live round in the chamber.

Over on the poker bunk, the Peacock boys were yelling again. Back in camp, they had been most peaceful when they were singing tunes from back in the red-clay-and-pine-tree country. In the evenings, the Peacocks and their good buddy, six-foot-five Skinny Lenny—his elongated Adam's apple jumping all over his throat—had serenaded us. Wiry Canny picked the guitar while squat, bull-shouldered Red Dog hunched over a footlocker and slapped spoons for rhythm.

43

They had both been hunters all their lives, with a lot of woods time, and were great shooters. In our squad, Canny played the M-79 grenade launcher with considerable skill (he claimed to have once put a round in a pisspot at 180 yards), and Red Dog was a demon drummer on the M-60 light machine gun. When riled up, blood gorging his face, Dog contained emotion the way a full bucket contains running water. Three more of Canny's aces had filled his bucket to the brim, and it was only the arrival of our platoon sergeant that kept peace in the ranks.

REWIND

The sight of our platoon sergeant would keep peace in most ranks. Such a big, smooth, pleasantly menacing hump of black stallion. A voice that sang at us with such deep, melodious, soldierly conviction. That still rang soft, rural-South soft, but hard and savvy enough at the edges to suggest it'd been some places and said some things. The merest flash of those large white teeth in that armorplated black face instantly achieving wonders of communication.

Called "a darn great soldier" by Captain Billy Wilson, "a bad motor scooter" by others—in admiration. Good dude to have with you in a firefight is what they meant. Even when someone whispered "Big Nigger," it came out heroic.

Sergeant First Class Odell "Cool Breeze" Carson. Born South and went North, graduate of Alabama and Harlem. Enlisted when he was seventeen. Soon found himself in the Valley of the Shadow: the Ia Drang, oh, shit. Made it out with the Silver Star and on through two Vietnam tours. Two lifetimes before he was old enough to vote.

Rained on and sunned on, war weathered, hard as a concrete telephone pole. VC heavy metal dented him on the last one though, did a number on his kneecap bad enough to tear cartilage and rip tendons, bad enough to butt-can his army career for a while. "I felt a li'l bit broken down. I was out the army and back home and got married and had some li'l crumb-snatchers and bounced from job to job. But my feets was burnin' to get back in."

When he made it back, that was merely wonderful. "Because I'm a soldier down to my . . . down to my . . . li'l ding-dong. You're lookin' at one. And I don't regret nothin'. Not even the knee. Because I can hump jus' fine. Sometimes in cold weather, the knee get kind of . . . kind of. . . . Anyway, it don't matter. It ain' that cold in Nam. And I can hop pretty good, too. People back home sayin', 'Hey, man, where you comin' from? You ain' gotta sacrifice your black nuts for nunna them white daddies. You don't gotta go back to no Vietnam. Jus' don't report back.' And I said, 'Don't give me that jive.' And I went. And I came back. And now I'm goin' again.

"You got to shake your head and just drive on. Listen, the army give me three meals a day, a place to stay, clothes on my back. You got to soldier to the max. You got to give one hundred per-cent out there. You got to have gen-u-wine sincerity. Listen, the people I was brung up with, I climbed out of a bucket of garbage back there. A bucket of slime. Okay, I'm in the army again. Now the rose is starting to blossom for me."

7

One Word or Two?

Cool Breeze Carson came gliding down the junky aisle, and Ching-Ching, joint snuffed out, waved his map and requested the sergeant to come over and share his expertise by explaining exactly where we were going in this Vietnam quagmire.

Easing between bunks, kneeling, the black man took hold of the map and flapped it out.

"We'll land at this cheerful place, name of Bien Hoa," he said, planting a big finger. "Then we'll truck on over to this cheerful place, name of Cu Chi."

"But how can you return to that dreaded place again, Sarge?" asked Ching-Ching.

"Oh, it's kind of pretty over there. Nothin' to get high blood about."

"And if you believe that. . . ," mumbled Ching-Ching. "Sarge, unless you really feel this war thing is your kind of thing, I definitely don't feel you should be letting yourself get killed or something."

Harry had raised up on one elbow. Breeze winked at him, then edged up on the end of Harry's sagging bunk.

46

"Well," crooned Breeze, "everybody got to get dinged someplace. It beat choppin' cotton."

"We owe God a ding," noted Harry, yawning.

Others were drifting over now. Too-Fat was telling Breeze how dangerous he had heard fooling around with Vietnam's female population was.

"I hear there's a fiendish fucking penis-paralyzing disease they give forth known as Saigon Rose that is mightier than man or medicine. Is that a true story, Sarge?"

"It is, Schwartzy." Breeze shook his head gravely. "One bad dose of the Rose, and they have to whack your poor whootie right off. Wrap it up in a little box and ship it home. It's sad to see."

"Yeowww!" yelled Red Dog. He and other warriors of Third Squad, First Platoon grabbed hold of themselves and started howling and jumping and flopping around.

"I hear a VC's so hardass one round won't even dent the rust on its butt," said Too-Fat. "You have to blow it apart to even make it bleed."

"Well, now, the VC, no matter how many times you kill him, he jus' don't die good," agreed the Breeze. "You can cut off the head, then the wings, and stomp on it awhile, but the mean li'l tail still keep hoppin' around tryin' to sting you."

"I hear the VC eat dogs and rats and bugs just like we eat beans," said Schwartz, who heard more than most.

"Yeah, they surely do spook the li'l doggies. You hear 'em whinin' and howlin' for miles across the paddies. Next mornin', you find the li'l doggies chewed right off the chain. When Charlie get a case of the hungries, do yourself a favor and *di di mau* out of there."

"Sergeant, what actually does this 'dee-dee mow-mow' mean?" inquired a boyish-looking medic with a missing front tooth.

"Well, *di di mau* is what we old veterans call a 'retrograde operation.' Mean 'shove the motha in reverse and jerk it on out of there.' First time you catch some incomin', Kelly, you know what it mean."

"How long will it take us actually to know the difference between the incoming and the outgoing?" asked Kelly, whom The Smoker called "Little Boy Blue," and who looked more like a flute player in the school band than a man going to war.

"Actually, Doc, once be enough. If it ain', you better go out for another sport."

"Is Vietnam actually one word or two, Sergeant?" asked Kelly, poking his tongue into his tooth gap. "It's for when I want to write home."

The Breeze offered us about five cents worth of his million-dollar smile and breathed a little sigh. "Well, the truth be, like everything else over there, I've seen it both ways. Listen, I don't care which way you spell it. What I care is, when you get out in that bush, goin' to school with Mr. Charlie, that's when I want you to be smart. When you boogie out in that bush. Natural, you can dig that. Ain' no way to figure it all the way, not out in that bush. It's kind of a game of skill and kind of a game of chance. But you owe it to yourself to don't take nothin' for granted. Not one minute of life out in that bush. Because out there, they's just two kinds of dudes: the dudes who gets Charlie, and the dudes Charlie gets."

"Aw, boo sheet," Red Dog announced. "I'm tired of hearin' how tough Charlie is. Give him a wet paper bag, and he'll break it in a week anyway." Jaw poked out, he unloosed a cloud of tobacco juice toward a butt can, just missing. "I'm ready to get on over yonder right damn now. 'At guy what humps a radio in second platoon, he says them VC ain't no big deal. And he's been there, too. Hell, let's get on to it. I'll fight any damn body. You can betcha booties on that. Them little fuckers ain't got the what-for to whip my ass."

"We bad," said Breeze.

"The baddest dudes around," said Skinny Lenny.

"We even smell bad," said Breeze.

"Nobody smells worse than us," said Harry.

"Bravo leads the way," said Breeze. "And First Platoon leads Bravo. Our morale is outstanding."

"You want morale?"—Red Dog leaped off his bunk, strangling air. "Aaaaaaagh—' *at's* morale."

"Infantry is the queen of battle," shouted Skinny Lenny.

"You just got to grab your nuts and drive on," said Breeze. "Without a doubt, we is the baddest queens in the battalion. Anybody doubt that?"

"Can I say a word about morale?" asked Roland, frowning. "Let me say a word about morale."

"Don't," said Harry.

"Just keep that happy smile upon your face," said Breeze.

"Here's morale!" whooped Red Dog, grabbing Roland by the neck.

"But what happens first time you come up against six *real* VC queens?" hollered Canny Peacock. "Oink, oink."

"I will close with the queens," drawled Red Dog, "and destroy them. I'll zap any muth'fucker I see."

Cool Breeze stood up. "Well, now. I tell the young troop to be observant, but you can be too observant. Eyes play tricks. If you keep on lookin' for somethin' to shoot, you keep on starin' out there, and you sure gonna see somethin' evil creepin' along out there. And ain' nothin' creepin' out there but *you*. I sure don't wanna see somebody get all shot up on 'count some humbug."

"I'll shoot 'at Humbug fucker first," growled Dog. "If he's in my sights, he's dead meat."

Breeze answered softly, "The young troop, he think it so easy to kill a man. I tell you, it really ain' that easy. You take the average line doggie and set an enemy out there and say, 'Okay, kill him.' He would be very leery to pull that trigger. And it only take two pounds of pressure to pull it. He maybe couldn't do it, just lookin' at him, you know. But if he got mad, he could do it easy. I explain that to some kid and he say, 'Hey, Sarge,

49

you ain' wrapped too tight.' And I say, 'That jus' be the way it is, you know.' "

Breeze gave off that soft chuckle. "I wouldn't let anything happen to him for nothin' in the world, you know."

Breeze handed back the map and eased away, saying he had to go hunt up the lieutenant of our platoon, a fresh bean sprout from college ROTC who depended on him almost completely.

Even Harry had listened to Breeze respectfully. The black sergeant had named Harry acting squad leader after our previous leader, Corporal Thursday, had fallen in action from overeating and hemorrhoids. Harry insisted he didn't want to lead this squad or anything, except maybe Roland's mind to reality.

"Just think, Rol," Harry said, as the others moved away, "your one big chance in life to fight killer communists with a gun, a knife, and your bare hands."

"Talk about mental illness," said Roland. "If you think I'm burning with desire to travel ten thousand miles to pat peasants on the head and shoot a commie for Mommie, you're sick."

"Don't you want to stop the Red Menace, Rol?"

"Who's going to stop *Boobus americanus?*"

"You sound like some of those patriots I used to work with."

"Well, maybe they had you figured out," said Roland, sitting down on the saggy end of Harry's bunk. "Thinking we're so superior to everybody else, going around spanking the world. I suppose you feel comfortable in the world with that kind of relationship."

"You want the truth, the very truth?" Harry said, grinning. "If it kicks a little commie ass. . . ."

"Oh, communism, smomunism. We're tired of hearing about it. Aren't we, Mike?"

"Ummm."

I lay there on my rack, eyes closed, drifting in and out, listening to the barracks' babble, life in the transient barracks.

"I hear they may let us go on twenty-four-hour pass," Too-Fat was saying.

"They ain't paid us in so long, we'll have to go to some town where everything is free," Canny was saying.

"Lotsa good free pussy in Vietnam," Red Dog was saying. "Hey, who's got my firing pin? Everything's missing."

"Well, when you make up a weapon with stolen parts, dipstick, they'll be gone just as quick," Canny said.

"Gimme that toothbrush, son. This weapon is gonna gleam."

"Anybody got a smoke?" Canny yelled. "Anybody got a free smoke?"

Ching-Ching wanted to know about Kelly's missing tooth.

"Did Sergeant Crazy do that?"

"Actually," Kelly said, "a truck did."

Before the army, Kelly had broadsided a truck with his motorcycle and been knocked out for three days. He had a lucky false tooth in his pocket, he said with a giggle, but only stuck it in when he wanted to feel lucky or look pretty. The reason he became a medic was because it might help him find interesting work when he got out of the service.

"I'm eighteen years old," Little Boy Blue told Ching-Ching solemnly, "and not getting any younger."

"Where we're going," sighed Ching-Ching, "we're not going to get any older."

"You can't assume the worst," put in Too-Fat. "You must have a little more faith in your politicians. You must believe the big guys in Washington wouldn't be sending you over there for nothing. You got to believe they know what they're doing. Surely, you believe that. . . ."

I was half asleep . . . neutralizing the Red Threat . . . sanitizing the Yellow Peril . . . standing tall against Saigon Rose . . . wondering about my wife and the horny pack. . . . (*"You will treasure your beautiful piece," my instructor instructed, jerking it out of my hands. "Your beautiful piece is your closest, most desirable companion, stupid one. This lovely piece is better for you than poontang and will save your stupid ass when nobody and nothing else will. You will sleep on the hard old ground with your beautiful piece, but you must never, never let your piece get too dirty to utilize. And may God help you if you ever lose your piece. The good soldier must know every beautiful inch of his beautiful piece and be able to strip her down in seconds and get the fucking best out of her. Now, in firing his piece, the good soldier must know that the only good battlefield is an empty battlefield. That could be significant to the soldier and his beautiful piece, begging his complete fucking attention. The good soldier must thus exercise clear thinking under all kinds of fucking pressure in order to maximize his performance and his fucking efficiency rating in the heat of fucking battle—that is, stay cool and not shoot his fucking buddies or his fucking dick off!"*)

"Awright, awright, yew sorry people. Clear the shit out of this aisle or your ass is grass and I'm your ass-kickin' lawn mower. And speaking of grass, who is puffing on that mind-rotting substance now?"

I opened my eyes and sat up on one elbow. The Smoker's nose was leading him back.

"Oh, Chrize," Ching-Ching muttered, pinching out fire and slipping the joint into the folds of his map. "Here comes The Crazed One."

"When I come in here I don't want to hear no laughing, and very little of that," bawled The Smoker. "I would hate to be the one who's puffing on that mind-rotting substance. Oh, how I would hate to be him."

Bravo's top sergeant, nostrils flaring, jerking his head left and right, kept coming, kicking gear out of the aisle.

"Yew people, yeww damn people. . . ." He stopped almost in front of Roland, who, talking to Harry, did not at once look up. "Let's just knock it off back here. Is that you smoking that mind-rotting substance, Private Donahoo?"

"What is this about rotting minds?" asked Harry from his bunk.

"Smoking?" Roland looked vaguely toward our top sergeant's formidable crotch.

"You heard me down there. Why are you always looking down, boy? Nobody wants to go to war with a dumbass who's always looking down."

"Do I look like I'm smoking?" Roland mumbled. In The Smoker's presence, he usually shut his mouth as carefully as a little old lady snaps shut her purse.

"I don't know what you look like. What's lower down than a pissant? Hey, when I speak to you, answer smartly. I want to hear those teeth clicking. I don't hear no teeth clicking."

"If you don't like my looks, I'm sorry. Please feel free to leave me here when you go to Vietnam."

Roland had only glanced up for one tortured moment at his top sergeant.

"*Please feeel freeeee*," mewled The Smoker. "From now on, all I want out of you is 'yes' and 'no' and blind fucking obedience, dirtbag, because for the next year I own your pissant soul. If I tell you to jump off a fucking building without breaking a leg, by all means you will so do as you have been so ordered."

"Without breaking a leg?" Harry mused aloud. "That's kind of hard to do, Sarge. Like fucking yourself."

"Knock it off, Hammarth, I'm warning you. Do you read me, Donahoo?"

Roland smiled wanly, still not looking up. "Yes, I certainly read you, Sergeant. But this is still not Prussia, I think, and individual worth and dignity should still mean something in the American Army. I'm sorry if you don't agree."

"*I'm sorreee if you don't agreeeee*," mewled The Smoker. "Oh, you're such a brilliant shit, aren't you? But when I look at you, I don't see no dignity worth a damn. All I see is a whining shit-turd who can't unroll toilet paper straight, who'd fuck up a steel ball with a rubber hammer, and who I guarantee is gonna get his butt killed the first day. You're gonna die the *first day*, Donahoo. The gooks are gonna getcha."

"Aw, ease off, Sarge," Harry said. "All this troop's been talking about is you. How eager he is to start defending the land of

Boobus americanus under your far-seeing and splendid guidance. How he's just balls-to-the-wall to get on over there in the great out-of-doors and start slaying Reds . . . utilizing your excellent training, Sergeant. And then"—Harry mustered up a look of hurt—"here you come talking as though there were users of cannabis among us, a substance about which we know little. You can imagine our dismay when—"

"Awright, awright, just knock off the goddamn funny shit, Hammarth. You're on my list too, wiseass, right on top. All you fartblossoms back here are. Whatta outfit. I sure don't want my life depending on one of you weirdos stoned-out in his guard tower. I don't need that fucking shit."

He gave something in the aisle a swipe with his boot and turned to go.

"Now, why's your lip dragging there, Ripp? Messing in your panties again? Crying for mama and not gone a week yet. Yes, sir, all you candy-asses rank very high on my list, I shit you not. You, too, there, Charlie Chan, and all your miserable ancestors. I know about you. I've instructed Sergeant Carson to keep a very close watch on you over there in case you decide to go over to the gooks."

"Jeez Chrize," mumbled Ching-Ching, who sat on a duffel bag staring at his map, "Vietnam sure looks pretty."

REWIND

The story went that Lieutenant Colonel Frederick Gutmann Gurgles had risen in the ranks the hard way. "I'll do anything you want me to, sir."

The professional ingratiator. The little fish who attached himself to the big fish. The sly little maneuvers, outflanking his peers, the small goose-steps and victory postures after lunch with the general. They extended even to the act of urinating, into the macho, triumphant up buttoning of the fly over the piss-tube. "I will do anything you want me to, sir." He liked to

talk in terms of how many people he had under him. His underlings. "I am the commander of this battalion, and you aren't."

He required of his underlings abject loyalty and obedience.
Fake abject loyalty and obedience would do nicely. Positive eye
contact, the gleaming smile of glass could win you his favor. In
the battalion, things had to go well on the surface, the ever-
polished spit-and-shine surface. Reports had to be especially
shiny, the numbers polished, the paper indices of success glittering. He put more into the bullshit machine than most. Lovely
bullshit in, lovely bullshit out. Bullshit, bullshit, bullshit.

You had to know him not to love him. But something good
must be said about him. In all fairness, *something* good must be
said about our colonel. What? What? He had a nice salute.
Some felt he spent so much time perfecting his nice salute and
covering his fine ass that somewhere along the line he had lost
his basic balls.

At first, he wore a small, blond, magical mustache. When he
shaved it off, his military image lost some of its attractiveness.
Revealed those thin lips, those piranha teeth, made his jaw seem
arrogant. If he had retained the magical mustache, he would
have presented a much sweeter military image. He was one of
those rare people who did not motivate you to want to get to
know him as a whole human being, whether under all that bullshit he liked puppies and babies and what have you. More than
anything, he seemed to need to impress you with his little power
—like a big kid kicking a small dog—and the power he would
like to have.

8

No Boohoo

We truck to the airfield in a sleepy, drizzly dawn, humpback shadows bulging with all the accouterments of modern zapping. We off-load and form up groggily, bitchily, to await the arrival of the battalion commander, who has a few thousand words for us. Cool Breeze Carson stands playfully before First Platoon, rubbing his hands together in the wet chill.

"Now, men." He grins and tries to talk like, and does a quick little strut like our Gurgles. "I sho am mighty pleased that old Hide-and-Slide Platoon has graciously volunteered for this-here thorny suicide mission. Would you like me to address myself to that before de shit hit de fan?"

"Hell, no—"

"Thank you, my men. Now, men, I be advised you can hardly wait to do your duty for me and the Lord God Almighty, to get yourself cheerfully blown up without no complaint. Because good grunts don't whine. Good grunts don't boohoo. Good grunts are *cheerful* grunts. Are you gettin' the picture, men? Are you? Don't be bashful. Let me hear from you this lovely morning. Louder!"

"Good morning, *sirrrr*," shrills Schwartz.

"It's always a pleasure to hear from you, my men."

Cool Breeze carries on like this until he sees one of the lesser commanding figures in the U.S. Infantry approaching. Second Lieutenant Art Rodeliano, our platoon officer, who until recently was majoring in business administration at Michigan U. He does not seem quite sure what marvelous accident of reasoning got him here, or that he is an actual leader of men going into an actual war zone. He is hawk-nosed, slim, dark, tense. He smokes a lot and his wires smoke. I wonder if he will burn out before he reaches the war. He picks The Breeze's brain constantly —"How does this work?" "How will that go?"—cramming for combat. He keeps worrying out loud how we will react under fire. We are beginning to worry out loud how he will react under fire. Each time I see the ROTC gee-whiz worrying, I am glad we have the old steady Breeze.

Head down, Rodeliano comes worrying toward us along with Captain Billy Wilson, Bravo's commander for two whole weeks now. Wilson is Liberty Bell, Texas. When he talks, that bell rings. When he passes through the ranks, here comes The Alamo. "You sons of guns are going to do all right over there." This is his first command, a rifle company bound for battle, hallelujah! He's squared away, sturdy looking, his brow furrowing earnestly over large brown eyes. He even tries to keep a lid on The Smoker, which should earn him a medal right there.

Then comes the main event, Frederick G. Gurgles, and we are commanded to sit in the grass near the flight line. We sit, slowly getting our asses wet listening to the bandy-legged, fighting-cock colonel who has not yet led men into real battle, who struts back and forth belting his battalion with words over a bull horn. The story that Bad News Benson has passed to Too-Fat Schwartz and Too-Fat has passed to us is that our commander just missed Korea and never forgave that inconsiderate war. At the time, he was a sergeant of some kind. This war has already jumped him from captain to lieutenant colonel and thrust upon him a battalion of infantry to lead into mortal combat. He strides back and forth, his jaw puffing up under his helmet, carrying the bull horn in one hand and a slender map case he switches back and forth like a swagger stick in the other.

"You men," he blares, "can I honestly call you that—men? Do I see some sleepy eyes out there? Are you awakening out there? Well, you'd better be, because you know what today is? Today is nitty-gritty day. Today you join the varsity, the first team, the *Always First Battalion*, by God, is what today is.

"Now, men. You better listen up out there. Are you getting the picture? WAKE YOUR ASSES UP! Now, the question of the day is: Are you *ready* to join the Always First Battalion? And the answer is—HELL, NO! One look at you and I can say without reservation, 'HELL, NO!' Do you read me? I said, 'HELL—'"

At that point, the colonel's bull horn goes off and he continues shouting, but no one can hear him clearly.

"What did he say?" Ching-Ching mutters. "Oh, gee, I can't hear what that man is saying. Am I missing anything? I would sure hate to miss anything that man is saying."

At that point, the bull horn returns to full volume.

"Now, you men. I ask you this morning: Why is that? Why is your performance so shoddy, so piss-poor? Why? I'll tell you why. Because you lack the necessary discipline"—his teeth are grinding at us—"because you lack the necessary aggressiveness. Because you lack—"

Again the bull horn is not working.

"What'd that man say we lacked?" says Ching-Ching. "I would sure wish to know what we lacked."

"Because when it comes to the fundamentals of soldiery"—the bull horn is again functioning—"your performance is pretty second rate. And that could be pretty inconvenient for you where you're going.

"Men of the Always First Battalion. I am not always the smiling specimen you see before you now. It pains me to tell you that many of the shining faces I am looking at in this sweet morning dew will *not* be coming back. Yes, *not* coming ba—"

Again the bull horn flakes out, and Gurgles shakes it viciously until once more it carries forth his sounds.

"Yes, you, you, and you"—he is pointing his map case at us like the staff of Moses summoning up the Furies—"and you, little Johnny, and you. Yes, many of those pretty faces will be kilt over there. I said *kilt*. Pretty heads will roll, lovely legs will sever, fingers will fly. And your remains, yes, your sad remains, litle Johnny, your pitiful remains, your poor, miserable little bits and pieces will be swept up and stuffed, scraped, and poured into what we call body bags."

It's raining now and we are getting steadily soaked, hundreds of huddled men getting all wet listening to our Moses. And now the rain falls harder, and there's a thrashing and flapping all around as the men struggle into ponchos. A jet goes ripping overhead as our Moses, jaw working, his little slit-trench mouth full of uneven yellow teeth grinding, raises his voice an octave into a near shriek as he tells us what will be expected of us when we reach the Promised Land.

Now Major Bradley Sheridan comes edging up to the left and rear of the colonel and lets his minnow eyes swim among us. These are our leaders. This pair will lead us to victory or death.

Sheridan and I have already had another brief altercation over my soldierly qualities. It happened on the last training day, as we were being shown film of American jets screaming over North Vietnam's Red River delta. They were diving into a sunset, strafing and going *boom, boom, boom* with their cannons and *shuuu, shuuu, shuuu* with their rockets at little brown blobs with legs scattering on a dirt road. Then this one blob—it was hard to tell whether it was a military blob or a civilian blob— stopped and turned as the plane bore down on him, stared frozenly as the plane came on, and in the final moment, threw his arms across his face, the jet's gun cameras catching him

perfectly as his top half flew off his bottom half. In the back-
ground, after the disintegration, the song *Red River Valley*
played hauntingly, sentimentally, as the sun-streaked planes
banked around toward the Gulf of Tonkin and their carrier. As
the music swelled gloriously, laying the message on us, I felt
this heavy gin-breath behind my left ear and turned to look into
my XO's odd little eyes, gleaming.

The lights came on, and the eyes had floated in my direction.

"There"—his lips moved like a whisper in church—"is *war*,
kid."

"It looked more like rabbit shooting to me," I said.

"You'll find those rabbits shoot back. Just where the hell is
your manhood anyway, Ripp?" He shook his head sadly, got up
and turned away.

Manhood. Maybe one day I would be bursting with the pride
and varicose veins of those aged Legionnaires I had seen tottering to the drum tap down Cherry Street, become a manhood
marching fool. Slay rabbits.

"Now, men. Listen up out there," called the bull-horn colonel.
"At this point in time, I am going to address myself to a most
thorny subject. We have been keeping close tabs on the multifarious crybabies and malingerers infesting the ranks, tearing
down the morale. That impacts me hard, men. We know who
you are and it will not, repeat not, be tolerated henceforth.
Henceforth, you are do-or-die grunts taking your orders from
the higher superiors as I take my orders. And happy to do it, by
God. Do you begin to get the picture out there, little Johnnies?
Now don't be bashful"—he whacks his map case against his hip
—"let me hear from you out there. Do you get the goddamn
picture? Is the picture coming through? Is it a good picture?
I'm not hearing you. I say I am not *hearing* you."

"Yeah, yeah," comes a smattering of voices, "we get it . . . we
got it."

"You had better, by God, because you are infantrymen. Do
you realize that you are infantrymen? Cheerful infantrymen?

Cheerful American infantrymen? Who don't whine? Who don't boohoo? Setting out on a do-or-die mission for your country? I say further, little Johnny, that if you are sitting out there wondering why poor little you is going to decommunize Vietnam . . . well, I fucking urge you to wonder silently. I say, if you are wondering why Lord God Almighty put you under my command, do it silently. I will not, repeat *not*, tolerate this battalion being screwed up by a lot of perfidious wondering.

"Now, men. On a more positive note . . . at this point in time, let me address myself to how you will perform when you come to grips with the communist enemy. Now war is the meanest contact support there is, by God. And the motto of my team is *'Ever Forward, Never Backward'!* What that means is we are going to fire up a lot of sonofabitchin' little Red assholes in the coming year. We are going to show them that this is the best battalion of the best brigade of the best division of the United States Army, who have nothing to offer but blood, sweat, tears, and so on and so forth. We kill more.

"Now, men. Let me close by telling you that upon your return from Vietnam you will live proud and tall the rest of your lives. Yes, that I personally guarantee. Because America never fails to stand foursquare behind her sons who fight the brave fight, who lay their lives on the line for her, and so on and so forth. So that should be a comfort to you over there.

"Men of the Always First Battalion. What have I said to you as we start our long journey? I have said that on my team the motto is 'Ever Forward, Never Backward'. So let me hear it from you loud and clear—WHAT IS OUR MOTTO?"

"Ever Forward, Never Backward," comes a small chorus in the drizzle.

"Now, men, don't be bashful, goddamnit. Let me hear from you, LOUDER!"

He is shouting as the sun comes up. It is still lightly raining and the sun is shining rainbows as we march to the fat-bellied transport planes. We strap into long lines of red nylon parachute seats as engines roar all across the field and lights blink inside the dim, sallow belly of our great stuffed bird, which starts to belch and gasp and whistle and then, shaking itself moves forward slowly, and with a roaring rush begins ponderously to rise, and there is a bump-thumping underneath and oh, lordy, here we go.

"Sure hope we earn our letter." Ching-Ching, stoned, giggles next to me. "Sure hope we make varsity."

"Ever Backward, Never Forward," somebody chants through the roaring.

Rocking upward, hugely soaring and smoothing out, curving out over an enormous blue universe of water with waves running like a cavalry charge, white banners flying, we go. Going to Asia.

"There it is," Ching-Ching sings, peering back through a porthole, *"there it is."*

Way off, stacked beautifully on hills, is romance city and the bridge of dreams swooping into mist. And then, dazzling, long-legged sprawling all over the sunrise in one last gorgeous showing off of her bountiful glories, America herself.

"Oh, yes," Ching-Ching rhapsodizes as we leave it. "My goodness, yes."

REWIND

Ching-Ching. Outcast son of a simple Chinaman and an unknown white lady. On the thin-chested, slightly slant-eyed side. "How did I get into this war? I am just a poor urchin from the streets of the San Francisco disadvantaged. I am peaceable folk. I do not hassle nor hurt nobody is what I am. How did I get into this war? I liked to play the saxophone once. Laying-on the sunny sounds, doing the soft blue notes, you dig? Only the fuzz wouldn't let me, you dig? They came in there freaking up the music and destabilizing the San Francisco poor is what they did. Searching for dope of all things. I had it hid in the sax of all things. Infamous scene. No serene home life at all after that.

The grim fuzz denying me my very bread, practically. I had to get it begging, borrowing, stealing, selling my small amount of blood that is left. But I'm all right now, pretty much, I'm alive, I'm cool.

"You know that, Mike. I can take it or leave it, practically, even as we travel to the cruel war scene, make the Big Trip, the Big Gig, the Final Wow. Bloody-toothed Armageddon over there waiting to swallow us like the giant-jawed shark. And us here, hitting the high notes, slow-starting but rallying with magnificent cool. Are you sure you don't want some of this, Mike? I've got enough, practically.

"Oh, Chrize. Shit. Here we go. We're really going. Men on a mission in defense of our country. Staving off the giant-jawed shark, and yet at the same time mainlining love and peace. Crumbling the Bad Machine—hack, slash, bleed—with simple flowers and music. My goodness, yes. Are you sure you don't want a smidge of this, Mike? Ninety-nine percent mean-ass world, Mike. It's just heinous out there. Oh, Chrize, shit, how did I get into this war? Just blows my mind. What am I doing here? It's just heinous in here."

His voice was beginning to clank through the roaring of the engines. His eyes were dark, leaky, slanted little rooms in a haunted house. Tears were trickling down his bony cheeks.

"Are you sure you don't want just a smidge of this?"

9

The First Increment

Cu Chi, Cu Chi,
Worst fucking place I ever did see
    Jodie—5/25/67

You ain't seen shit
    Al—5/26/67

—Scribblings on outhouse door

"*Goooooood* morning Vietnamm. . . ."

It came in darkly, usually down on dream layer three or four, my erotic-exotic channels—nudity, language, violence—but it wasn't that good of a morning ever. The cheerful, good-soldier, can-do, asshole voice of Armed Forces Network Vietnam Radio shrieked us out of our holes, abysses, and deathbeds with the news that this was the kickoff of another wow-now day in one's beautiful life (Impending demise? Hey, troopie, not on the old morning show). in Vietnam Cong Hoa, which was the Republic of South Vietnam, which was ten thousand miles from what I dreamed of.

The Smoker had cunningly taped the greeting part. And with the dawn of each new day, sometimes in dark rain pounding like kettle drums under speakers bleating out manic good mornings over and over, he would be hunched outside our tents, his lip and gut poked out, rain dropping off his nose, to warmly welcome us.

"Move! Move! Yew damn people had the good life just *teww* long."

And kept on braying as we slipped and slid through dark

downpours along slimy paths made of wooden ammo casings and out across mud wallows, a pound of gunk on each foot, learning about Vietnam rain ("I'm gettin' wet," says Dog. "You should. Your poncho's on inside out," says Canny), squishing on until boots, britches, everything finally just wet, wet, sticky wet, falling-apart wet, paper-disintegrating wet, my letter from Char disintegrating. Mud and rain, rain and mud. Living on the ground, go to sleep in a drizzle, wake up in a waterfall.

These little rehearsals for battle made Sergeant Smoker smile, seeming to be his lonely pleasure in the early days before he could lead us to even better places. He ambled around, muttering grouchily, "They call this war? They call these worn-out scumballs (old Vietnamese mama- and papa-san janitorial types) the rough, rough enemy?"

"No, top, they're the friendlies," Harry offered.

"A zip is a zip, freckle-nuts, and don't ever forget it."

Or he would see some ARVN, South Vietnamese soldiers, go sidling past, maybe holding hands.

"Just look at that pitiful performance, will you. You can see right there why they ain't much on fighting."

So far, it was an easy war. Flying in, I had braced to nose-dive into instant epic battle against screaming armies of Viet Cong human-waving at us. We flew over watery bomb and shell holes, thousands of them, each shining up from the deep, dark greenness as ominous as the eye of Cyclops. But down on the ground nothing scarier than The Smoker's yawning maw. Nothing more threatening than our colonel's climbing calculations for mass Cong homicides with our bodies as his adding machines. Nothing more discomforting than being rained on five times a day, monsoon skyfloods followed by sunbursts of heat and humidity that could break a sweat in three minutes and boil you in thirty if you were as pale green and runny at the center as we were.

We weren't getting shot at, but we heard American artillery firing from inside our base camp at Cu Chi, followed by muffled crunchings miles away in the jungled *out there*. Sometimes there were other crunchings out there, not so big, strong, and earth-moving as ours, but small, nasty crunchings, such as our still-unseen foe might make.

Cu Chi was this big, messy alternating mud and dust sprawl of tents, bunkers, plywood huts, shit houses, a growing number of more-solid structures, big-gun positions, small-gun positions, rolls and rolls of concertina wire, endless sandbags, and helicopter pads nineteen miles northwest of the land called Saigon. My main suffering was heat rash and gas pains, mosquito bites and long rainy dream-soaked nights without Charlotte.

Colonel Gurgles, meanwhile, was "delighted" that we were the first "increment" of infantry representing Old Lightning Blue to set foot in the war zone, a "signal honor."

But down in the ranks, Red Dog was disgruntled. "I came here to fight these bing-bang-bungs, not honor no increment."

Cousin Canny was restless. "We're here to do good, ain't we? Where's all 'at good poontang I heard about? Where's all them little brown fuckin' machines we was promised?"

Roland dragged around, jaw hung lower than the brooding skies that kept dumping on us. "God, this is oppressive, Mike. How can you stand it?"

Too-Fat Schwartz, belly bobbing, sweating heavily, went around smiling at things. He smiled at rain. He smiled at mosquitos. "Hello, sirrr." He smiled at Gurgles.

Harry was eager: Custer ready to ride. Once a column of black smoke appeared very close in the sky, and Harry was up instantly, jumping for his rifle. "Let's do it!" Someone was burning feces.

Our squad, too, was briefly blessed with burning great humps of the lovely stuff, whose fierce smoke spirals could be seen for miles. The Smoker trooped over to favor us with a rare belly laugh.

"Yeww people are scaring hell out of the gooks. Best damn feces squad we ever had. Gonna change your MOS to permanent feces fighter. Private Donahoo, I now gaze upon exactly what it is you remind me of, I shit you not."

As we settled in, Captain Billy Wilson gave an orientation talk on how we servicemembers were to conduct ourselves in our new environment. He read a few lines from a paper, shrugged, and looked up.

"Basically, what it says here is that we are in Vietnam to help out, men. Cripes, anybody out there who doesn't know that? We're here to assist these Vietnam people in their valiant struggle against communist aggression. Okay? But just remember, when we're not out fighting, we're being afforded the opportunity of being kind of ambassadors for America, of building the American image. By that I mean there's more to this war than killing, and as servicemembers, we're expected to be friendly and to help these common Vietnam people out. Hey, I'm serious about that. I want you to mingle with the good people on our side and make friends when you can. We've got to win some hearts and minds out there. And here's something else. Treat their womenfolk with *respect*. Hey, I'm serious. Even if you're feelin' sorta—" His eyes crinkled warmly. "Well, you know how you feel."

"Oh, sirrr," called out Too-Fat, "that's how we feel, sir. But we don't know what to do about it, sir."

"Well, anyway," Wilson said, looking at the paper, "this stuff goes on and on. Suffice it to say, just use your common sense. Like when you're out on the roads, give these Vietnam people the right of way. Little things like that. Don't run over them with a truck or anything. And like in a public place, don't be loud or rude, hit anybody over the head with a bottle or something dumb. And listen, men, try to learn the language if you have time. Some nice words. What do you think *nuoc mam* is, for example? No, Ching, not 'nuke bomb.' It's a fishy stuff these Vietnam people dab all over what they eat. And it smells pretty terrible, okay? Could be that's worth knowing."

Ching-Ching still wasn't wholly with us. He had come down

with a feverish malady shortly after arrival and spent days shivering and giggling in his rack, smoking dew and listening to The Grateful Dead and other spirits. "This tent life ain't bad, men."

"Okay," Wilson was saying, "it goes without saying that we don't want you messing around in any black market, or illegal money changing, or buying dope, or brawling with the local people and the like when you're off duty. I just pass that on from our local provost marshal. What it says here I should encourage you to do—and I do—should you find yourself in Saigon or one of the other cities with a little free time on your hands, go visit the fine zoo, or seek out some of the better restaurants, or go take a gander at some of the exotic Buddhist-type temples they have over here, and absorb some of the culture of this land. And you can always visit the USO and the like. That's all good stuff. It also says here that from time to time there will be excellent outdoor floor shows right here at Cu Chi base camp brought in by the USO and the like. Once it stops raining. There will also be some outdoor movies right here at Cu Chi base camp, and you will be happy to know that we have been promised excellent mail service at old Cu Chi base camp. So all in all, things look pretty A-OK as far as the amenities go."

Bad Company, one hundred thirty-one strong, sitting and squatting in a semicircle between mud puddles, generously applauded the amenities. Wilson was winning us over. But now came Colonel Gurgles, a disturbed-looking Gurgles striding before us. He had been standing off to the side, listening and looking fierce. Grinding his teeth. Now here he came glowering and whacking his map case in the palm of his hand. He assumed the legs-spread, hands-on-hips position to address us.

"Men of Bravo. Your company commander has given you a superb account of how to spend your leisure time in this war zone. But I am here to tell you how you will spend the other ninety-nine percent of your time. Now, it behooves you to know that we have over here in this war zone what is known as the search-and-destroy maneuver. Men, make no mistake about what is your prime mission over here, which is to search and destroy the communist enemy—yes, search and destroy, search and destroy. We will let those REMFs, those rear-echelon mother-fucker punks, concentrate on soaking up the magnificent culture of the land, will we not? Because we are the straightlegs, the do-or-die grunts, looking for little Red assholes to aggress, aren't we? We will be taking a few hikes in the jungle, won't we?

"Now, men. I know that you are straining at the bit to get on with the job of defeating our raggedy-ass opposition. I like that. I like that look of ferocious determination I see out there. And, by God, we *will* defeat them, because we've got them number-wise, digitally speaking, out-tanked about two thousand to zip, out-helicoptered about four thousand to zip, out-gunned by no-telling-what to zip, and so on and so forth.

"Men of Bravo. Now that we've fixed our main mission firmly in mind, a brief word concerning intermingling with the locals— a thorny subject. It is all well and good talking about becoming palsy-walsy with a lot of strange-looking characters trotting around in black pajamas and what have you. But easier said than done, right? Am I right? Yes, easier said than done. Because who's to say whether those are our little Vietnamese running around or Ho Chi Minh's little farts? Who's to say? Now, do you begin to get the picture?

"So, men, what have I said? I have said that my advice to you —and I'm sure Captain Wilson concurs—is just don't associate with these suspicious locals as much as possible. Be security-conscious at all times. Now, men. Just a word more on the so-called amenities of this place. As far as I'm concerned, this war zone has no goddamned amenities. And one more thing— for those of you who might eventually have sexual desires—I know, I know, it happens, and we've got to be right out front with this—I know from time to time you will tend to get, well . . . it's a force that rears its ugly head in the night, ha, as sneaky as the enemy, ha. But I say to you, I want you to defeat it, men. Put it down. Do it for your country. Fight it, fight it, fight it. I say—and without being facetious—it *can* be done.

"Men of Bravo. What I am saying is that I strongly urge you to save yourself for the battlefield. Because you are going to need everything you got. At this point in time, I am banning any messing around with the local femmes, the local young yummy-butts you may stumble upon in our area of operations. So, men, save it, save your precious energy for the battlefield.

"Now, men. Are you getting the picture? Let me hear from you on that. Let me hear from you, damn it! Are you GETTING THE FUCKING PICTURE?"

"Yes," shrilled Schwartz. "Oh, it's coming in. We got it, sirrr."

"All right then. So far, so good. So now we're getting down to crunch time. So now the game gets a little more interesting, eh? Now, futurewise, here's what comes next."

Next would come an eighty-hour combat orientation course in what was known as Jungle Demon School. In Jungle Demon School, we would take cram courses in "The Art of Jungle Fighting," "Ambush and Counter Ambush," "Knowing the Enemy," "Mines and Booby Traps," "Tunnel Destruction," and other topical subjects that, said the colonel, "will stand you in good stead as you rev up to run the raggedy-ass opposition right back to Hanoi."

The snake-lean officer in the green beret stood under a wet banana tree lecturing us on "how to survive in the jungle, gentlemen. You are going to have to live like the animals, gentlemen: head close to the ground, eyes and ears open, mind clean and mean, moving quietly, stealthily, developing woodsman expertise, and killer's instinct, gentlemen. I can see in your plump, pleasant faces that you are going to become very fierce jungle killers, gentlemen. You are going to become masters of surprise and concealment as you go out to combat the most deadly beast in the forest. Very cunning, very tenacious is this beast. Don't listen to mental defectives who say otherwise. The method of this beast is that when you advance, he withdraws; when you defend, he harasses; when you are tired, he attacks; when you withdraw, he pursues. Thus, you must become even more dangerous and sly than he is. You must out-beast him, gentlemen."

Snake man slithered among us, eyes glinting like razor blades that slashed at first this one of us and then that one, his head swinging slowly side to side as he spoke to us as gentlemen and beasts.

"But right now, you are a little too civilized-looking to go swishing off into the scratchy jungle, gentlemen. That must change. So we are about to lift your rock, gentlemen. Let the creatures crawl out. See the lovely underside of who you are. Because in the jungle in the dark with the beast moving around you, life is very different from what you were taught back in Niceville. Yes, indeed. In the jungle in the dark, gentlemen . . . in the jungle in the dark. . . ."

The officer talked on darkly for a while and then weaved back to his banana tree, a weary, almost resigned look crossing the thin, yellow face in the fading light.

"So there you are, troops. You will certainly find all this out for yourselves. To help you survive, gentlemen, I would like to introduce you to another gentleman whom, if I were you, I would avoid ever meeting in the jungle in the dark."

The officer turned and gabbled something in Vietnamese. A man quickly emerged from a nearby patch of trees, hunkered down barefoot before us, butt resting on his heels, arms dangling in front of his knees. He was built like twists of wire, wore only shorts, and his skin was streaked with red clay. Speaking in a singsong voice and looking toward us with zero emotion, he identified himself as a former Viet Cong sapper who had *chieu hoi*'d, come over to our side, for reasons he did not go into. What he went into was how he and his former comrades had outwitted and slain the enemy by sneaking through their defenses and blowing them up with satchel charges. As the officer stood beside him interpreting, he described a typical sapper mission aimed at a typical American position protected by the typical concertina wire, claymore mines, trip flares, and clumsy, slow American boys.

". . . by now, the barbs of the wire were caught in my body, in my abdomen. And then, while among the wires, my hand touched something. When I saw that it was a mine, I shivered. The mine was there, the trip string was there, and there was only the thickness of a simple hair between me and death.

"If I shivered strongly, I would set off the mine. I had to be very calm. I used my hand to detect the string attached to the mine. I could feel the coolness of the mine's metal. I had to be very careful . . . very calm. . . . Slowly, on my belly sliding, fingers pulling, toes pushing forward inch by inch, I worked my way through the mines and the wire which was so thickly constructed it might seem that a rat couldn't wriggle through. And yet, I did, disarming the claymores and trip flares as I went. And then I was ready to unsling the satchel charges from around my neck, pick myself up, charge forward, and explode the enemy."

"That would be you," interjected the officer, "you pleasant-faced gentlemen out there."

"Sometimes there were sentry dogs present," the ex-sapper continued, "and so we must attack his weak points. The weakest point of the sentry dog is his fear of the tiger. Thus each of us took along a piece of tiger fat, or tiger skin soaked in fat. Fresh tiger fat was best, and if you planted tiger mustache hairs in it and threw it at the dog, he was terrified. He would not bark or run at you. I once killed such a dog in place. When I took its legs off the ground, the dog was considered as dead. I killed the dog and brought it back to our camp and ate it.

"Sometimes, also, there is the problem of the goose or duck, which will quack noisily at strangers. In order to overcome the goose or the duck, you must roast the stem of a large taro leaf, tie it to a stick, push it toward the feet of the goose or the duck, and shake it. They will think it is the snake. They will not quack, their necks will droop, and they are as paralyzed. You must also

72

be careful to walk against the wind, or smear your bodies with onion and garlic—which is as a snake to the goose or the duck."

At that point, someone—it sounded like The Smoker—called out that this fine group was not composed of geese or ducks, but of dumb jackasses, and what advice did he have for jackasses? The officer chuckled and spoke again in Vietnamese. The ex-sapper nodded and continued his discourse.

"The weak points of the American jackasses on perimeter guard are that they stand up and sit down too much, talk too much, cough too much, flash their lights too much, smoke too much, and concentrate their forces too much. That makes it very easy. Six of us could get inside a position and cause much confusion and explode many enemy. I myself have seen a sentinel only eight meters from me fire a flare and then look directly at me without seeing me. He was considered as dead. . . ."

The reformed sapper spoke impassively for the most part, but at this last, he seemed to permit himself the very slightest of smiles. Or perhaps it was only a twitch.

" 'At old boy looks meaner'n a striped snake," muttered Canny Peacock.

Bad Company was primed to go aggress somebody. Graduation from Jungle Demon School was to be the occasion for our first live combat mission. The evening before this happened, Lieutenant Rodeliano and Cool Breeze Carson hiked part of the platoon to the camp's edge. We looked out over rusty rolls of wire and fields studded with claymores toward where we would be marching. It was scraggly, mean-looking, mostly flat terrain with little slopes and swells, lots of elephant grass, smashed rubber trees, and much half-burnt, half-exploded forest.

"Jeez Chrize, why would anybody want to go out there?" said Ching-Ching.

"Boo sheet," Red Dog said, waving at it contemptuously. "Don't look no worse'n Georgia to me. Let's get on out 'ere. Let's get some."

"Not what it look like," cautioned Breeze. "What it don't look like you got to watch out for."

"Well, it don't look like much," sneered Red Dog.

"Onliest thing to remember is, lay your eyes down before you lays your feets down," said Breeze. "Charlie's dug thousands of tunnels out there. You liable to fall in on ol' grandpaps Ho Chi Minh hisself, you don't step lightly."

"Good," grunted Red Dog. "Saves buryin' the fucker."

"Irregardless, you be huntin' on his turf. The little man can mess on you pretty bad he take a mind to."

"Suicide mission," said Ching-Ching, sighing. "This army. All they want is spit-shine boots, pressed fatigues, and go catch some bullets."

"Everyone look the same in combat," said Breeze. "Smell the same, too. Like mud and shit."

Roland shook his head. "Let them have their turf. It's stupid going out there."

"Very strange, very spooky," Ching-Ching said, looking spooked. "Don't feel nothing but negatives coming out of that old burnt forest, Sarge. Know you have great savvy of the entire situation, Sarge, but something whispering to me, 'Hey, man, don't go.' Curse of the born loser, Sarge."

Breeze smiled beautifully. "Oh yeah, I have that curse myself. 'Don't go, don't go.' Always say that. Don't mean nothin'. Irregardless, what we're gonna do tomorrow is sweep out that way about ten or fifteen clicks." He pointed due north. "We'll hump from sun to sun and dine out by the Ho Bo Woods 'morrow evenin'."

"Ho Bo Woods," Too-Fat was laughing. "Is that who we're fighting, Sarge, hobo commies?"

"You'll see for yourself, Schwartzy. You'll soon be gettin' the picture."

Too-Fat smiled. "Here we go, in the flower of our youth, out to search for the dreaded insurgents."

"I just hope it's a place what gets us some war," grumped

Red Dog. "Got to stop all the dang yak and find us a little dang war. Ain't 'at right, Canny?"

"Well," said Canny, squinting warily toward the darkening forest, "can't say I got any big fat hard-on to hurry out there myself."

"Don't see why we do all this trainin' stuff back here," said Red Dog. "'Cause when you get out there, it ain't the same. Ain't nothin' the same."

"How many times you been out there?" asked Canny.

"None, acehole. But you know it ain't the same."

"First booby trap you hit, you'll be long gone," said Canny.

"Bet I last longer'n you do."

"Sure, 'cause you'll be back in the barracks watchin' the tube, watchin' *I Love Lucy.*"

"Maybe," said Red Dog, slapping his M-60, "I'll just go on out yonder right now and get the job done. Save yaw the trouble."

"You ain' got live rounds in there now?" asked Breeze.

"Man, I'll tell you, there'd be some dead peckerwoods out there if I had live rounds," said Red Dog, swaggering around, swinging his gun toward the sky as though ready to drop a few birds. "You can bet yer booties on that."

"And over that way's what we call the Iron Triangle," Breeze hummed on. "Oh, yeah, we gonna have some nice times in there."

"My servicemember hurts," said Too-Fat, staring toward the shadowy trees.

I was checking it all out on the little compass that hung from my neck. Harry, looking keen to get going, was doing the same with his.

Rodeliano, Breeze's shadow, had stood by rather stiffly, smoking, saying little as he stared through the wire, concern creasing his face, which seemed to have grown thinner each day and in the last five minutes. His back seemed a little more hunched, as though the weight of command as we neared combat was bending our lieutenant steadily earthward.

"Sergeant Carson," he said, "if we do get hit tomorrow—get contact—there is that possibility—a word to the men on how best to react—you know—when that first shot is fired—"

"Men," said Breeze, "best reaction is to fire *back.*"

"But if we should, say, get ambushed," pressed Rodeliano, unfolding his map, tracing the route of the operation, "the men should know, you know, what it's like—what the odds are—what the enemy is likely to—most likely to—"

"Well, it is jus' like an atheist all his life, when the ground start shakin', he gonna look up to the sky," said the black sergeant, kneeling, drawing his own battle map in the dirt with a stick. "Serusly now, if you survive the first thirty seconds of a bushwhack, my computer calcalations say you got it made. That's in your plain, everyday, day bushwhack. Thirty seconds—the main killin' time. And then Charlie will probably *di di* less'n he got you in a tight—sewed up in a real bad place, and he be out to make a point, which sometime he do."

"Thirty seconds," guffawed Red Dog. "Hell, back home I pee longer'n 'at."

"Well, you in Vietnam now, mister," said Breeze. "Don't do no good to sing *Dixie* in Vietnam. Irregardless, once we get to operatin' down at the platoon level out in that bush, we gonna do jus' fine. Gonna move like smoke. Surprise and concealment, all that good junk. Only time we walks trails is at night, when we be ordered to go in and help somebody caught in the *deep* shit. Elsewise, we use the bush. Keep our ass in the grass. You got to know Charlie is waiting for us on the trails. We got to *hear* Charlie first. Little birds and monkeys get real quiet. But when we walk the bush, *we* be the hunters. We won't stay nowhere long. Don't wanna sit in no bull's-eyes. We pick it up and move it around, right, Harry?"

"Right, Cool," said Harry, totally absorbed, the good reporter in him missing none of the expert testimony.

"We move it around, here, there. Don't want Charlie zingin' us no big stuff. Mortars ain' no big sweat though, men, 'cause we'll set up in the thick stuff with overhead cover, and we know how to dig in mighty fine, right, grunts?"

"Mighty fine," said Harry.

"Oh, yeah," went on Breeze. "Best hunter wins. Even their scouts up in the trees won't see the silent cats of First Platoon glidin' along. 'Cause we *bad*. I just wish it was us, the platoon goin' out tomorrow 'stead of the whole big-ass battalion. Less chance to fuck up."

"I don't think anybody should go out there," Roland blurted. "Us skulking after them, them skulking after us. I don't care how much propaganda I hear, I'm not shooting anybody."

"Sure, man," said the Breeze soothingly. "Nobody gonna hit you on the head and make you pull no trigger. But what people don't know is, you don' have to feel too terrible bad doin' it to a man who's tryin' to do it to you first. Out there, the ones you ding must not be real people to you. But then, they are dudes tryin' to kill you. Tryin' to *kill* you, man. You musn't feel prayerful about it. You mustn't feel your soul is in damnation. Best thing in the bush, man, is jus' not get froze up with that kind of thinkin'."

"Well, I'm not shooting anybody," insisted Roland. "I mean them no harm, and I'm sure they mean me no harm."

"You don't need to shoot anybody," Harry said, patting Roland's shoulder. "They've probably laughed themselves bonkers just listening to you."

That night in Third Squad's tent, I wished somebody would laugh a little. Men sat and knelt and squatted around, quietly checking weapons, doing last things with equipment in the dim, yellowish glow.

Kelly, the boy medic, came around, handing out malaria pills. Then Lieutenant Rodeliano came in for the last inspection looking like he was point man in a funeral, with Cool Breeze behind him.

"Squad, ten-shun. Stand at ease."

There wasn't much ease either as Rodeliano worried all over us. He didn't want any bang-bang cities out there. He didn't want—and emphasized that Captain Wilson didn't want and Colonel Gurgles didn't want—us to think of this as some wild, nervous, crazy adventure out there. He didn't want any hot-dogging or messing up or lame-braining out there. He really didn't. And the captain didn't, and the colonel didn't. He wanted total professionality, well-programmed precision.

"Isn't that right, Sergeant Carson?"

"Be cool," said the Breeze, watching a mosquito float sluggishly in front of his face.

"And don't get all upset if you get a sighting and don't get permission to fire," said Rodeliano. "This is a strange war, and we can't go out there expecting to shoot everything on sight. Often our mere presence will be enough to do the job."

"Whadda fuck you talkin' about, Lootenant?" asked Red Dog.

"Fire discipline. Isn't that right, Sergeant Carson."

"Damn straight, Lieutenant. Be nice to go out there and kill everything in the forest, but we ain' gotta do it. Listen, when you go out there, do the same thing I been—the lieutenant and me been—tellin' you. Be cool, don't get excited, don't lose control, and we'll have us a very enjoyable, well-programmed time out there."

"Aw, fuck," groused Red Dog, slapping on mosquito repellent after our platoon leaders had left. "Don't do this. Don't do that. Whadda fuck we fightin' for?"

"Pussy," said Canny. "Hey, Skin, tell ol' Dog about 'at good car-wash boom-boom we got outside camp this morning."

"She was really sumpin'," said Skinny Lenny, Adam's apple bobbing, long neck craning. "I swear to gosh, after two Coca-Colas, she was really gettin' into it. Got out right in front of us and started flippin' around and *whoooo*. Suzie Nguyen's her name. I don't know what her real name was. Suzie, I guess. Or Miss Nguyen. Who cares. Numba waann. I'm in luuv."

"I'm in luuv, too," said Canny. "Oink, oink."

"Boo sheet," said Red Dog. "Y'all didn't get no real pussy."

"Hell, we didn't," said Canny, raising his right hand into the swearing position. "Ask ol' Mike. You can't beat 'at ol' car-wash boom-boom, can you, Mike?"

I laughed and pulled from my wallet a picture of Charlotte, overflowing a bikini.

"No car wash for me, pal."

"*Yahooooo!*" Red Dog went mad. "*Yahooooo!* Yow! Yow! Yow! Cranks my tractor! No wonder you din' wanna come to no Nam. No wonder. No wonder. Can I borrow this for tonight? Can I keep this? *Yahoooooo!*"

"Here comes the rain," Harry said.

It came twenty seconds later and seemed about to blow Bad Company away. Tents billowed, flapped, and sagged from the drumbeat of wind and water. Lightning forked around us. The lights went off in the tent.

"*Turn on the lights!*" Harry yelled. Instantly, the lights flashed back on.

"Thank you," Harry said.

But soon the tent went dark again.

"*Turn on the fucking lights!*" Harry yelled again.

It took longer this time, but they popped back on.

"Thank you."

Red Dog thought Harry's command of the elements was marvelous.

"Sheet, troops. With old Hare guidin' us, we ain't got nothin' to worry 'bout out 'ere. Right, Hare?"

"Right as rain, Dog."

Too-Fat leaned over his belly and sagely advised Red Dog, "Well, if that lightning starts crackin' around you, just get away from your metal."

"Whaddaya mean, my metal—my *weapon*?"

"Get on away from it. You're no good to yourself dead, man."

"Why come I should? Soldier don't get away from his weapon. Whoever heard of a soldier gettin' away from his weapon? Suppose one of them li'l VCs come around while I'm away from my weapon?"

Over in a corner, Roland lay on his cot staring at the tent top, sagging from the weight of collected water. He had been there all evening, saying nothing, his gear in disarray around him, and finally Harry went over and got him organized.

Next to him, Kelly, not getting any younger, sat steadily, avidly writing letters back home. About tomorrow's big adventure, I guessed. Whistling through the gap in his teeth, he would finish one page and start another. Even when the lights went out for good, he flicked on his flashlight and went on writing to Mississippi.

Much later, I'm thrashing around on my cot, listening to the bumps in the night *out there*. Something dreadful and fundamental is finally seeping through my mental mummy wrappings. It's really going to happen. *They* have put me in the position to go out there and *kill* actual people. People out there are waiting to *kill* me. That is too strange. That is fantastic.

I'm feeling dank inside. Outside, too, this odd, oily, deep-shit sweat. Maybe Sheridan was right. I feel my legs twitching, practicing the Hail Mary retreat. He died with his boots on and never got out of his cot. They're all doing better than me, even Roland. At least he's unconscious. They're all sleeping. Except someone down at the end. I see the cigarette moving. Soon, even his light goes out.

I lay there, staring up through the mosquito netting, smelling rain, boots, gun oil, wet canvas, mildew—mostly myself. Hearing the rain come softly tapping across the tent, men grunting and tossing, farting and sleep-mumbling, a generator humming somewhere . . . the rain seeming to stop, then the tapping again. Glancing over at Harry, snoring Harry. What was he afraid of? I had asked him earlier. "What am I afraid of?" he said slowly. "Nothin'." He had laughed. We all had laughed.

Now I lay me down to sleep, I pray the Lord my soul. . . .

And still can't sleep. Once Roland wakes up yelling, "Get these poison lizards off me!" and throws a boot into the side of the tent. Didn't know he had that much violence in him.

It's 2 a.m., and I'm still running, wrestling my demon cot, attacking the night . . . summoning up visions of Char again . . . bikini goddess, proud-tailed, pompous-breasted, striding golden through the grossness, flying her bod like a flag, like a victory banner flapping in the faces of merely mortal women . . . now she's sitting at the edge of the banging surf, digging her heels into the wet, soft sand . . . moving those electric hips, that rambunctious rear, those dancer's legs in the old thrilling rhythm . . . Lord, she's making it with the sea, big Neptune himself . . . now she's . . . I wish she would write more . . . what's she doing in wacko California anyway? Why doesn't she write more?

BAROOOM! BAROOOM! A battery of 175s, ours, H & I— harassing and interdicting—distributing steel into the wild black out there . . . giant members, long as telephone poles, lining up to service my sea goddess . . . and I'm flinching with every eruption now, every roaring ejaculation ("Oh, fight it, men, put it down, defeat it, save your energy for the battlefield. That's an order! I'm not being facetious, har. . . .").

Fading again . . . remembering my first act of war, the time I chased down and gave the dastardly coward, Wellsby Aimswood III, known as Speedie, his just deserts, potted him in the ass with a BB gun after he shot Aunt Tettie in the eye with a rubber arrow. I was her avenging hero, Little Mike, sharpshooter, driving off the bad kid . . . search and destroy. . . .

Reaching down under the cot, fingers groping around. My boots are still there, in the same place. My rifle and pack are still there; they have not moved. And I'm still here, in this place. It's really going to happen. Almost three now. It keeps raining, lightly drumming. The artillery rumblethumps on for a while, then ceases. Harry, probably dreaming of charging up a mountain with a bayonet between his teeth, finally shuts his teeth and stops snoring. Then just the rain.

10

Curse of the Born Loser

"Oh, I may hurt and I may cry,
But I know damn well I won't die,
'Cause Bravo leads the way. . ."

Until now, it had all been play war. Our green young men would run down the rain-pooled road toward chow, and Breeze would bark things like, "Hey, you animals, let me hear you roar!" And we would go, "ROWWR!"

"Hey, you animals, do you love your jobs?"

"YES, WE LOVE OUR JOBS!"

"Are we bad?"

"We BAD, we BAD, we BAD. . . ."

But there was little roaring on this morning by The Bad Ones. Very early, before Harry stirred, I numbly pawed for my boots ("the durable jungle boot with the deep mud cleats and the spike retarding sole, gentlemen. . . ."), which had not moved. And then I began the long climb upward, heavily, mechanically, grudgingly, left foot, right foot, staggering from my coffin to face this day.

At 0500 hours, after a ritual nauseous breakfast—hasty, gummy swallows in the dark—"What was that stuff?"—we came slowly out of our tents, filled up several canteens each, loaded up with C-rations, scooped up extra ammo from boxes broken open in a clearing, clipped on fragmentation and smoke grenades, packed on mortar tubes and shells and extra grenade launchers, loaded ourselves with radios, signal mirrors, handguns for shooting star clusters, starlight scopes for seeing at night, a strobe light for signaling at night, and looped on extra bandoliers of ammo for the M-60s.

Breeze thought we were traveling about three times too heavy for our initial mission, which was to simply tromp around for a few days in an area where the enemy hung out and see what we could stir up. But Colonel Gurgles thought it would be nice to put "the fear of God in Charlie first time out of the blocks, if he's got the balls to stand up and face us," as well as "being prepared for any and all contingencies."

Gleaming with bandoliers, Red Dog looked like a walking ammo dump. He cradled his machine gun in his arms like a bear rifle, plopped on his helmet at an angle so that it nearly covered one eye, glared out of his other eye with great menace, staggered a few steps forward, and announced himself ready for the hunt.

"How you gone move under that mountain o' shit, peckernose?" Canny wanted to know.

"My plan is them VC peckernoses doin' the movin' while *I'm* doin' the shootin'," replied Red Dog, scowling.

It was one of the few notes of Bad Company bravado sounded as we prepared to see how bad we really were.

Of course, there was Harry. He had gotten up humming and whistling, gobbled down bacon lumps and grease, swigged coffee, gone back for seconds, whipped his gear into shape like the happy housewife preparing to go to market, whistled on over to Roland to get him going, and generally rub-a-dub-dubbed through the squad trying to scrub our dreads away.

As The Bad Ones slowly formed into platoons, The Smoker came plunging through, looking us over, gazing deep into the death masks of Roland and Ching-Ching, who were obviously having a hard time getting going, maybe as hard as me.

"What's wrong with these troops, Sergeant Carson? Some of

your people look a little sick. Look at Private Ching there. Is he gonna faint out on us? Hell, I'm counting on him to give us timely tips on how to fight his fellow gooks. And what's with Roland there? Looks like he done been smoked and stepped on. Like his asshole done shrunk up inside his navel. Or maybe he's gonna have a baby. Okay, girls, let's vote on it, who don't want to die today?"

Rodeliano, who had been rather nervously supervising the distribution of ammo, went over for perhaps the fifth time to consult with Captain Billy Wilson, and Breeze moved among us, talking easily and checking our gear and our pulse.

"We got to drive on now. We got to keep that happy smile upon our face. . . ."

"Tell us the scoop—" Harry said, smiling, "how we're going to bong the Cong."

"Absolutely. Listen here, grunts. In this American Army, we don't run and we don't quit. We win. Leastwise, that's what I run across, and I run across some of it."

"That's the scoop," Harry said. He smacked me on the butt and gave me that fire-engine grin.

At 0600 hours, in a light rain, Captain Billy Wilson shouted the order: "Right about, face!" Then: "Move out in a column of fours."

A short time later, the platoons of Bravo, leading the battalion, went out in three horseshoe formations from the camp, slopping through the rain-sodden red earth of Vietnam. Ours was the point platoon, and much of the time, Cool Breeze Carson was in front of it all.

"Here it starts, grunts," he called, popping a clip into his M-16.

A few times, The Smoker came tromping up. "Awright, awright, get that rifle off your shoulder!" he bellowed at Roland from behind. "And screw that steel pot down on your marijuana head, shitsnapper."

"What you think you got there, a bag of oranges?" he yelled at Ching-Ching, who was carrying extra ammo in one hand in a paper sack. "How you gonna shoot your fellow gooks like that? Yew people . . . don't *yeww* ignorant people realize *yeww* are now in a combat situation?"

Cool Breeze moved the platoon along smoothly, but behind us, the parade of miserable people into the badlands was in danger of disintegrating. The Always First Battalion was marching to war—crash, bam, the Riverdale Boys Band—surprising no one and concealing nothing. Breeze looked toward the rear and shook his head, "Lawdy, lawdy."

I looked back at Schwartz and was amazed to see that he was carrying to war, of all things, a covered bird cage. A soldier going home had given him a homing pigeon, and at the last minute, Too-Fat had talked Breeze into letting him carry the bird into the boonies.

"Secret weapon, Sarge. You never know, we might be surrounded somewhere without a radio. And this baby, Red Eagle, could be our last link with the outside world. Let me test it out, Sarge. You never know, Sarge."

"But the bird ain' red."

Too-Fat kept peeking at the pigeon under the cover, telling it everything was fine and he was sorry if he was jarring it, or if the weather was too muggy, or if the bad language was disturbing it, but that things would get better.

The sun nudged through the clouds, and things got hotter and worse. Harry's thermometer said 105.

"But it can't be that hot," gasped Skinny Lenny, gurgling water from his canteen.

Urging us onward, from two thousand feet up in his command-and-control helicopter, was Colonel Gurgles. But down on the ground, the tactical sweep had become a mad march that kept bunching up too much or straggling out too much and finally just buggered to a halt.

"It's just too damn sloppy," snapped a voice hurrying past. There went Major Sheridan, sweat rolling down his face. Bad News Benson and a troop packing a radio trotted at his heels. According to Bad News, Watson had been determined to go with the troops on the ground rather than remain in battalion rear. But things weren't going right. His radioman was having a time relaying the deluge of messages and instructions raining down from Gurgles in the clouds. I saw the major consulting with Billy Wilson and Rodeliano and then go up to talk to Breeze. He was imparting the colonel's latest advice. They were both laughing.

Commands flowed, and we heaved forward again. Next to me, Kelly grimaced. He took out his false tooth and slipped it into a little box in his pocket. "It sorta makes my head hurt when I walk," he said. I asked him who he was writing all those letters to last night. "Oh," he said softly, grinning, "I got me a girl-friend kinna. . . ."

All around came the crunching of boots, the tapping of rifle slings, the bumps and rattles of equipment, young men carrying firepower like most people carried pocket change, and every step loaded with strange menace. And after a while, too, there was this growing feeling of camaraderie and even collective power, of many armed men moving together like a human battleship, ever deeper into mystery.

It went on for hours. Bent under the big packs, guns ready, we watched for some sign of what was called the enemy, and kept going through blistering-hot, thorny, thick-brushed, broken-treed flatlands. It rained hard on and off, and between gully washers, the sun switched on fiercely. Like marching through tunnels of fire and water: Everything steamed, my saliva thickened, my uniform grew wet and heavy. I raked my fingernails across sudden skin rashes, and kept knocking off little stinging things, blood-gorged mosquitos and slow fat flies that stuck in my sweat. ("*. . . and a word about the environment, gentlemen. When the beast is not after you, beware of the ubiquitous*

*malaria, which we have in several deadly flavors over here. Also,
the debilitating cholera, the unpleasant plague, the nasty, cruddy
jungle rot, the un-American fevers and shits. You sporting gentlemen will notice as you prance about in the streams and paddies
that your feet will tend to crack and swell and rot. As you cavort
through the bush, you may feel itching and bleeding, blistering
and festering among your bodily parts, gentlemen of the jungle,
strange fungal cysts popping out all over your soft skin, even
your defenseless genitalia. You will be attacked by all sorts of
unclean flying, crawling, hopping, biting, stinging, sucking
things . . . because the jungle sucks, gentlemen, your blood and
your lives. . . ."*)

Ahead, a soldier screamed. As he brushed under a tree, a
column of ants had attacked down his shirt, blowing up his neck
so big with red welts that a dust-off (medical evacuation
chopper) had to fly in and lift him and several other grunts,
sagging from the heat, back to Cu Chi.

Red Dog, staggering under his load, looked a little less
ferocious, too. "I'm tired," he said, spitting a blob of tobacco
juice, "but I'll make it, 'cause I'm kickin' ass and takin' names
out here and that's it."

But finally, reluctantly, he had to redistribute some of his load
and let Canny carry his twenty-three-pound machine gun for a
while. " 'At's all right, I'll hep you," Canny said, grinning slyly.
"Just lean on me, Dog."

"The worst thing is we ain't got attacked yet," said Red Dog.
"I'm really pissed about 'at."

Harry looked over at me, winked, and bounced forward. Too-
Fat got Kelly to carry his bird for a while. Roland and Ching-
Ching exchanged glazed looks, gulped water, and hobbled on.
Our colonel, flying buzzy little circles high above, kept urging
us ever forward. He was impatient for contact with the foe.
Where was the foe? Why wouldn't the foe come out and swap
a little firepower? There were supposed to be at least five
hundred of the foe, main force and local guerilla types, operat-

ing on the very ground on which we were walking. They were clearly marked with red grease pencil on the plastic stretched across the colonel's big map. Clearly. But the raggedy-ass foe wouldn't come out and face the wrath of the Always First. We saw plenty of tunnels, some fresh, many old and crumbled, thrice destroyed, but no foe.

Following the ant crisis came the crisis of Skinny Lenny. His long body suddenly sank from view as he dropped his rifle, grabbed wildly at blades of elephant grass, and dangled over eighteen-inch bamboo spikes dipped in animal dung. It was a not-totally-defanged punji pit, and we pulled Skinny up before he got pricked. Breeze went back and dropped a grenade into the pit.

Gurgles, aloft, wanted to know if we had yet made contact with the foe. After more instructions from the colonel, we continued the march, boot following boot, walking in each other's footsteps as much as possible to avoid mines, the marching becoming hypnotic . . . wading through terrain now as sloppy as a bayou . . . ankles twisting, staggering, losing our footing . . . wobbling from fatigue . . . radiomen with their heavy equipment going down and being helped up . . . and now we're out into another stretch of the sharp-edged, fifteen-foot-high, mean-green elephant grass, wall-to-wall razor blades.

There's no band, but Breeze is moving to his own drum, swinging those arms. One minute he's snapping, "Okay, move those feet, step along, tighten it up." The next, he's laughing, "Hot damn, here we go, hot, hot, hot. . . ."

He's the only one talking now. Our breath is for breathing. Breeze keeps cheering us on.

"We're The Bad Ones," he chants through rivulets of sweat, "baddest of the bad . . . puff . . . 'cause we're rompin', stompin', ass-kickin' grunts . . . puff . . . and grunts don't whine . . . puff . . . grunts don't boohoo . . . puff . . . grunts don't even grunt . . . puff, puff . . . come on back there, you stragglers, straighten it up . . . come on, you people . . . drive on, drive on. . . ."

Skinny Lenny, our long tall Sally from South Carolina, begins to sag, begins to weave, reels on rubber legs out to the side as the column moves on past.

"Doc, get him! Need some help, Doc!"

"Doc! Doc!"

"Right here!" yells Kelly.

Harry is already back there, dousing Skinny with water. He takes his weapon and carries it for him. Skinny doggedly tries to reclaim his rifle, insists on carrying it, but his eyes roll and he starts to stagger again. Breeze hurries back, takes his rucksack, and slings it over one shoulder. Others, carrying the heavy stuff, swap loads. I'm shifting my pack, left shoulder, right shoulder. . . .

Breeze swings by me. "How you feelin', Jack?"

He calls me Jack. "Okay, Sarge."

"Keep those feet movin'," he shouts to the rest, "straight on. Don't stop. Drive on, you cheerful grunts, drive on."

"How can you carry all that, Sarge?" gasps Ching-Ching.

"Just carry it," drawls Breeze. "Have to break your mind in. Hey, after awhile it begins to feel good."

And our colonel buzzes around and around above us like a mad bee in search of combat honey.

But it was all tension and bull labor, no great battles. Finally, for me, it wasn't even tension, just weariness. Even Lieutenant Rodeliano, the business grad, cum laude, who had surrendered management of his business to the cotton-field sergeant, ceased worrying what-if about hordes of wild-eyed Viet Cong overrunning us and just dragged on after Breeze with the rest of the troops. On through the bush to the next mud wallow, squishing along, dripping along. It's raining again.

During a break, I felt so boiled out, so becalmed, and so silly over the fear of the morning, that I walked—boldly strode, really—right out into a clearing and stepped up on a little rise so that I could see things better. Sometimes I did things like that. My purpose was to urinate. Everyone was down in the grass behind me, and I stood out there, the lone representative of the American Way, doing my business and daring the entire VC military might, wherever it was, to try and stop me. It was like times back at the old Bitter Inn, and I thought of this as a defiant, even courageous, act and wished Char was present to witness this radical event, urinating not only on war but on fear. Staring at a treeline that offered fine cover for a regiment of snipers, I gave a little shrug—screw it—and felt right on top of things.

"I found my thrill . . . on old Cu Chi Hill," a voice crooned behind me.

"Hey, Jack," Cool Breeze called softly, "you really oughtn't to be dancin' around out there."

"How's it going, Sarge?"

"Just gruntin' along," sighed Breeze, "bitin' bullets and walkin' on water."

Squatting shirtless in his flak jacket, a towel wrapped around his neck, his eyes cocked toward the treeline, he said, "Jack, you know I been here before. I had a buddy killed right over there. Right *there*. He wasn't 'fraid of nothin'. I watched him one day chase a VC down the rice paddies. Just chased him down. Wore his butt out. And then he got killed. He was a good man. A good man but a sorry soldier. . . ."

"Are you trying to tell me something, Sarge?"

"How'd you guess? Tryin' to tell you that out here you gotta be better'n good. You got to be near 'bout purr-fect. And then you're all the way up to fifty-fifty."

"Well, we've certainly been perfect today."

Breeze laughed. His eyes followed the flight of the sun through the heavy clouds, nosediving toward the trees. "Stop soon," he said.

"When?"

"Depend on the colonel."

"Speaking of perfection, Sarge. Does he know what he's doing?"

Breeze's big white teeth gleamed. He poured some water on his towel, lifted it high, wrung it out, and let the drops roll down his face.

"Well," he said, "you got to do what the heavies say. That's discipline. That's part of it. Man say boogie, we got to boogie."

"Yeah, but does he know what he's doing?"

Breeze chuckled. He began to laugh until his big shoulders shook. "You can't jive the troops, can you? They'll smell it that quick. You got to lead from the front. You got to have gen-u-wine sincerity out here."

We got moving again and humped on till we came to another stretch of elephant grass mixed with big swaths of burnt black grass. Here, out in the wide-open, the order came down from Gurgles to dig in for the night. We heaved down packs and weapons, stripped off our blouses, drank deep from warm canteens, got out entrenching tools for digging foxholes and filling sandbags, sat down, sprawled down, laughed, cussed.

"Is this piece of shit-ground what we been marchin' to conquer all day?" grumbled Red Dog.

"That's war," kidded Harry, rummaging through his pack. He had a large rip in his trousers through which half a leg protruded.

"I suggest you red-blooded American boys use your bug juice tonight," hollered Captain Wilson, "because we're surrounded by stagnant waters."

"I hope that's all we're surrounded by," said Roland weakly, looking even more exhausted than he sounded.

"It's snakes I'm worried about," said Ching-Ching, "those terrible kraits." He had crawled into a patch of grass, seeking rest.

"I got a hunnert rounds right here 'at says ain't no krait gone bite my butt," announced Red Dog.

"This man's got a bad rash, a dripping rash," said Kelly, bending over Canny. "Is that an infection there?"

"Naw, just pus."

"Anybody else got blisters while I got this stuff out?" called Kelly.

"Let him check your feet," Harry yelled at Roland and Ching-Ching. "Go ahead and let him check your feet. Hey, Doc, check their feet."

"How're you feelin', Skin?" asked Red Dog. "You okay now?"

"Ohhh, me," moaned Skinny. "I ate them beans again. Beans with apple jelly. I guess that's what it was."

"You're sick, man," said Harry.

"Apple jelly? He ate beans with his apple jelly?" Ching-Ching shook his head. "I prefer the baloney, peanut butter, and banana sandwich myself. Something you have to taste to believe."

"You're all sick," said Harry. "Okay, let's dig."

"I don't trust anybody that eats pork and beans and jelly," said Too-Fat, petting his white pigeon, Red Eagle.

"Don't be funny," said Skinny. "There weren't no pork in there. Ohh, I got to get medevacced out of here. Ohh, I'm hurtin' bad. I need emergency leave. I know they just gonna let me expire. I know they just gonna forget me and leave me behind the lines and let me die . . . a slow, cruel death."

"Fuck that shit," said Red Dog. "You goin', I'm goin'."

"If you're going, I'm going," said Too-Fat. "I think Eagle's not feeling too well."

"Fuck that," said Harry. "Hey, get those holes finished. Get those bags filled."

"Be compassionate, man," said Too-Fat.

"I *am* compassionate," said Harry.

"Where is all them field women I heard about?" yelled Canny. "Where's all 'at good field pussy?"

"You don't want any of those *field* women," warned Harry. "Stay away from those *field* women."

"After eight beers, who cares?"

"Your pecker cares," said Harry, "when it splits down the center."

"Have a lemon drop."

"Thanks."

"Are there any swamp women around?" asked Canny. "Has anybody seen any of those *beeyooootiful* swamp women?"

"Where's 'at pitcher, Mike?" Red Dog wanted to know. "I got to see that pitcher again. Reminds me of my recruiter. Tits way out to here. Blond hair. Legs ten feet long up to her ass. She was female. She wasn't too dumb either. Fuck. I was gone be a Marine, and she talked me inna this dumb shit."

"How long we staying out here, Harry?" asked Ching-Ching.

"Saturday, I think."

"Man, we're going to be some stinky boys come Saturday."

"Hey, Harry," called Canny, "what's the password tonight?"

"Halt, dimbulb, or I'll blow you away."

"That usually works."

It had turned into just another field problem. Enemy territory was just territory. I saw Major Sheridan puffing by like a sunburnt blowfish, Bad News trudging at his heels. Sheridan was rendez-vousing with Gurgles, whose helicopter was settling to earth now out in the grass. One of the big Chinook choppers rattled over, dangling a portable water tank under its belly, and men hurried with their canteens through the bright, waving grass toward it, bunching up nicely out in the open for anyone who might wish to blow them up. Another of the Chinooks thudded down, hauling Turnip Green's field kitchen. There was to be hot chow in the boonies tonight, by gosh, in celebration of something.

Now Smoker came blowing our way, calling for "volunteers" to dig the company latrine ditch. Looking for an ace shit detail, he jabbed his finger at Roland, Ching-Ching, and me, as well as a new sergeant named Horny Wheeler to oversee us. Harry had gone off with Rodeliano to the briefing for the night ambushes.

Cool Breeze, setting up the platoon's defensive position facing a thick line of nipa palms, looked up at the sky and told The Smoker, "Bad illumn tonight. A real dark night." Then he started demonstrating the art of digging to some fagged-out greenies. Humming, with sweat shining on the big humps of muscles in his back and shoulders, he was a digging machine.

We walked on with The Smoker as he and Horny Wheeler debated where to dig the latrine.

"Oh, Serrr-geant," called Too-Fat as we passed, "any important messages for the Eagle to carry back to camp?"

"Gonna eat that turdbird you don't get rid of it," hooted The Smoker over his shoulder.

"Don't worry, fella," cooed Too-Fat to the pigeon, "I'll protect you."

About five hundred meters out, well beyond our perimeter, there sounded artillery bursts. Some of us jumped a little, then relaxed. It was only our stuff back at Cu Chi, zeroing in around the battalion in case the VC hit during the night.

"Well, Sergeant," Wheeler was explaining to The Smoker, "we got swamp over here and swamp over there. And the brush over there is just too fuckin' thick for a decent shit hole. Nobody's gonna be goin' through there. We got troops all the way around here. There just ain't no place to dig it. Unless you want to dig up to your ankles in mud. Ain't no place to dig it."

"Are you suggesting we all just crap in our pants, Sergeant?" countered The Smoker as the great debate went on.

"Well, only place is about three hundred yards down there. Who's gonna walk three hundred yards at night? Nobody's gonna use the damn thing anyway. Probably get snakebit anyway. Frankly, I've dug six or seven of these things, and nobody ever uses them. Course, I'll dig it anyway just to be SOP. If you insist. Frankly, I prefer cattholes."

The rain was starting again, and Ching-Ching, perhaps the most bedraggled-looking soldier in the history of the U.S. Army, sighed at the heavens and said, "I don't care how blue the sky is, it always rains on me wherever I go."

Though no one has ever returned from the dead to verify it, the old saying holds that you never hear the one that gets you. I heard this one. It came rushing downward through the air like a locomotive sliding into a station with its brakes on, and my head seemed already down and touching the ground before the explosion. There was this bursting, shocking sensation all around, and I was rolling in a great, smacking wave of sound and smoke. And then it went over me.

The next thing I saw was white knuckles clutching blades of grass, holding on like a man going overboard. A voice to my left was saying, "What the hell, what the hell"—and then the voice was furious, unbelieving—"that was one of *ours!*"

There was another explosion farther away, and then another, and I heard the same voice—it was The Smoker—shouting, "TELL THAT GODDAMNED ARTILLERY TO CEASE!"

I looked up and saw the smoke from the first explosion: a rising black umbrella over where we had just walked. All around, men were yelling, "Medic! Medic!" And at the same time, there came screams, ungodly screams.

I rolled over and saw Roland stretched out flat in the grass. "Are you hit?"

He just lay there, rigidly flat, eyeballs bulging, his dimpled face dead-meat white—even his gums had turned white. I got to my knees and bent over him and saw his temples throbbing. Then his eyes rolled. He wasn't dead—or even hit—just close to concrete. Beside him, Ching-Ching sat up in a blinking daze, his newly broken glasses hanging off one ear, "Chrize, oh, Chrize. . . ."

My legs got me up somehow, seeming to think on their own, moving me toward the smoke, where I stepped on something, something of flesh. It was an arm from the elbow down, a pale hand making a fist.

The armless man lay in the dirt and smoke. It was our pigeon soldier, Too-Fat. His eyes and mouth were wide open, as though he had died shouting. I saw the cage twisted in the grass, but the pigeon was gone.

Not far away, spread-eagled near my own foxhole, was The Great Soldier: Cool Breeze Carson lay on his back on a hump of red earth, the loser of his head. Where his left shoulder and arm had been, there were just bloody rags of cloth and flesh, little strings of meat and stuff hanging out.

In the next minutes, Kelly and the other medics worked furiously in the blood and howls. Captain Billy Wilson and The Smoker rushed around shouting orders. Rodeliano kept telling us we ought to find our sergeant's head. Harry picked up Schwartz's arm and placed it across his chest. I couldn't find the pigeon. Five men worked with morphine and bandages over a screaming soldier whose leg was half severed at the knee, the foot still doing a little dance in the boot.

We kept beating away huge ants, big black ones and bigger red ones. Insects crawled and hopped all over a helmet spattered with blood and wet meat. Scrawled across the front were the words "Big Zapper"—across the side, "329-to-go." Big Zapper was going home early, the parts of him we could police up and collect in a poncho anyway, which wasn't too much and maybe not all his.

On seeing Cool Breeze, Roland—who had been quiet for hours and now looked as though he had washed his fatigues in a bucket of guts—exploded in sobs, "Where is that major? I want Major Sheridan. I want that major to come here and view this and lecture me on the great learning experience of war. I want him to explain to me the profound meaning of this. Where is the President of the United States? I want the President of the United States to stand here and view this and—"

"Aw, shad the fuck up!" roared The Smoker. "Shad that garbage up and find that troop's head!"

Staring at the bugs swarming into Breeze's oozing neck, Roland started vomiting.

Kelly, bloody to his elbows, not getting any younger, reported to Wilson on the dead and wounded. There were eight dead in Bravo—killed in action, as they say—six more that could go either way, and ten others with lesser wounds. It was our own Cu Chi artillery, firing short, a small technological, probably perfectly explainable, fuck-up.

"Oh, what a thing to happen," Ching-Ching said over and over, fighting back tears. "Oh, what a thing to happen."

I just stood there, swallowing hard, eyes blinking, head shaking, "Boy, that was really . . . that was really. . . ."

Rodeliano bent over, looking down unbelievingly at Breeze. "Some of these men had wives and kids," he mumbled to Wilson.

"Sergeant Carson was a good man, Cap'n," The Smoker said to Wilson, "and a good damn soldier."

"The best," Billy Wilson replied softly, "the very best."

A little later, four men rushed over, picked up Breeze's body by his two legs and one arm, and dropped him bumping onto a stretcher.

"Hey, motherfucks, you don't have to treat him like that!" Harry yelled. "That's no damn sandbag you're throwing around there!"

"You think he *felt* that?" one of the soldiers muttered. "You wanna us stand around and cry? You wanna play some music?"

So now The Bad Ones had reached the strange Vietnam War, down and dirty. I never did find out about Schwartzy's pigeon. But I guess it got the message. It was never seen again, not a feather.

11

In the Jungle in the Dark

"Jumpfrog: This is Eagle Six. Have you recovered that man's missing member yet? Over."

"Negative, Six. Still unable comply on that. It's pretty dark out here. Over."

"Urnghk—Say again. I want that man's member located. Are you reading me? Over."

"Roger. But there's the possibility that the missing . . . uh . . . member is no more. But will press the search at first light. Over."

"Urge you definitely do that, Frog. Imperative I hear from you on that. Over and out."

Colonel Gurgles, spending his night back at Cu Chi, was in a terrible stew—his first combat mission turned inglorious because of self-inflicted wounds. All evening, Bravo's radios smoked with messages from The Eagle. Not a promising start for the men of the Always First, a poor team effort, chided The Eagle as we groped in darkness for some remnant of Cool Breeze Carson's head.

"Jeez Chrize," said Ching-Ching, down on his hands and knees, feeling around in the grass. "If the mighty Breeze couldn't make it, what chance do we got?"

"Our only hope is them VCs is more screwed up than we are," grunted Canny Peacock, who was crawling and cussing beside him. "Let's just call it a draw and go home."

"We have been shot to pieces," lamented Roland on his knees. "We have seen lives taken, and nobody has shot at us but us."

"Hide that butt!" Harry yelled at someone smoking in the grass. "Put a poncho over it before you light that fucking cigarette!"

The darker it got, the more jittery the battalion got. Every so often, a section of our loosely positioned perimeter would unloose a little orgasm of small-arms fire. Each time a few rounds would pop off, Eagle would be on the radio inquiring whether we had yet begun to annihilate Victor Charlie. "Sorry we keeping you awake," Billy Wilson would reply. "Buncha shadows, noises out there, but no confirmed Victor Charlie. Guess the men are a little spooked."

We were spaced out in shallow, one-man holes mostly, with many breaks in our lines. Victor Charlie could easily come slithering through, it seemed to me, slashing one throat after another, or however Victor Charlie chose to do it. But what did I know?

For a while, I had stayed with Harry, listening to the squad radio; then I reluctantly retired to my own hole. I lay there on my belly, the smell of freshly butchered human in my nose. Reaching out, I could touch the very spot where poor Breeze had lain headless. When the moon came out briefly, I could just make out Harry's bulk in his hole. When the moon disappeared, I couldn't make out anything human.

Stretched out now, exhausted, trying to sleep, but jerking awake to peer around dopily and slap at whining mosquitos that ferociously attacked everything: eyelids, ears, the inside of my nose. Then smearing on more bug juice until I stank with it, felt it dribbling off my chin. Finally, pulling my poncho liner over my head and greasy, itching hands and just lying there lumped in that primordial hole like a miserable bag of laundry. Why couldn't I sleep? I chased sleep but couldn't catch it. I had seen Ching-Ching so tired he had rolled half upside down into his hole and never knew it, snoring in seconds. Roland had gone to sleep sitting up, mumbling.

Noises again . . . *clankety, brrp, scruff, scritch* over in the high grass . . . *ska-yoww, ska-yoww* from the trees. I saw a huge bat-like something swoop over, its wings waving wider than my arms, watched it float off over the grass. . . .

The far side of night now, heavy clouds rolling over the moon, rain coming and going, nothing now but darkness and alone-ness. Can't see Harry, can hardly see my own hand, as raindrops plink on my helmet. What's that moving in the grass there? That long gray thing? My God, it looks like. . . . Is it moving this way? Yes? No?

Big-eyed, hard-eyed staring, blinking in the rain . . . the gray menace seeming to dissolve . . . but not the dread . . . so ele-mental it's as if my bones have already begun a slow, inexorable merging with the blood-lapping earth that has lapped up Breeze and is waiting for us all. . . .

I feel for my rifle, small comfort. Before retiring, I had care-fully laid out my gear (*"The good soldier is always prepared. The good soldier leaves nothing to chance"*), rifle to the right, clips of ammo and a few grenades to the left, like a very good soldier.

Lot of good being good did poor Breeze. One minute he's good, the next, he's ant meat.

Artillery is firing out of Cu Chi again. Maybe they know what they're firing at this time. Maybe it was only a little screw-up of coordinates or a small trick of weather that had done it. (*"Weather is tricky, men. Wind speed and direction can have a destabilizing effect on an artillery round, men."*) Maybe it was only that, the wind . . . what wind? I don't remember any wind . . . here comes another . . . high and smooth and humming, like wind around a house. . . .

(*A soldier who knew the shell game better than most had once spent some time explaining it to us newbies. He was well seasoned in combat and could isolate the sounds of guns as the firing shifted and alternated, sometimes heavy from the left, other times solid from the right, as though they were instruments in some ferocious jazz band. If you had been fired on enough—and survived—he maintained, your ears could become as finely tuned as some ace musician's, able to instantly classify every faraway pop, crump, and thump, every close-in whine, whistle, and boom, just like they were drums, piano, and trumpet—and this could increase your chances of going home a whole lot. "But I heard you never hear the one that gets you," Too-Fat Schwartz had said. "Well, then, that's just plain old bad luck and shouldn't reflect no discredit upon you," Cool Breeze Carson had noted. "Either that or Jesus wants to talk to you. Nothin' to feel bad about."*)

"Harry," I call through the rain, which has disintegrated into a chill, misty dribble that makes my teeth chatter, "Harry . . ."

No answer . . . can't see my hand two feet away now . . . nothing . . . now I'm up on my knees, groping toward Harry's hole less than ten meters away . . . feeling around . . . only Harry isn't in his hole . . . has the American Army packed up and gone home while I dawdled? I crawl on, panicky, faster now. . . .

"Who goes?" comes a startled whisper.

"Me, Ripp."

"Ripp where?"

"Here."

"Here where? Make a noise."

I tap my rifle. "I *am* making a noise. Who're you?"

"Who goes 'ere?" rasps another voice harshly, just to the left of the first. "Identify or I'm agonna grease your gook ass!"

Suddenly, a shadow looms over me in the mist, flapping out in its poncho like a giant bird. There is the glint of a weapon jammed down at my gut, and I can almost feel the slugs ripping in.

"It's me! Ripp! Ripp! Get that thing off me, bastard!"

"Ripp? What you doin' over here, ol' Ripp? I thought I seen a shadow or sumpin."

Red Dog Peacock's own shadow sinks back to the ground. He's built like a sawed-off shotgun and he's acting like one. But I crawl toward him. He and Canny overlap the sides of their little hole like baby hippos in a bathtub.

"What're you maniacs doing together?" I whisper.

"Purly got lonesome," snickers Canny. "Wanted to hold hands."

"We come out here to get some Charlie," whispers Red Dog, "and two guns are better'n one."

"Can't sleep noways," says Canny.

"Me either. Swear I just saw a fifteen-foot anaconda go by," I whisper.

"An ana-what?" yelps Red Dog.

"I got bit by a fifteen-foot skeeter," says Canny. "Skeeters eatin' us alive."

"I'm swole up all over," whispers Red Dog. "Even my dong's swole up."

"Bug juice don't do no good," says Canny. "They suck it right up. This is the longest night I ever lived."

"We need to get to some high ground," I mutter as the rain peppers us harder. "I'm swimming out here."

"Ain't no more high ground," says Canny. "Done all washed away."

"I almost let you have it a little, Mike," says Red Dog, giggling. "Can't see doodly squat, though I seen sumpin. Don't make me no never mind. I was kinna out reconnin' for some of them Veetneeze bing-bang-bungs."

"Where the hell's Harry?"

"Dunno, Mike. Can't see doodly squat. They come sneakin' around here, I'm agonna rip off a burst."

"Well, don't do it my way. Let's see, where's my hole?"

"Just tell ol' America don't worry, Mike. Ol' Dog's on the job."

"Not going to America. Where's my hole?"

"Where'd they dig our shit hole," asks Canny. "I got to shit bad."

"Down in the bushes somewhere."

"What bushes?"

"Any bushes."

It's just past 0400 when the floor show breaks out along our line. There's a lot of yelling that the VC are coming in. Bodies have been heard swishing through the grass. Suddenly, it's old Chicago, tracers and all kinds of steel shit flying around. Red Dog leaps straight up, hollering and firing his machine gun from the hip at the whole wonderful world. Three mad minutes and things cool down, a few final rounds popping off, last licks. I haven't fired a shot. Just pressing my bones deeper into the suddenly motherly earth, staring bug-eyed and gripping my rifle.

Someone shouts for everyone to stop firing, for everyone to stay in their holes—illumination rounds are going up. Anyone seen moving out of his fucking hole will be regarded as the fucking enemy.

A mortar team pops up flares that never reach beyond our perimeter, bursting straight overhead, night sunshine in the drizzle. Seeing no enemy in the drifting gunsmoke, only ourselves staring at ourselves.

As morning breaks, Harry, who has been with Rodeliano, passes word that what the Always First has blasted is one of the Always First's own ambush patrols, trying to return to the perimeter before light. But such was the ferocity and accuracy of our firepower, three more KIAs have been added to the Ever Forward, Never Backward battalion's unique and burgeoning body count.

REWIND

Leaning back expansively in his leather swivel chair behind the great mahogany desk, the old gentleman himself had strongly counseled me, been very much in favor of it.

Uncle Ned had played a little tune on his belly with his chubby fingers, peered at me over his bifocals, scooted his chair around close to mine, and leaned forward confidentially. Tapping my knee with his knuckles, the underwear king had advised me to "answer the call. That's the stuff that made America great.

"Hell's bells—" He started, coughing, then broke into a fit of wheezy laughter as he lit up another Lucky, "There's no good reason for you not to go on over there and wrap this pip-squeak war up for us. Gee whiz, if we let these Nervous Nellies run things, there's no telling who'll do us in first, the commanists or our esteemed black brethren. Hell's bells, bring on those one billion little commanist monkeys and I'll sell 'em all underwear. Course we could ship all our niggers over there and let them and the other monkeys cut up on each other if it didn't cost too much. . . .

"All in all, I think it will be a profitable experience for you. Bring us back some glory. Bring us back a hero. This damn town could sure use a new hero. Hell, maybe I'll build you a doggone monument, stick you up on a horse or something. Do they have horses over there? But you'd better hurry. From what I've seen of it, this Veetnam deal could peter out before you get there."

Even Aunt Tettie, between her cat shows, crying jags, weddings, funerals, teas, tête-à-têtes, chargings up the courthouse steps with the flag of the Confederacy, bridge parties, garden parties, trips to her multifarious doctors for the nineteen different kinds of pills for her nineteen different kinds of miseries, her religious life, and manifold other activities in the community, had been summoned by the old gentleman to share his enthusiasm. Even childless Aunt Tettie, who had tried so hard to unleash a version of motherhood on me after the deaths of my parents, had been moved to beaming affirmation when Uncle Ned, balling his fists, cheerily exclaimed, "By golly, I only wish I was your age again. Every man should serve the colors. I just missed my war, but if I was a young buck again, I sure wouldn't miss this one."

Aunt Tettie had immediately launched herself into organizing a send-off gala for me. The big doings were held in the historic house on Jackson Hill overlooking the river. Built of slave-made bricks and purchased several underwear factories ago, it was the preeminent dwelling in all of Larchmont, the site the Yankees had captured and established as their headquarters before being counterattacked and routed in pitched battle. Out back was the old cistern where they found the Union cannonballs. In the house's great oaken doors were Larchmont's last surviving Yankee bullet holes. Adorning its ornate ceiling were marks said to be the last traces of Yankee brains splattered there in the final charge led by General Jackson himself. It was also said that Yankee ghosts still prowled in the cellar where so many had died. This was attested to by Aunt Tettie, who quite regularly heard their groanings and knockings in the night.

Everyone drank up at my farewell, even Aunt Tettie— especially Aunt Tettie, sometimes sliding off to starboard in her chair. Uncle Ned, Aunt Tettie, all of them were football crazy, so the more they drank, the more my departure to military service took on the jolly flavor of a pregame bash, with everybody going around calling the moose, the university's famous mascot. Dinner got ever louder. Faces became flushed and merry.

Presiding at the head of the historic table under the revered vestiges of Yankee brains, Uncle Ned began to sing the university's famous fight song. Soon the whole table, with the exception of Charlotte, burst into song. It was the voice of rock 'em, sock 'em America, and one could imagine the war being triumphantly played out in the Vietnam Bowl, with Michael Ripp, now entering the game, scoring the winning touchdown.

Cheers for me. Uncle Ned lifting his goblet in my direction. All the rest, except for my wife, lifting their goblets in my direction. Everything was carrying on in this gay, smashed fashion when Char—the young lady with the magnificent mammary overhang and the unchallenged center of male rapid eye movement—grown increasingly nauseated with it all, strongly suggested that we depart my spirited farewell early. We left Uncle Ned, with his borderline emphysema, going around calling the mighty moose. We left Aunt Tettie, glassy-eyed, draped on the edge of her chair, listing to port.

12

Splendid News

"At 0400 hours, elements of First Battalion, Second Brigade were hit with 18 rounds of mixed enemy rocket and mortar fire in operations 17 miles northwest of Cu Chi. Casualties were light. . . ."

For Colonel Gurgles, numerous such reports comprised the stuff of unsatisfactory combat over the next few months, an altogether frustrating, even maddening, set of circumstances at the command level.

Down at the grunt level, the enemy would fire off a few rounds at us and phase immediately into his *di di* maneuver. Led by the cautious Lieutenant Rodeliano, our platoon would leisurely follow in the enemy's wake, if there was any, at a most respectable distance. If we could have continued this tactic of gentlemanly pursuit, with nobody getting hurt much, it would surely have contributed to a breakthrough in nonviolent warfare, but our colonel strongly objected. He fretted about other American units fighting big headline battles at Loc Ninh, only fifty miles from our AO (area of operations), and at Con Thien up near the DMZ.

Meanwhile, the Always First Battalion engaged in desultory

sweeps through villages, rice paddies, jungle, and shot-up rubber plantations—searching, searching, but not destroying. Sometimes we would chase the muzzle flashes of our foe flush to the Cambodian border, across which we were not allowed to pass because, well, Cambodia was classified as neutral. The Smoker really got to roaring one day when we took a KIA from a group of enemy who then pranced across the border—he swore —thumbing their noses at him.

I never saw a Vietnamese thumb his nose, and nothing much that bothered The Smoker bothered me. Nevertheless, these nickel-and-dime potshots had increased the Always First's casualty list so high that we had the distinction of leading the entire division, all of Old Lightning Blue, in reverse kill ratio.

Colonel Gurgles's concern—indeed, his shame—over his battalion's backward image was communicated to us daily in pugnacious little bulletins. To uphold the flagging Ever Forward tradition, we were exhorted to react vigorously to even the smell of Charlie within our AO, to "pursue him and pursue him until he drops . . . and then to grind him up."

Grinding up Charlie certainly looked simple enough on the briefing maps. Here and there, clearly fixed by red-*x*'d rectangles, were the points of last contact with the enemy. By the time we arrived, however, Charlie might be miles away in any direction in the jungle or under the jungle or having tea back in Cambodia, which was *neutral*.

But we pursued ever-more vigorously. Even Lieutenant Rodeliano was getting into it. Sometimes, closing in breathlessly on a hot target, we would hear bamboo clackers signaling in the bush. If we were very, very vigorous, we might find cook fires still smoking, fresh deep-dug bunkers, weapons, uniforms, and anything from medical supplies from France to Florida orange juice from Florida.

Once in the rain we came upon a rice cache the size of a huge, rectangular room, the rice piled up nine feet high and contained by big, bulging bamboo mats. Gurgles got on the horn and ordered us to destroy the rice forthwith.

Rodeliano thought on how to do that, and then we spread it all out as much as we could through the woods, and everybody waded through it and stomped and tromped around on the rice for hours. And then another message came crackling from the colonel: "Do *not* destroy the rice. We have decided to evacuate it."

"Roger . . ." replied Rodeliano, staring wet-eyed at the rice.

It was really raining, with torrents of water and muck running all over the rice, and we started blowing up trees to make an LZ for choppers to come in and carry away the remains of the drowned rice. Then Gurgles messaged us again, advising that we should, after all, destroy the rice.

"It *is* destroyed . . ."

"Well, how did you destroy it?"

"Well, sir, we walked on it, you know. We spread it out all over the place and stepped on it and blew some of it up and let the rain fall on it."

"That's not good enough."

"Tell him to come out here," sniggered Canny, "and pee on it."

It was raining, raining and we had been dicking around with and destroying this rice for eleven hours.

"Burn it!" ordered Gurgles.

"Well, it's sort of raining too much for that. Maybe you could come out here for a few minutes and just look at it, sir."

All night we guarded the rice in the deluge, and the next day our colonel flew out, looked at it, and said, "Well, I guess it is destroyed."

And that much was true.

In those days, we would come humping out of the bush into places with names like Ap Bap or Trang Bang, classified as pacified, semipacified, or plain hit-the-ground. In the better ones, the kids would appear, barefoot, in shorts or pajamas, fizzing over with life juice, climbing all over us, hollering, "Hallo, hallo, you—" not seeming much impressed with our fierce mien.

Captain Wilson and Rodeliano liked to say that we were winning hearts and minds and that it was better to plant good feelings than people. We found ourselves passing out Kool-Aid and cookies, and Doctor Kelly would be out there in the middle of some ville looking down throats and recommending toothpaste.

"Oh, hell yes, the civic-action garbage looks good on paper," our colonel told Wilson, "so see that you keep it on paper." But it was hardly hardballs orthodox infantry, and the colonel tolerated it only because word came down from the superiors to show some results. He tolerated it with a wink.

"If I want bodies to pass out cookies and engage in area beautification, I will summon the sweet Doughnut Dollies of the Red Cross, who are probably a hell of a lot more aggressive than the dollies masquerading as soldiers in this battalion."

Inspiring as these words were, however, Bad Company kept its gun hand mostly dormant, even in places where the receptions were nervous blips between looks of darkness. We were going back into villes now where people lived very schizo lives, switching smiles and flags to match the sentiments of the gentlemen packing the hardware.

And then there were those times when we would come filing off a narrow footpath into some Spartan little hamlet that snaked back into the jungle, the hair already at attention on the backs of our necks; where the *presence* grew so thick with every step that we could smell it, slice it with our bayonets, lick it off the trees; where nobody smiled at you for real or for fake. Plain old bare-ass VC country: No men around at all, except for a few ancients too wasted to move, staring at the new saviors, the new bright boys, the studs having recently exited, maybe ten, maybe two minutes in front of us, maybe watching from a tunnel opening fifty meters away, fingers curling on triggers.

The women would just gaze on through us in blinky-eyed

hate-fright-cunning that came out as hard blankness, pretending not to notice as we poked into corners and under cookpots, even that we existed; or they would go scrambling out to snatch children back into their hootches and then squat on earthen floors, gazing downward fixedly at ants or dead ashes or their interesting toenails. There was no "Hallo, hallo," just "Watch where you're dancing, Jack."

Straying from the Ho Chi Minh–loving revolutionary path could also be hard on villagers' nerves. This one little place perched on the bank of a canal had recently been reclassified by the American-computed Hamlet Evaluation System (HES) as "currently secure and friendly." We had patrolled through it the week before, and Harry and Roland had even sipped tea with the smiling village chief, sipping and smiling with the bulge of a .45 under his shirt.

Going back through, we found the chief and his wife with their smiles wiped away, their heads stuck out to dry on booby-trapped stakes in a rice paddy, a sign hung underneath admonishing the chief for playing ball with the "American imperialists and the traitorous Saigon puppet regime. . . ." A nurse and school teacher had been taken away at gunpoint along with fifteen fighting-age males. Twenty-nine defenders had been slain. And HES would have to reevaluate.

It was near this place that we captured our first live "gorilla." We saw him bat-assing across a paddy dike, then dodging in and out of palm trees along the narrow, muddy canal that ran to the headless chief's village. A gunship working with us went fanning over the treetops, knocking fronds off flapping palms, and the runner kept glancing back over his shoulder at the bird demon that came on and on and finally cornered him, just after he jumped out of his khaki pants and flung them in the canal.

He looked about twenty, with grizzly-bear-thick black hair that seemed to sprout up from his eyebrows, burning little spider eyes over cheekbones like brown rocks, body strung like barbed wire, bruised and dirty bare feet tough as my boots, and scars on his back that looped and swirled like a child's fingerpainting or a bad blast.

"You ain't gonna believe this," a gunner on the helicopter said to Rodeliano, "but this character says he no can see. Says he's a *blind* man."

"Yes, it's hard to believe," said Rodeliano, pawing the ground with his boot.

"We chased that *blind* man for fifteen minutes. Nearly ran out of gas chasing that *blind* man."

"Hey, looka here," yelled Canny Peacock, holding out the dripping khakis and a G.I.'s dog tags. "Found these in old race-hoss's pocket."

"Why 'at zip bastid!" blurted Red Dog, jerking up his M-60. "Whyn't I just grease his ol' zip butt right now, Lieutenant?"

Rodeliano examined the tags and shook his head. "No, he's a detainee, and we'll hold him for questioning. Now let's sweep that ville."

"He's a *what*?" yelled Red Dog.

"The man has no weapon, Peacock. Now I said, let's sweep that ville. You men spread out now. And look sharp!"

Slowly we worked through a line of huts stuck together with mud, bamboo, rice straw, and palm leaves, finding stone-faced women mumbling, "No *biet*" ("I don't understand").

"No *biet*, shit," hollered Red Dog, smashing at a big jar set out to catch rain water, knocking around pots and pans, a small Buddha statue, anything he could lay his hands or his gun butt on, inviting a couple of other grunts to join in.

"You men cut that out!" yelled Rodeliano. "Just cut that crap out!"

"Hey, it's a gorilla village, ain't it?" fumed Red Dog. "We're here to ding gorillas, ain't we? Why don't we just blow this pigpen right off the world, Lieutenant, huh? Hell, these people ain't even civilized. Come on, Lieutenant, let me smoke that 'tainee's ass. He's so ignert he don't know he's alive anyway."

"You heard me, Peacock! Back off now! That's an order!"

"Aw, Lieutenant, ain't we here to ding these dang Veetneeze gorillas? Why come we let them ding us Americans all the time, and we don't ding nobody back?"

"Just back off now, Peacock. Hammarth, get that man under control and acting like a soldier instead of a hooligan."

"A what?" said Red Dog with a snort. "What's a hooligan? Hear 'at shit, Canny? Hear 'at shit, Mike? Hear 'at shit, Skin? I'm a *hooooligan*, and I guess 'at maggot mouth's gone get a medal for what he did."

Red Dog suddenly jammed his machine gun squarely between the detainee's eyes, and this led to the sudden admission by the detainee that he was not blind and a lot of jumping around and hollering and cussing until we got Dog under control.

"Come on, Dog," Harry said, pulling the Georgian away. "We'll find you a war yet."

An intelligence officer later told us that this tough combat cookie had finally crumbled under questioning, confessed that he was a main-force guerilla, and revealed to them very good information about an impending attack on a nearby village. As it happened, however, the very good information turned out to be a fraction off—about eighteen *miles* off—the revolutionary path. Another village got hit that night, got the HES kicked out of it, and more paper work for the antigorillas.

Back at Cu Chi, I did not get a letter from Char. I miss her like hell. I wonder what the situation with the baby is? Why doesn't she write? I wonder where she is exactly? I wonder what she's doing exactly? I wonder who she's with exactly? Why doesn't she write?

I sat down and wrote a long, impassioned, inquisitive letter, asking her about the baby and telling her I loved her and hoped she would soon be settling down in a good place to have the baby, and fired it off in a sentimental sweat.

That afternoon, Colonel Gurgles called us out and advised us that the day we had been waiting for was at hand. Major

Sheridan, who by now had steamed off a good ten pounds of gut, stood by smiling as the colonel conveyed with undisguised glee the gravity of the situation into which we were being thrust. Our brigade was being op/conned as reinforcements to a rapidly expanding, fierce new front raging around Dak Toy in the Central Highlands, perhaps the biggest infantry battle of the war.

"Men of the Always First," the colonel, radiating cheer, practically yodeled at us. "At this point in time, let us honestly face our situation. In all candor, I have not kept my promise to you. I know, I know. I promised you we were coming to a *war*. I, too, came to fight a war, but so far, I have not been able to find that war. What *I* call a war. I know it's over here, because I keep reading about it. But I do not call sitting around base camp a war. I do not call taking little strolls in the flora and fauna and pausing to pass out cookies to dumb peasants a war. I do not call chasing around a few raggedy-tailed, so-called guerillas who are too chicken to stand and fight like a man a war. . . ."

Colonel Gurgles, who had been practically in hiding of late, was really grooving again, stepping back and forth, poking out his jaw, his whole being snapping with excitement and anticipation.

"You men. The thorny truth of it is: The real war has been passing us by, leaving us spinning our wheels. And to speak frankly on that, our performance in the field has been—what? What has our performance been? The answer to that is—and Major Sheridan here will agree—our performance has been piss-poor, a very piss-poor team effort. But under my command, a fighting command, the road ahead is brightening.

"Now, men. It behooves you to listen closely. I have some really splendid news for you. We couldn't ask for a better opportunity to strut our stuff. Thousands of the enemy are massing up in the Central Highlands. I have just returned from a briefing with the general, and he tells me the enemy is trying to cut South Vietnam in half. And these are not your raggedy-butt

Viet Cong, these are your big-time North Vietnamese regulars, Hanoi's finest.

"Men. Are you getting the picture? Now comes the time we shall show the people who the hell we are! Now comes the time we shall establish our *fighting identity*! Because we came here to attrit the enemy, and now is the hour, by God! Because we shall pursue the enemy without surcease! We shall make them pay! We shall kick their ass! We shall grind them up! We shall—"

I grabbed my fluttering belly and made a run for it, a small outbreak of Ho Chi Minh's revenge taking a bit of the shine off this truly splendid news.

REWIND

We were alone that spring in her father the pig's beach house beside the Gulf, watching the power of waves sweeping in and rushing up under the pilings and shaking the house. We gazed at the Florida sea and drank coffee and ate eggs the color of the sun, and then, with the blood pulling to our bellies in the chill early morning, she whispered, "Come on, let's go back to bed." She had been frightened during the storm, and then she pulled me back and pressed very close, her eyes half-closed but wild and glittery as the galloping green sea, whispering, "Come on, say it to me," and I said it, and she said, "Come on, right now, do it now." Those were our first times, and the house shook, and the sea raged, and I knew that no one was ever going to love her but me.

"Disillusionment," expounded the professor of literature, one year later, "is rampant in the world today." And so, wow, was this professor. This mind-beautiful, oldish-youngish, carefully coiffed, wild-haired prof, how he did go on, weaving wonderful tales of where it was all at and where it was all going to, ladies and gentlemen; opening up these glowing vistas of our sophomoric imagination, flinging open challenging new doors of the liberated mind for us, the traditionally shackled, to step through. Especially the young ladies. When he got to going on about bodies flowing together, lip upon lip, belly upon belly, and the love juices exploding, the white-hot, scalding liberated juices, his eyes blazed, his nostrils flared, and he just rolled on and on, raging, raging in splendid resonance and marvelous rhythms.

He had confined himself at first to the excusable, playful little displays of interest: the now-and-then tug at her provocative earlobe; tracing with his little finger the exciting change since yesterday in her nose or mouth, that pouty mouth; removing with appropriate cluckings of concern the terrible speck in her right eye—or was it the left? And then one night, tracking them down at one of the highway joints, I stepped quietly through this rather seedy old motel doorway, saw their clothes (off duty, he wore sandals) scattered across the floor, and then the outside light cutting across the bed like a sword. No words, just a noise that started from my feet and rushed up through the fire of my belly and came tearing out of my throat, a half-howl, half-roaring that shook that room. There was the suction sound of parting love juices as the humping sheet collapsed. And out of the sheet came this arm-flapping blur, this apparition of a naked professor, not so spellbinding without his clothes on actually. I didn't touch him, but he fell down anyway and then scrambled by me like a four-legged thing out of there. No attempt to scoop up his sandals, no pause to explain, no dallying to deliver an illuminating remark on modern sexual orientation, not even a backward glance to see who or what it was after him.

Char had raised up, big-eyed, moist-nippled, breasts trembling straight out, jerking up the sheet, beginning to cry, then going on hysterically, crying and talking in a torrent about why she had done it, was in the process of doing it, how the prof had word-painted it as a soul thing that could never die, how it had seemed so right and so relevant, as he gazed at her with his erudite eyes. How what he said had seemed so right and so relevant as he began kissing her all over with his scholar's lips.

And I replied almost groggily that it was okay, it was all okay, that sure I understood, sure things happen, and happen, sure I understood. An she again swore unending fidelity for sure this time from this moment forward, nevermore to violate our relationship, nevermore to succumb to any mouthy poetic Professor Raging Dick panting under the sheet, "You have the most radiantly lovely hair, dear, and your cheekbones, God, I love your cheekbones. Would you like to go to Mexico City with me and eat a little iguana?" "Iguana, Mike. He was an iguana freak." And then after the tears and the make-up and the talking about it and more tears, she began to urge me to complete in the bed of higher purpose the great mystical fuck the professor had commenced. "*Now*, Mike, if that's what you want, right *now*." Pushing those big, creamy, tear-wet blossoms up in my face. And of course I wanted it right then, and later we both dropped English Lit.

13

Boxed In

Bad News Benson sucked like a baby on his religious medal. Canny Peacock looked down, breathed deep, tried to whistle. Harry Hammarth peered through a porthole of the C-130 and said, "How charming. I think I'll go back to newspaper work."

It was the jungle we were flying into, mean like we'd never seen, triple-canopy spooksville, primeval down there. We banked over incredible towering trees that rolled over great battle-smogged hills that plunged into gloom-and-doom-soaked valleys, full of dark and mist and death-rattling. Wild, crawling with North Vietnamese regiments. Now we saw fires in the hills, the lightning bursts of artillery, and then we flew down through the smoke pall toward *real* war. And Bad News was about to get religion.

"Hey, youse guys," he had cackled earlier, "have no fear, our colonel is here. He says this is gonna be a Diebienphuse in reverse."

Only it didn't seem like Dien Bien Phu in reverse when we tried to land. There were flashes across the primitive Dak Toy airstrip like giant matches being struck and snuffed out. As we leveled off to touch down, a C-130 taxiing along the runway took a direct hit, a bumping burst that shook us all over. And then, in a great, groaning, last-second maneuver, we heaved back upward, scudding as straight up as the plane could go.

"Let's get offa this bomb!" Bad News was grabbing at his safety belt and screaming over the plane's thunder, "Let's get outta here! Let's say goodby to all this!"

When we got on the ground, it seemed as though every bird in-country had been diverted to rush men and supplies to Dak Toy: another hasty sprawl of tents and bunkers around an airstrip, swelling with troops, jumping with war nerves. And all around, the smoke-blowing hills were making noises like live volcanos.

The sky had turned dark red; it seemed to be raining red, all day and all night. Ching-Ching, licking the big drops running down into his mouth, croaked, "The rain over here *is* wetter, men."

We temporarily settled into tents next to a company of paratroopers just pulled off the line, a blood-and-water-streaked bunch, many walking-wounded among them, their outfit hit a little too hard, their eyes staring into spaces I hadn't visited yet.

A blond trooper, resplendent in rags, stepped out of the big, saggy tent next to us, both knees ripped out of his fatigues, so glazed with mud that he looked like a half-chewed gingerbread man. He stood there haggard and unsteady, gazing at the new guys, smiling his knowing little smile and smoking his bamboo pipe, oblivious to the rain, the sweet smell of staying alive enveloping him.

"Doesn't it ever stop raining up here, man?" inquired Ching-Ching.

"Shit," said the staying-alive trooper with a giggle, "this here's your dry season. S'posed to be, anyway."

Inside, a tentload of them didn't seem to know or particularly care what season it was or where they were, tripping off somewhere in funky blue heaven, far from war.

"Need some?" asked the trooper.

"Don't mind if I do," said Ching-Ching.

"No thanks," I said. "It just gets me to going sideways."

"I'd rather go anyways than where I been," said the paratrooper. "Guess we're about the mellowest bunch in the army by now. Guess if you're gonna hang it up, might's well feel good about it."

"Your first sergeant don't care?" inquired Ching-Ching, peering into the tent. "Our first sergeant cares deeply."

"Nope, he don't. Least, when I helped scrape him off that tree back there, he didn't make no big fuss. And who gives a fuck? Just who gives a duck-fuck who cares?"

"Not me, man," said Ching-Ching.

A black soldier with huge bare feet was down on his knees just inside the tent. I thought he might be praying, but he was washing his socks in his helmet. First time he'd had his boots off in four days, he laughed, holding up a dripping sock. His outfit had come off that hill with such dispatch, they'd even had to leave the scrapings of their poor top sergeant up there. "And that's terrible," he said pleasantly.

"Cocksucking dinks swarmin' all over us," said the blond one. "Couldn't get no resupply in, couldn't get no help, nothin'. Finally, we just had to come on down from there. Just give that hill away. And who gives a royal duck-fuck? Dinks got that hill now, those duckfuckers."

"Neva goin' back up that hill. Neva, neva," said the big-footed black guy, looking for a place to hang his socks.

"Which hill's that?" I asked.

"Old 711," he said, shaking his head. "Old lucky 711, the meanest motha in the mountains. Neva was no hill like old—"

There was a *whoooo* in the sky and shouts of incoming, and suddenly men running, diving, crawling. Something hitting very close, a hot wind rushing, a busting sound like a kick in the ear. Red dirt went up, and the paratrooper tent came down, bumped off cloud city. Troopers came crawling, clawing wildly out from under. Explosions all over, and I went flopping down hard in a hole on my face in the red, sucking goo. "You all right?" Harry helped me up, got me going again. Then kneeing up and plunging ahead, *schulck, schulck,* cordite burning my nose, a wild shrapnel singing in my ears, shells rattling down from that red sky and blowing stuff all over us.

Muddy-faced Harry kept pushing me, pointing toward a bunker entrance ahead. Dizzily, I went in past a water can, down narrow, slimy sandbag steps, stumbling into a dim, low dirt room with cots, gas masks, boxes of C-rations, a chirping field telephone, and a single candle burning. Then on into a deeper, darker hole, heads down, helmets banging, tangled equipment bumping. Crammed into a hole five-by-five now, five of us, popping sweat, kneecap to kneecap.

Faces flickered into view as somebody lit a candle. Harry was to the right. Bad News Benson, working his spastic elbows, was on my left. Straight across was the bootless black, and next to him, eyes upraised, was the no-longer-mellow blond.

Inches over our head was a ceiling of dirt, planks, shell casings, sandbags. It seemed a good hole, but there it was again outside, thundering, the hole shuddering. Chunks of mud spat down. The candle blew out. I thought of being buried alive.

"Close," Harry said.

"What's it, rockets?" rasped Bad News, squirming in the dark.

"Arty—130s, maybe," said the black trooper. "Oh, they brung the world down on us that time."

"Charlie's not supposed to have that bigga stuff up here," said Bad News, poking my ribs with his elbow, "not supposed to—"

"S'posed to *shit!*" said the no-longer-mellow trooper. "Tired of hearin' all this *s'posed-to* shit. *Really* tired of hearin' all that s'posed-to shit."

"Listen at that," whistled the black trooper. "Damn, they done done it to the ammo dump."

The candle, a fat yellow one, was relit as we sat there with our tails pressed into the cold, muddy water, feeling the earth tremble.

"What the hell you sucking on there?" I muttered to Bad News, who was sucking and biting on his medal until his teeth seemed about to crack.

Bad News started to babble: "St. Jude. Youse ain't never hoida St. Jude? The saint of impossible things and stuff like that? Youse fucking-A I suck on it. Youse fucking-A."

"I thought that was St. Christopher."

"Fuck, no."

"Well, what does St. Christopher do?"

"Hey, what do youse care anywise? Who the fuck cares? I just wanna get outta here alive."

"Stay active in your old age," Harry said. "That's the answer."

"What?" babbled Bad News. "What's he talking about?"

"When you get old, stay active," Harry said. "It's the secret of long life. I read that yesterday. Just stay active."

"*Old*? Did that crazy fuck say *old*? Who in here's gonna get *old*?"

We sat there for a long time in the deep hole, watching the candle dance.

"So who's winning?" Harry asked the paratroopers after a while.

"The general says *we* are," said the black trooper with a tired little chuckle. "He says we've got them boxed in."

14

What We Came For

"Men of the Always First Battalion. It is Hill 711 that we are bound for. They've got it, and we're going to get it. Are you hearing me, men? Do you get the picture? We're going up there. We're going to kick their ass. We're going to seize it from their grasp. We're going to grind them up. Because we're First Battalion. Because we're Lightning Blue. Remember— Ever Forward, Never Backward. Forward Ever, Backward Never. Now let me hear from you, men. Let me hear from you louder. What is our motto? I can barely HEAR you! I will stand out here until I HEAR from you!"

By now, everyone had heard of Hill 711. It was being called by some the epic hill battle of the war—and other things by other experts: The Enemy's Last Gasp, An American Tragedy, Dien Bien Phu in Reverse, Dien Bien Phu Two, Our Supreme Challenge, Our Darkest Hour . . . and a bad place to spend the night.

The NVA, infiltrating off the Ho Chi Minh Trail from Laos (neutral) and Cambodia (neutral), had driven outnumbered American and ARVN troops off the hill and then began to dig. Hill 711, said to be beehived with tunnels and bunkers. The enemy dug in deep, deep, the hill fought over and refought over, blown up and reblown up, smoking, half–tree-denuded, dead piling upon dead, a questionable place for a young man to make a living. Old 711. The numbers alone enough to send shivers down the spine of anyone who came within smelling distance: "711 . . . oh, my Lord. . . ."

And now came The Bad Ones.

We were being "accorded the incredible honor," shouted our colonel, of spearheading the final assault. A contrary view was that Always First was the most expendable collection of future dead meat available at the moment. Gurgles laughed at that. It was a commander's dream battle, a chapter of warfare that would not soon be forgotten, a turning point. The light at the top of the hill beckoned, and we would take that hill "at all costs."

At all costs? "Why the fuck for, Captain?" Ching-Ching asked Billy Wilson during a briefing. "Why we need that crappy old hill *at all costs?*"

Wilson relayed the command view. The command view emanated from COMUSMACV in Saigon and came right on down the slide: that the foe was trying to cut the country in half. But this time, went the command view, the foe had rolled the dice wrong. Instead of hitting and running, the foe was trying to fight in set-piece battles through those hills, exposing his massed infantry (if you could call fighting under cover of that ferocious forest exposing and massing) to superior American firepower that would ultimately chew him to pieces.

Now Hill 711 had become the largest and most terrible of those set-piece battles. The enemy was on that hill. All we had to do was go up there and seize it from his grasp. The dice were loaded in our favor, went the command view.

"If the dice are loaded in our favor, Captain," said Ching-Ching, "then what's that they're stuffing in those bags over there, sir?"

We saw what they were stuffing as we moved out very early the next morning past the graves-registration tent. There were new green body bags and new stuffings from the night's action all around. The relatively-whole dead were being zipped in snugly against the morning dew, while some of the latest arrivees, and pieces of arrivees, were still on stretchers or scattered about haphazardly, being hastily tagged and bagged. We trudged on past the portable outdoor refrigeration units for the deceased, which—like the dice—were heavily loaded (overloaded now) in our favor. The area was in total disarray. A rocket had hit during the night, zapping some of them the second time around.

Farther on, a sign outside the emergency tent said:

DAK TOY HILTON
No Vacancy

Through the open tent flap, I saw figures working in a dull reddish glow over a soldier laid out on a stretcher propped on sawhorses. A maze of tubes and bottles hung over the soldier. Shadows danced across the sides of the tent. The shadows held the soldier's arms down. They had slit his trousers and were pulling off his boots, and the soldier, head back, chin thrust up, howled and howled through the dark morning rain as we moved on away from there.

By 0600, the rain had stopped. The sun probed and filtered through the heavy haze, steadily burned brighter and brighter, and in an hour, the sky had cleared blazingly. The mud hardened as we waited for the fleet of choppers that would carry us into the hills. We waited for eight hours at an LZ, a landing zone, that by afternoon was just a stretch of blowing dust, ammo and C-ration crates, and the sun-dried raisins of First Battalion. We sprawled around in three or four inches of shade, listening to the racketing in the hills, watching a Spooky gunship banking slowly round and round in the distance, its miniguns grinding *brrrrrp! brrrrrp!* like some apeshit dentist drilling serious cavities down in the trees.

Hours in the sun drained out tension like dirty bathwater. And then came some murderous *brrrrrp!* or *brrraaap!* or *crr-rummpbump!* out there, and you started filling up all over again. Imagining what those hard noises were doing to soft flesh could make a soldier feel dead before he really was. Feeling alive was better, even if you were slumped against the hot crates with resupply choppers whipping around in little dust cyclones that dusted your C-rations and turned spit red, blew your hair into a grainy goo that snapped teeth out of combs, that was all over you, gritty in your lungs, and caused you to shut your eyes tight, cussing, "Fuck this shit."

Except for Roland, gentle Roland in his daze, like a transcendental baked potato. It was all getting worse with Roland. I offered him a can of C's, but he just shook his head. He didn't want any of the ham and beans and dust, and he didn't want any of the beans and franks and dust. I told him he ought to eat something, and then I washed some down myself with warm water and dust, and my belly juices were singing *ping-a-ring-ding.*

I sat there, eyes half-closed, nestled among boxes of "chicken loaf, chopped," and "grenades, yellow smoke," listening to the hills flying apart, watching Char march down Cherry Street in my head. I wondered if she could picture what I was doing. And I tried to picture what *she* was doing, but I couldn't get the picture.

"Marching, marching," I sang softly, stuporously in the sun.

"Who's marching?" mumbled Harry in the dust, a damp towel over his face.

"Awright, awright!" bawled The Smoker, hurrying toward us in that pigeon-toed gallop. "Here come the slicks! You down there, fighting fairies of First Platoon—off and on! Second platoon—get those lead asses moving! Third platoon—saddle up! I say, saddle up! We're going to war!"

Char marched out of my head as the choppers that would carry us approached in a long, low, undulating line just over the trees, then weaved and half-circled away, and finally moved toward us again, dragonlike, curving and clattering and blowing up wild, dancing dust.

Then they settled down, and I saw that they had taken a lot of hits. Heavy fire from Hill 711 had been knocking down choppers for days, and we were to be inserted farther away on another hill, a secured hill. Then, if things went well, we would make the short march through the jungle to link up with troops already positioned near the base of 711. We would then have the incredible honor of taking that hill.

On signal, we made the run in under the rotors through the biting dust and jammed into choppers that were already starting to lift. Only mine was too packed. I couldn't squeeze in. Then this door gunner was waving me on. I jumped up beside him in his little side compartment. He was belted in behind his machine gun, wearing thick body armor, and I hung onto him with one arm and onto my rifle and pack with the other as the skids left the ground. At the last second, a soldier came waving and yelling through the dust storm and pitched a can of Carling Black Label straight up. The gunner leaned out and caught it, juggled it, caught it again, and gave the soldier below thumbs-up. The gunner was laughing and drinking and talking through the rising scream of the rotors and didn't seem scared a bit.

Then we were sweeping forward, nose dipping, gaining speed, rolling up fast over small trees and then on up over two-hundred-foot trees spreading out like great green-dark umbrellas over the smoking earth and then on up over ridges and knobs and saddles of those forbidding hills. We were really stuffed in, and I was hanging onto the gunner's neck, and all the time he jovially swigged beer and pointed out tourist attractions below.

Battles seemed to be going on everywhere. Smoke curled up as though from a hundred giant campfires. A column of red smoke popped up through the trees, and then a jet, a Phantom streak, roared down almost on top of us. The gunner, who had a bunch of teeth missing, laughed as the chopper shuddered and tilted sideways, and the beer went spinning, fizzing down, down, swallowed by the dark trees. And for a blood-rushing moment, I almost followed it.

"Charlie's gonna have a good time tonight," shouted the gunner, leaning out and rolling his head to watch the flight of his beer bomb. "Hang on, hang on," he yelled in my ear. "Dinks get *beaucoup* pissed off when grunts fall on their head."

Minutes later, we jumped off along the slopes of what was supposed to be the secured hill and watched the choppers, never quite touching down, rattle the hell out of there. I waved goodby to the gunner and stood in the explosive stink rising out of the craters of this very-smashed-up secured hill. Shirtless paratroopers were digging furiously.

"Welcome, welcome," said a tall soldier, planting a foot on his shovel. "Who the fuck are you?"

"Lightning Blue," yelled Harry. "Where the hell is 711?"

The tall soldier pointed over toward trees looming solid as a box of monster toothpicks, then up toward big, roiling clouds of smoke.

"That noisy fucker over there. Ain't no red carpet leading to it though," he replied, digging away, seeming pretty happy about something.

"Why you digging so fast?" I asked.

"So's I won't get myself messed up," he said, laughing.

"Shit, man, we just got hit again, eighty rounds," laughed a short Chicano soldier, who looked as though he had been sweeping chimneys. He held out pieces of his broken rifle. "A four-deucer hit it. Like to blowed me up, man. Like to blowed me far, far up into heaven."

"Hey, José, you got the hoe?" hollered the tall soldier.

"Do I look like a home gardener?" chortled the short soldier.

Roland, who just wasn't comprehending, shook his head. "Just what—." He looked strangely around. "What—is so funny here?"

"You don't know?" laughed José. "The fucking sun, it is shining, man, that's all."

Soon we were breaking trail through what the newspapers were always calling the "impenetrable jungle." Less than four miles to go, hacking with machetes the whole way, the thorny brush cutting us up, through mazes of vines and tangled skyscraper trees. It was prehistoric in there, some stretches so dark and dense, with so many layers of growth, you couldn't glimpse the sky. In other places, the sun filtered through and played off the leaves like little green faces, twinkling and darting just beyond us in the twilight.

One hundred percent humidity, water dripping off purple and yellow jungle flowers. Leech infested, dank in there. It stank in there. Heat that wrapped around me like a python and squeezed out clammy sweat in fat drops. Big black mosquitoes floating sluggishly in front of my eyes like dizzy spots. Long green lizards scurrying around trees that ran sap the color of blood.

We would be moving in silence, and suddenly the forest would erupt, one creature echoing another in a great yawping, croaking, screeching, yowling chain of sound, and then it would all just as suddenly, mysteriously hush, leaving only hundreds of boots moving hypnotically in rhythm, twigs and leaves crunching, dog tags clinking, packs bumping, mess gear rattling, men stumbling and cursing softly, a rifle banging against a tree, men blowing hard under rucksack straps cutting into shoulders . . . and on and on like a forest locomotive in the growing dark. . . .

Our short march was turning into hours. American boys learning the mysteries of deepest nature. Roland wobbling along ahead, carrying his M-16 by the sights like a suitcase. Gangling, one-hundred-fifty-pound Skinny Lenny lurching along behind, helmet slipping down over his eyes, taking big sucking breaths, wheezing and drooling like an exhausted giraffe.

We were getting close to 711—you could hear machine guns. The march came to a temporary halt, and I sat down heavily, swatting away mosquitos. Some men sagged against trees. Others took off their boots to let their blistered feet hang out for a minute, fumbled in their packs for foot powder, dry socks, Band-Aids. Damn if I was taking off my boots out here. Kelly came through, warning us to be sure and take our malaria pills, the usual big fat orange one and also the little teeny white one. "Don't forget the little white one. Malaria is very dangerous up here, actually. Yes, very dangerous."

"Fuck malaria," said Red Dog, thumping his forefinger at a blood-bloated leech clinging to his leg just above the boot top.

"Kill it with mosquito spray," cautioned Kelly, "so you won't get infected."

"Oh, Chrize, no," said Ching-Ching. "We surely don't want to get infected or anything out here."

Red Dog spat tobacco juice and slicked it over the wriggling leech's back. "This slant-eyed fucker's got to burn." He snapped out his Zippo, set the flame close, and watched the creature sizzle on his leg. "Fuckin' VC."

"I used to like to play animal in the woods," said Canny, head on his pack, grimacing and rubbing his back. "Not no more."

"Whatsa matter?" asked Red Dog. "Ol' yella streak actin' up again?"

"Believe it," said Canny, "but otherwise than that, Purly, I got *my* shit together."

"Well, 'at's all right, Cousin. Just lean on me, heh, heh. I'll tote the weary load. Just lean on ol' Dog. Fuckin' hill don't scare my rusty butt none. Boo sheet, I been on coon hunts worse 'n this."

Not far away, Billy Wilson, Rodeliano, The Smoker, and Major Sheridan were huddling over a map. The XO was again walking in with the grunts while Gurgles commanded from above. Sheridan turned and came trooping down the column, injecting eleventh-hour élan into his Samurai. He spied me, stopped, bent over, mustache flying at me in the dusk.

"How's it going, Roland?"

"Still humping, Major. I'm Ripp."

"Listen"—he leaned close, skin around his eyes jumping, voice an excited whisper, the only time he had spoken to me in months—"this is what I was telling you about back there, remember? It's what we came for. We're going up that hill, kid. Just wanted to say good luck."

What *you* came for, I wanted to say, but didn't, as he wheeled and went on down the column, the old Banzai Kid, trailing clouds of gin and glory. In that moment, he seemed to have forgiven me my military trespasses before Armageddon.

The Smoker, loping along behind, leering like some malevolent ape finally at home in his jungle, was forgiving nothing. He got down close to my face with his cancer of the breath, whispering, "Still crying over your little mama, titty-sucker? Or can we depend on you tonight?"

Before I could think up an answer, he was gone, launching himself over to lay a last love tap on Roland, slumped against a tree, rubbing his temples.

"Well, what's wrong now?" He hulked over Roland. "Still on that damn locoweed? Listen, *yeww* fuck us up on that hill and I promise to personally save the gooks a two-cent bullet and end your misery. Before this day is done, I wanta see you eating lightning and crapping thunder, shitbird. And that ain't no shit."

"Thank you, Top Sergeant," Roland said miserably. "I don't care what you do."

When The Smoker turned away, Roland's shoulders twitched slightly, and then he shook himself like a dog shaking off water, or something worse.

A fierce *shoooosh* came over the top, and there was a sudden banging so close that the trees trembled all around and leaves came fluttering down over us. Everyone hit the deck, waiting for the next one. Everyone except Ernest Smoker, who stood there observing us with some disdain. And then his lips curled back in the human smile, showing the gums, the yellowed teeth.

15

Brave Hearts to the Front

Now in the dark, we moved through the remnants of an ARVN battalion and almost got shot, and then on through the green tangle into jump-off positions at the base of Hill 711, vacated by punch-drunk airborne.

Rodeliano and our new platoon sergeant, Horny Wheeler, ordered us to deepen our holes, chop down saplings for overhead cover, and clear fields of fire. There wasn't that much to do, though. Everybody's shelling had already chopped and cleared the position to pieces. And the holes were already deep, bloody deep.

Then I took a good look up those 711 meters for the first time, and "forbidding" didn't cover it, not what was coming off that hill. I could feel them up there, the eyes of Indochina, watching from their bunkers and spider holes, ready to die the glorious death, the Dragons of Dien Bien Phu, felt their breathing, felt their fingers caressing their triggers. . . .

It was fairly quiet now, and parachute flares came floating down, two million candle power, trailing smoke and running out eerie, jumping shadows over thousands of watery, scummy bomb and shell holes, over smoldering stumps and charred, topless trees, over corpses littering the slope like broken bags of forgotten garbage. I'd finally reached it, the back of beyond, the end of the earth.

The squad was hunched down in a section of zigzag trench, dug by the NVA, eating what Roland kept saying was our last meal. I ate peaches, tilting the can up, sipping the juice, thinking how nice it would be to be back in my good old safe cot back at good old Cu Chi. Compared to this, Cu Chi seemed like rear-echelon motherfucker heaven.

Off to the right, a puff of yellow smoke cracked open in the sky like a runny egg. There were more puffs—a steadily increasing volume of U.S. eggs—breaking across the hill, helping to drown out Roland.

Harry jumped down beside us. Wonderful news. We had three whole hours to rest and get ready, and then we were to proceed up the hill. It seemed nothing was ever so bad as it was going to get. It would be a night attack. That was what the wonderful fucking plan was. *They* had decided. I put down the peaches. I had hoped it would come tomorrow, or some far, far day in the future, or that the NVA would fade away. They were always said to be fading away, why in hell didn't they do it?

"Chrize, man," fretted Ching-Ching, staring up the hill, "I don't dig working this hoot-owl shift. When I agreed to come over here, I was assured the night belonged to Charlie. That was in the contract, man. I definitely think somebody has made a big mistake on this. Shouldn't we ask Gurgles about this? Just where is that Gurgles man, anyhow?"

"Frederick the Great is elsewhere," Harry said. "He sends cheers."

"But why is our commander not down here with us?"

"If he's a commander," Harry said, "I'm a prima ballerina in the Hanoi Ballet."

"Well, where's that Sheridan man?"

"He's with us. He's got his pecker up for this one, all the way."

Ching-Ching stared hypnotically up the hill as another flare drifted over our hole. "All I know is, if a poor dude keeps walking around out here, he's going to get himself badly harmed. I been scared over here maybe three hundred times already, man. But this is a lot more scarier. I mean there it *is*, man."

"And we should let it stay there," Roland said. "I know I'm not going up there."

"Sure you are," Harry grunted, punching open a can of C's with his knife. "What is this shit I'm eating?"

"No way," Roland said, gritting his teeth. "Not this time."

"Sure you will"—Harry jammed his knife in the side of the trench—"got to, got to."

"No, I don't got to." Roland clenched his fists. "Not anymore."

"Hey, so we've got this little hill to climb," Harry said, eating ravenously. "We'll whip right on up there and have a leisurely hilltop breakfast in the morning. I hate these meals on the run. Who's not eating those peaches?"

"Eat them," I said. "I've had enough."

"The thing is," Harry said, slurping down the peaches, "this could turn into a mildly eventful evening. So eat up, Rol. We need our strength for our little hike."

"It's going to be bad, Harry," Roland said. "It's really bad karma tonight. Don't you feel it?"

"It's going to be interesting," Harry said. "Tell him, Mike."

"Interesting," I said.

"I wanted to go to India," Roland said vaguely, shaking his head. "There are good things going on in India, Mike."

"Sure," Harry said, smiling. "India. Right after the hill."

"I wanted to go to Japan," Roland said. "I wanted to experience the tea ceremony."

"You will," Harry assured him. "We'll all go. We'll drink seventeen different fucking kinds of tea."

Harry had finished the peaches and was rummaging around for something else. "You're sitting on the food, Rol, enough to feed half of India."

"God, how can you sit down here in this grave and stuff yourself like a pig?" Roland blurted. "What good is eating when you're not going to be alive in the morning?"

"At ease, tiger. Go to sleep. Get some rest."

"Sleep? What good is sleeping when I'll be in a body bag before the sun comes up?"

"Bullshit. Hey, Canny, Dog—escort our buddy here up that hill, will you? Shoo all the bad guys away."

"It would be gettin' me a little bit upset escortin' him," said Canny from down the trench, "when I ain't even wantin' to escort myself."

"Sheet, yeah, I'll escort him," said Dog from the shadows, the sound of tobacco juice spatting mud. "I'll shoo 'em old karmas away. Do I look scared? Do I look beduffled? Ain't no karma make me piss my pants. Get outta the way up there, slope-karma assholes. Ol' Roland is coming up, heh, heh."

"Maybe they don't know they're slopes," Roland said. "Maybe they think they're actual human beings like you."

"They're fuckin' dog meat when I get through with 'em is what they fuckin' are. Sorry about 'at, old karma buddies!" Red Dog suddenly yahooed up the hill, sticking his arm up and giving the hill the finger.

"Quiet down," Harry said. "Get some rest."

"How does it feel inside a body bag?" Roland rambled on. "That's the relevant question here. What are civilized people doing out here climbing these miserable bloody hills anyway? Why doesn't somebody answer me that question? All we hear before we die is, 'Be gutsy! Go kick ass!' What would Breeze say about that now if he could come back? Somebody answer me that."

"He'd say, 'Fuck you, Roland,' " answered Red Dog.

Roland did not like being unable to make plans for tomorrow. He had not enjoyed the haphazardness of being a hippie, he once told me, and he certainly did not like the haphazardness of combat. He had been trying so hard to structure his life. He had embraced all the new California higher consciousnesses he could find in order to cement his center together. But something would always happen, and it would come loose and begin to shake around inside him. And now Hill 711 was happening. Earlier in the day, he had confided to me that he was thinking of becoming a Catholic again. But at the moment, he was getting ready to become whatever substance it was Ching-Ching had just passed on to him.

"Oh, Chrize," Ching-Ching was moaning, "listen to that up there. There can't be nothing left breathing up there. We might as well go home, men."

Our artillery was giving the hill a thunderous last prepping before our advance up the western slope. There were two beat-up battalions of South Vietnamese paratroopers to our left and a thinned-out battalion of American paratroopers on our right. These were the forces with which we would coordinate to make our presumed conquest of the hill. We were close to two thousand men concentrating on taking this single hill, on which sat an estimated one thousand of the enemy, with many more thousands at large in the hills and jungle around us.

Harry told us that the South Vietnamese had started up the northern slope earlier in the day, but after a few hours had fallen back, observing that today was not a good day to die either, although a lot of them did. Our airborne had followed in a second wave, had been met with fierce fire, and had also retired. Tonight, with the fresh Always First leading off the attack—his blue lightning, Gurgles called us—we would hit them from three sides.

"It sounds okay," Harry said. "We'll make it. We'll probably get medals for going up there."

"Horray for Harry," Roland said. "Harry's going up there. Harry's stopping a little communism today. Harry's carving up the Cong. Harry's kicking ass in Vietnam. Harry's not going to leave even one little grandma hag communist alive. Isn't that great?"

Our artillery barrages continued until near midnight, pounding the NVA mole men and trying to grind their tunnels, caves, trench systems, and catacomb bunkers to dust—conquest by awesome firepower. But some of us, not all of us awesome, still had to climb up there and go nose to nose with the moles.

Rodeliano came visiting and, as usual, there were too many variables in this combat problem for his liking. As usual, he gave us the feeling we were about to flunk out of life. But he liked to talk to Harry; he seemed to draw boldness from Harry the way he once had from Breeze.

In the light of a flare, the lieutenant's face looked like a man who was born not to lead, who had learned the words to somebody else's music. He dutifully tried to impress upon us the need for absolute discipline in this kind of night attack, of advancing by fire and maneuver, of squads leapfrogging squads, of platoons protecting platoons, of maintaining the momentum of the attack, of keeping the volume of fire up, of not wandering around and getting lost and shooting each other in the back and getting panicky and screwing up, just so many ways to screw up. "And most of all," he said almost desperately, "discipline, discipline, discipline."

"Yes, yes," Ching-Ching whispered back, "discipline. I got that. But I can't see in the *dark*, Lieutenant."

When the artillery stopped, the planes started, making pass after pass, dumping last payloads, quicksilver streaking from behind, sweptback wings, banshee howling down your brain and out your ass. Banging away with steel bombs with air brakes for maximum accuracy, then icing it over with fire, skipping, twisting napalm. Below, kneeling in that trench, squinting from the flashing, I saw other things looming up there, like the gates of hell, beckoning.

Roland, gazing pie-eyed up the hill, shouted to Harry over the explosions, "You've really got to feel pity for those poor people up there."

"Pity the poor people down here!" Harry shouted back.

"Just because they might shoot me," Roland shouted, poking

his head well above the trench top, "doesn't mean I abandon my sense of perspective."

"Quit hating yourself. Hate them."

"What's wrong with a little self-hatred? We've done so much to earn it. It'll be fine here when we're gone."

Between these observations, he was dragging deeply on a joint, and I don't know what else he was inputting, or exactly where he was in his inner kingdom, but he no longer seemed terrified by the hill. He stuck his head up like a bottle begging to be shot off a fence, watching the planes, bombs expended, return for a last round of aerial rocketry and incendiary cannon fire, that kept the hill cooking.

"This is not the America I believe in!" Roland wailed, shaking his exposed head in the negative. "Not this bomber of poor Southern peasants who only want to be free in their own land!"

"That's *not* poor Southern peasants," Harry shouted back. "That's fucking poor North Vietnamese, some of the best killers in the world up there!"

"This is not my vision of America." Roland suddenly stood grandly all the way up and seemed about to launch into an oration on his vision of America.

"Screw a lid on it, tiger!" Harry jerked him back down. "You're not *in* America!"

"Mike," Harry called, "gotta go see the lieutenant. Sit on his head till I get back."

"Oh, me," said Ching-Ching, gazing up the hill with terrible fascination, fires dancing across the cracks of his glasses, "before I was in this army, I kept reading about push-button warfare. All I would have to do was sit around pushing these little buttons. But, man, *where* are the buttons?"

It was getting close to time to go up when Harry came back. He had a look on his face.

"Are we ready?" He glanced around. "Brave balls to the front." Harry the Hammer.

"I've got to peepee," Ching-Ching said, "real bad."

"Let's get some," growled Red Dog. "You ready, Skin?"

"Yuuh," mumbled Skinny.

"Are we bad?" growled Red Dog.

"Yuuh . . . I guess."

I nodded that I was ready. But whatever the word *brave* meant, I wondered whether it included what was oozing off me now like some primal fluid leaking out of my deeps, that felt like grease and stank more like a swamp or one of the lower cesspools than anything human (*Were sweat glands the mirror of the soul?*), and maybe I would have to Zippo this uniform to ever get it out. . . .

Crouching, waiting in this glorious stink-cloud of myself, sinking deeper into my funk-hole, feeling a tremendous, heavy, sodden, already-dead-and-embalmed unwillingness to move (except for the racket that moved in my chest *ba-thump ba-thump*), I functioned in semiparalysis; *semi* because when Harry gave me the old can-do smile, I smiled vacantly back, because at that moment, I was wondering what a body bag did feel like inside (*smooth*, baby, or a little rough?).

Ba-thump, ba-thump—

(*Be quiet in there. Dear Lord, just get us out of here safe— just watch over us and keep us alive and—*)

"Hey," Harry said, fumbling in his pocket, "this might cheer you up. Almost forgot." He handed me a letter our mail clerk had asked him to pass on, a letter from Charlotte, the first in a long time. I looked at it and didn't want to read it, then desperately did want to read it—ripped it open, reading by flashlight, scrunched down in the mud—suddenly reading that we were no longer of the same essence, that we were no longer one.

"*People do change. I mean, not all the way, but in some ways. Have you ever thought back: Why did I ever want to do that? Was that me? How could I have ever wanted to be that, or think that, or do that?*"

Ba-thump, ba-thump, ba-thump . . .

My eyes scanned the letter, jumped forward, backward, *". . . miscarriage . . . one little boy who will never have to go to Vietnam . . . I didn't want to tell you, but now I have to . . . What held us together is gone . . . He never saw the light, never laughed a laugh, never cried a tear. . . ."*

She went on to say that I, Michael, had made my choice and left her, and that now she, Charlotte, was making her choice and leaving me. She was not *"cut out to play the submissive cow contentedly chewing her cud until her hero returned."* She had washed that *"whole dismal Southern swamp scene where we grew up"* from her completely. I was the last link in that decadent, smothering chain. She had unshackled. She was striding out. She was marching with wonderful new people, great anti-war heroes with brave ideas on how to save the country before it was too late, *"who are working as hard at peace as you are at war. Because you've also changed, Mike. Your letters show that you've become one of them. So forget me, Mike. Don't try to find me. We had a thing, but it wasn't the real thing. It was another kind of thing, a lust thing. We were both such warm, touching people. But it wasn't Me you loved. Me. I'm tired of being Miss Peachy Yum Yum. Oh, it was sweet with you once, Mike, so sweet. We could have been such an attractive couple in Larchmont, as they say. Only all that is so nowhere and nothing now. I guess we blew it. We couldn't just go through life endlessly copulating, without speaking. I wish you luck. I would say 'love,' only I can't anymore. Crying time is over. Our time is over. Stay alive. And let those poor people stay alive. The ruling pigs can't make you kill if you don't want to. This has to be it for us, Mike."*

She signed it "Charlotte."

And I could feel something warm releasing in my head.

Crazy, fucking crazy. It was postmarked San Francisco, where they wore flowers in their hair.

And then, "Awright, Bad Ass Company. Get up! Stand up! Up! Up! Let's go . . . go . . . up that fucking hill!" The Smoker.

"First Platoon! Rise and shine! Let's sock it to 'em!" That was Horny Wheeler.

And then Harry: Make sure you fixed your bayonet—make sure you clicked off safety—make sure there was a round in the chamber of your weapon—make sure you and your weapon were pointed in the proper direction. Looking down, I saw my hands, strange filthy things, crushing the letter in one hand, grabbing my beautiful piece with the other.

Harry was leading us out, *jug, jug, slop, slop* through mud-mushy holes, with Rodeliano waving us on. Roland came, zombie-eyed, trudging behind Harry. He had said he wasn't going, but there he was. Here came Red Dog in his eager dogtrot. Here came cousin Canny, far from eager. Here came Kelly, tongue jammed in the space between his teeth. Here came visibly shaking Skinny Lenny, stumbling over the stump everybody else had walked around, losing his helmet. Here came Ching-Ching, blowing last-second dope, losing parts of his pack, which Harry picked up and carried, lightening his heavy load as he dragged his bones toward bad vibrations. And here I came, something hot releasing in my head. Mike the Mad, because after the letter, I started losing it. I was not exactly concentrating on the task at hand, not exactly giving all that much of a flying duck-fuck about what happened to my precious body.

In the light of the simmering napalm, I could see many figures moving, many shadows, many fire-dancing bayonets, all moving in the proper direction, 711 meters to go. Just old-time hardballs straight-on big-dick infantry, ramming it up into the whites of their eyes. I wonder who's fucking her now . . . I hear somebody cussing and somebody praying . . . firing short bursts between prayers and curses as we go.

It's hard going, but good going for me . . . out of one mucky crater and down into another . . . over and around smashed trees . . . men falling, getting up . . . hearing Captain Wilson yelling now, "Form a wedge. Move toward the objective. Second, damnit, where are those machine guns? Jammed? Jammed, hell! Do any of those 60s work? Fire those 60s! Fire those weapons!"

Suddenly, the machine guns on the right start clattering, and Wilson cheers.

"Straighten up those flanks!" bawls The Smoker over the bopping of the guns.

"First Platoon, drive on!" Wilson hollers, waving us forward.

Rodeliano is on the radio: "Big Bill . . . This is Rodeo . . . Rodeo . . . What kind of sitrep have you got? Over . . . Say again . . . Again . . . That's a roger. That's a copy. Over."

We keep going, nothing tricky, just up, up, waiting, waiting . . . not a thing from the enemy, and then, suddenly, shrill bugling up there . . . a bugle freak up there, and then thunder on the left, little blips of light flickering as the firing starts.

"I need one element to go forward!" Wilson is yelling. "First, go forward! Drop rucks and go forward! Others secure the low areas!"

First Platoon keeps going, moving lighter now, *jug, jug, slop, slop.* . . . We had been maintaining a proper skirmish line, we had been going beautifully. It was only when the firing started that the small confusions began: problems of timing, occupying the wrong positions in the dark, mechanical malfunctions, uncoordinated grid coordinates, moving when you're supposed to be waiting, waiting when you're supposed to be moving. . . .

Many muzzle flashes straight ahead now . . . many smoke puffs rising . . . falling down in a hole and getting up in slop so deep it's like swimming in a swamp . . . the hammering of their machine guns on the ridge to the right. . . .

Bad news for Bad Company. We are scattering and scrambling. "Sanders is down . . . Sanders is down . . . Medic! Medic!"

Hard breathing, tripping forward, crunching upward, then down on the ground (*ba-thump, ba-thump*). Somebody's boot jamming my gut, but that's okay, it's all okay. It's Red Dog, "I got 'at fucker, I got 'em for sure!" And right beside him, huddling close, Skinny Lenny. "They're shootin' down our throats! We ain't gonna make it! Dog, you ain't dead are you?"

"If I'm dead, why you talkin' to me?"

And now it's raining mortars, thunder-clapping all around. The moment between maintaining forward motion and mad *di di mau* backward is upon us. Bravo goes down and seems ready to stay down, some of them become digging fools, burrowing blindly, looking for Sweet Mother Earth's womb to crawl into, some of them curling up and just staying curled up like little roly-poly bugs waiting for the shrieking and crashing to pass. Skinny Lenny seized in wet-dog shivering, little whines and whimpers coming out of a big man at two o'clock in the morning. . . .

And then someone makes a sound that seems to rise up out of the cracks of the smoking earth. That hellhound howling, Bravo's inspiration: Ernest Smoker.

"Let's *goooo*, let's *goooo*, let's *goooo!*" And all around, dead legs are churning again, men are driving up the hill again, bent under their packs, firing their weapons as automatic fire snaps around us like a thousand whips, red tracers richocheting a hundred feet in the air.

Dreamlike, I hear that bugle going again, much closer. I jog past blasted, burning bunkers, past burnt, broken trees reaching out with blackened fingers, hear a machine gun, not one of ours, coughing up stuff to my right, and another, pumping out big slugs *bum-bum-bum* from the left, see grenades, not ours, bouncing down the hill like a family of coconuts. At one point, I am picking up grenades and throwing them back up the hill. At another point, there is a stunning rainbowish flash and a sound like a rock spinning in a teakettle.

I am belly-down, all-tangled-up down in a watery bomb crater with Eve of Destruction—that's what's written on his helmet—and he is on top of me, screaming down in my face, "Get the fuck out of my face!"

"Get the fuck out of mine!"

I feel for mine, and it's all there. I feel for other things, and they're all there. My helmet a few feet away has a jagged hole in the side. There's another soldier down there, his helmet over his face. He rolls over slowly, sits up in the slimy water, blowing blood out his nose. He holds up what had been his whole right hand. Blood is flowing from his half fingers as though from wine spigots. It's poor Horny Wheeler, called Horny because that's what he always is. Horny as in got-to-have-it, needing-it-always, the gnawing between his legs driving him hungrily morning, noon, night. The eternal Horny, got-to-have-it Wheeler. Ask him if it's raining out, and he would talk about *it*. Ask him what's two and two, he would talk about *it*. Until now. Now he's staring at his fingers, which have beat his poor got-to-have-it-even-when-it's-not-there meat to an orgasmic pulp so many times. But never again.

"You'll be okay, Horny."

I slosh over, pull his head out of the water, prop him up, jam a compress against his neck.

"Sure as shit, grunt." Horny is grinning his famous silly grin. "Ain't no big deal here." Two seconds later, he falls over dead. No more talk of women who drive men wild. No more pussy forever. Our latest platoon sergeant slides down into the water.

This terrifies Eve of Destruction. He claws his way crazily out of the crater. Hardly is he over the top than there come sounds like bricks hitting a mattress. And Eve is up there screaming. I go hand-over-hand out of the hole, find Eve twisted over, holding his leg. Bullets snap like dry sticks past our ears.

"Can you crawl back to the hole?" I shout.

"I'm all busted!" he gurgles. "I can't move!"

"You got to crawl a little!"

"Oh, shit, I can't crawl! My leg—*ayeeeeeee!*"

"They're shooting right over our heads!"

"I need morphine!"

"I don't *have* any morphine!"

"Well, get a medic who does—*ayeeeeeee!*"

I tried to drag him, but all he did was holler and kick me in the face. And then I picked him up on my shoulder—what the fuck—and he was babbling and bawling, and I stumbled and slid, plunged and tripped—*ayeeeeeee!*—and now I really didn't give a fuck, and I finally crashed into a wide-eyed Rodeliano. Together, we got screaming Eve into a hole stacked with wounded, where blood-dazed Kelly wasn't getting any younger.

I turned and started back up.

The lieutenant blinked. "Where're you going?"

"To get my rifle."

"We're too spread out. Where's Harry? We're too spread out. Where's your squad? We have to get this coordinated. We have to get this under control. We have to—"

The lieutenant was a very methodical fellow. He preferred to set his life as carefully as a thermostat, no wild highs and lows for him. But this, now, was very unthermostatical. This was shitty chaos.

I told him I was going to retrieve my rifle, but really I was just going. Nearby, I saw The Smoker prowling through the smoke and fire, pausing to kick a soldier in the rump.

The startled grunt rolled over, "God, Top, I think I'm the last man left alive in my squad!"

"Then find a new squad, fudgenuts!" And booted him forward.

A shimmering flare broke overhead, and I glimpsed Roland, down on his knees. He seemed to be both sobbing and making a speech. But at the same time, he was actually firing his rifle in the general direction of the NVA. And beside him knelt Harry, shaking a fist, shouting in his ear.

From between two shrapnel-hacked tree trunks, Red Dog plodded into view, firing his machine gun from the hip, just mucking along, roaming in the gloaming, as though it was nothing but a wee-hours stroll through a field of Georgia cowshit.

But then another mortar barrage bracketed us, and everyone went down. Everyone but me. I was up fighting the Vietnam War all alone, and I didn't even have my piece.

I find my piece by the bomb crater. I see Horny down in the crater. I go down to see if there's anything I can do for him, and then I remember old Super Sperm is dead. I prop his head up out of the slime. I pick up my own helmet with the hole in it, place it on my head, goo dripping out of it, and with my piece firmly in hand, climb up out of the crater. It is important to keep one's piece close, so much closer to one than one's wife ever was, and I am going up that hill, and the thing is, frankly, my dear, I don't give a muck-fuck what happens. Floating free, feeling this immunity, no consequences, the immortal Private Crazy Fuck, one-time riser in the underwear ranks. I'm all pumped up, chemically primed, boiling in my own bitter juice.

Some part of my great brain has separated off. . . . I'm my own fucking picture show, seeing my boots stepping in the lovely shit of war, watching my arms thrashing forward, seeing more of myself than I have ever seen or bad-dreamed.

Then, beside a big rock ahead, there is a muffled explosion. NVA. Dragons of Dien Bien Phu. They come staggering out of the mouth of a smoke-belching little cave. The first one runs bowlegged crazy right at me like he knows me, hello . . . blood and noises running out of his mouth, an AK-47 in his hands. I am spitting adrenaline, and I shoot him before he shoots me, if that is his intention. My first sure kill, and from that moment on, I no longer come close to understanding what I am doing in any neat, cogitative, is-this-a-wise-and-prudent-course, will-I-get-hurt sore of way. Because here comes the second one, like a napalm apparition, jumping wildly, uniform on fire, his pith helmet spinning out in front of him. He goes, rolling, yowling, right past me down the hill. I see The Smoker standing over that burning, kicking ghost for a long moment, then a short thrust, a little satisfied jerking of his bayonet. Got some. Then he is yelling something at me, waving his arms. . . . Long may he wave. We're not even fighting the same war. . . .

Out front now, they're crawling out of holes everywhere. I hear that spastic bugler, very close now . . . only they're scrambling not forward but backward up the hill away from us as fast as they can go, and I'm going after them. I am taking that hill. Shooting them better, faster than I have ever done anything.

Gone ape with audacity, fifty billion nerve cells firing off. I am going up that hill. Emotions, instincts hitting me too fast, unrecordable, just a raging rushing manic close-to-ecstatic killing blur, all of it finally just shoved up there in my throat, and I heard a sound that could have come out of The Beast, or Ernest Smoker, exploding out of me as they fled before me toward the Gates of Hell, where they belonged.

In fact, at just past sunrise on that morning, we stood at the top of Hill 711, staring down over what we had come up through, eyes not focusing too clearly, ears still ringing, shell drunk, reeking of gunpowder and blood, all bone and muscle exhausted, but kings of that hill, and we whooped and hollered, we made strange sounds never before recorded, not for tender ears, not for apple-pie society, not for psychiatric scrutiny. Because what shrink had ever made it up Hill 711? We stood up there fiercely, joyously, every filthy, stinking, smoking hair of us, yelling and roaring at that murderous bitch of an impenetrable jungle down there.

"We did it! We did it!" burbled Rodeliano, with much shaking of hands and slapping of butts.

"Real fine, you people did real fine!" yelled Captain Billy Wilson. "Oh, real fine. Where is Mike Ripp? Let me shake the hand of Mike Ripp."

They all wanted to shake the hand of Mike Ripp. "Where is the real Mike Ripp?" I heard Harry shouting. "Where is that mysterious fucker?" And he came over and embraced me.

" 'Cause the early bird gets the worm," Red Dog was going around yelping, "ever time, ever time. *Yahooo! Yahooo!*"

"Oh, we hung in there, did we not?" roared a black radioman called Willie the Moose. "We showed *all* the cats. Oh, rat on! Rat on! Hallelujah!"

We were up there flying, riding clouds of power, lords of that murderous bitch jungle. I got up high on some NVA sandbags at the edge of the hill, looking out over it all. Somebody down there could easily pick me off. Just daring it to happen. Well, piss on it, it won't happen. No way today, José. Piss on you, forest. And piss on you, Charlotte. Piss on you, underwear. Piss on it. Harry started singing. The Bad Ones were singing. We were alive, on top of the hill singing our bad song:

> "Oh I may hurt and I may cry,
> But I know damn well I won't die,
> 'Cause Bravo leads the way. . . ."

REWIND

Skinny Lenny. "I admit it. I used to fear certain stuff, heights and stuff. Gettin' killed and stuff. But I figured if I could go up this hill, it makes me something different, you know. Like back in South Carolina, I never went up no hills like this.

"I mean, a guy says, 'I'm not gonna go up this hill, it's gonna kill me.' So the only way you can do it is stop bein' afraid of nothin' or anything, and just go up the hill. I tell you, goin' up this hill will get you away from bein' afraid of nothin' or anything. It scares you no more, you know. Not darkness, alligators, anything.

"Just forget it. Go up the hill. Get the idear? It's a good game for your mind. Lot of work, lot of pain. What scares me is waitin' to do it. I never coulda thought the sound of shells and bombs are so loud. The most fun is when you do it with your eyes open. When the incomin's comin' in, some guys keep them shut.

"Now I'm not scared like I was of stuff. I'm not scared to volunteer for stuff anymore. I mean, I feel I can do anything. From up here, I can see everything. More than the guy walkin' around on the ground. Hell, I come up this hill. I feel good. I feel happy. I feel like I don't have nothin' wrong with me no more. It comes from the heart, you know. It feels good."

16

Victory Party

*"In the Central Highlands there are
many wild animals, such as elephants,
tigers, and monkeys. . . . Hunters, with
either camera or rifle, are at all
times surrounded by scenery of
breathtaking beauty. . . ."*

—OLD VIETNAM TRAVEL FOLDER

The sun is high, and the hill steams. I feel way low down.
Peaked out. All shot-down cold turkey from Armageddon, and
the whole place stunk up with cordite and death. But it's victory,
all right. The message from the general confirms it:

"Heartiest congratulations for your magnificent display of
teamwork and aggressiveness in the taking of Hill 711. In addi-
tion to the large number of enemy KIA and weapons seized,
the number of POWs taken merits highest praise. Well done on
a great victory. Lightning Blue all the way!"

This is read to us, or rather crowed to us, by Frederick G.
Gurgles, who—one hand tucked in his webbed pistol belt, the
other, the one with the message, scratching his crotch—stands
on some sandbags on the hilltop eroticizing the thrill of victory.

"Men of the Always First Battalion. By God, the general
knows it was us who took this hill. I made sure of that. Not the
ARVN. Not the airborne. They tried, but by God *we* took it.
We furnished the momentum. Big Mo was on our side. We led
the assault. We mounted this cherry. We busted this baby wide
open. We creamed this baby good.

"Now, men. Just as soon as we can haul some beer up here,

we're going to have us a victory party. You have my word on that. I don't think these hotshots want any more of what we've got to offer for a while."

Gurgles jerks his thumb toward an NVA corpse jackknifed over a stump. It doesn't look too tough dead.

"Now what am I trying to say? I'm trying to say that I know you men better than your own fathers. I have always believed in you, and I know you have always believed in me. I have always prided myself in being tough-but-fair with you. I have never asked anything of you that I wouldn't do myself, and so on and so forth.

"Men, I now know that you can cut the mustard for me. That we can play against *any* team. As a great old coach used to say, 'I think we established our running game up here last night.'

"Now, men, why is that? Well, I'll tell you why. It is because, by God, we are winners—*big* winners, by God. Because *I* am a winner and *you*, my men, have caught the winning spirit, and now you are also winners. Now let me hear from you, men. Are we winners or are we not winners?"

There is some response to the effect that we are winners, and then a little black soldier, pissing on a log, his head wrapped in about six pounds of bandages, drawls out, "Sho 'nuff, we's big winnuhs, coach. When can the big winnuhs get a little sleep?"

"Now, men. We are winners and we should properly project the image of winners. But some of you men look a little hang-dog out there."

"We's *tired* dogs, coach," says the little black soldier standing there, head down, pissing on the log.

The colonel looks sympathetic and goes on to say that it is regrettable that some of the troops of the Always First had to give the last, full measure of their devotion in order that this cherry might be mounted. But he is pleased that our casualties are only light to moderate. He is also pleased that representatives of the media will soon be choppering in to record this event. He orders us to quickly finish policing up our KIA and start laying out their KIA for best visual effect. Our bods are being shuttled out by Chinook, but there is some debate as to whether their bods are to be bulldozed into mass graves after viewing by the media, burned, or loaded in slings under helicopters, flown out over the jungle and dumped. He strongly desires that we impress the press, but to watch our words so that we convey only positive images. He urges us to spruce up and shave if we can, scrape off the crud, and generally try to radiate images of victory for the television cameras. He reminds us that this, as much as anything, is a media war, and those pictures will go back to an America that is an image-conscious country, a win-oriented country.

"So, men, let's put our best boot forward when we're on prime time, ha, ha. So loosen up out there. Rare up on your hind legs, by God. Show them what winners look like. Because, by God, I have conquered a damn mountain out here, and I will not be defeated by any sorry little molehills. So clean yourselves up, men, clean yourselves up. . . ."

He becomes exuberant again, and we learn that it is not the worst thing to be a KIA in the Always First Battalion. "Because anybody who died in this outfit has no reason for shame. I can tell the world—by God, I *will* tell the world—that the men of the Always First went down with snarls on their faces, that their fighting image is unsullied, that they will lie in heroes' graves, and so on and so forth. Now, men. You have my word on that. So you don't need to worry on that score. . . ."

But later, with rags tied around our noses, with the sweet, choking flesh-fog rising around us as we clean our dead off the hill and drag their dead out of the bunkers we're moving into, I could tell the colonel that men went down with many things on their faces, those that still had them.

Some of their dead left this world mashed so flat by great blast forces that they seemed only painted on trees and rocks, plastered across sandbags, or just sprayed into corners of bunkers and trenches, nothing left but a little flesh and cloth, often footless or handless, still vaguely in the general human shape, about an inch thick.

The old dead hump around like rotting scarecrows, their faces eaten off by rats and things. Some of the new dead seem more active. One of our guys is kicking high, maybe a fifty-yarder. Like he won the game. So winning-looking, in fact, that I carefully nudged his spine with my boot . . . and feel that he's all stiffed out . . . see a piece of thighbone rammed like a spear into his groin. Close by, four NVA prance beside a trench, nicely in step, arms spread, mouths open, faces so napalm-blackened they looked like a chorus of mammy singers. Others blossom frozenly around the edges of a mustard-colored crater. One blossom clutches a grenade high up between the remains of its jellied brains and two burnt tins of American pound cake. Another blossom, helmet cocked back jauntily, seems about to scratch its nose, only no nose.

Sometimes, they are blown free of their clothes, and their flesh has so grayed or yellowed or blackened or become barbecue-colored that it is difficult to tell whether they are friends or foes, much less whether they have snarls on their faces.

Now I move as if entranced down the hill, trying to remember things from the night, looking for the first man I shot. I'm shooing away rats, picking my way around tail fins of half-buried mortar shells, grenades with the pins pulled, an unexploded five-hundred-pound bomb stuck straight up in the mud, stepping over smashed AK-47s, cracked helmets, burnt packs, shot-up canteens, and Ho Chi Minh sandals scattered over the hill like battlefield confetti. I look for him—I know I dinged him—but I can't find him.

Then Skinny Lenny yells for me to come see what he's found. He's found a G.I. in an NVA bunker with his hands tied behind him, a long rope tight around his neck, his legs spread wide and tied by the ankles. He's naked except for one sock. There's also this obscenely fat, red-eyed rat with its head poked halfway into the soldier's gut. A ripping noise, and the rat is tearing out bunches of intestines, his jaws jerking back and forth like a dog with an old sock. Skinny pitches clods of dirt at the huge rat, which ignores him. I kick dirt and hear myself saying "huh, huh" at the rat in the manner of a bullfighter to a bull, and the rat seems to laugh. Then it stares at me balefully, as though I am the one who is supposed to retreat. At this point, Red Dog arrives. He takes one wild look and attacks with his bare hands, seizing the rat by its tail and flinging it far down the hill.

All the while, he's bellowing that he knows the dead soldier. His name is New, ol' Spec-4 New, a fellow Georgian. Good ol' New. Poor ol' New. Red Dog bellows for Canny to get his ass down here.

"Ain't 'at ol' New from Valdosta?"

Canny shakes his head. "Naw, 'at ain't New. New was from Waycross."

"Hell it ain't, peckerhead," hollers Red Dog, whose filthy face seems to be sweating blood. "You can tell what's went on by the way the bastids got him tied."

He and Canny seem ready to fight over whether it's ol' New from Valdosta or Waycross. Whoever it is, what he's been through has taken off one ear and one testicle. Something like cigarette burns polka-dot his body. He seems to have suffered not only rat bites, but also random pokings with a bayonet. In another bunker, three more grunts are found in similar condition. None appear to be snarling much.

"Just wait I get aholt me a gook!" shouts Red Dog, raging around, finally kicking out at an NVA corpse slumped over a machine gun. The corpse's head rolls sideways, the top sliding off as neatly as the lid of a broken coffeepot. Red Dog slaps a Lightning Blue patch into the open brain of the NVA, then, not satisfied, jerks at the man's gear, seizes his knapsack and shakes out paper all over the corpse. A picture of a frail, demure young Vietnamese woman falls out. And then a picture of the soldier with the woman and two children, one of those family photos. They were all very well dressed. And the soldier looked proud of a family that he cared for, very proud. Then another picture tumbles out: a large, naked *Playboy* white lady with breasts as big as cataloupes. Red Dog flaps out the centerfold and jumps around howling and yelling.

While this is going on, I squat down beside New's bunker and pick up a letter written in English, just as someone taps me on the shoulder.

"What's the matter with that man?" asks Major Sheridan, who is trooping the hill to survey the victory.

"Well, he's dead, Major."

"No, I mean that man jumping up and down over there."

"I don't know for sure, Major."

Sheridan crouches and looks at New, or whoever he is, and says he has to be airborne, he's not one of ours.

"I try to know every face in the battalion," the major says, fiddling with his mustache. "And I don't know that face."

Sheridan stuffs a cigar in his mouth and tells me what we did during the night was "damn fucking terrific." He notes that some lucky folks are going to be up for something very, very heavy in the medal department. He looks at me warmly.

"I'm amazed at you, Roland, just *amaaaazed*. What you did was just—"

"Ripp, Major. I'm not sure what I did. It's mostly a blur."

"Keep on blurring, kid. We can use all the blurs like you we can get."

He gives his mustache a twist. In the major's eyes, I have finally lost my civilian cherryhood and joined the boys on the road to Valhalla. He claps me on the shoulder before moving off. "Be talking to you, kid."

He doesn't get far, however. There, plopped before him, is Roland on a stump, looking gray-faced at the ground, looking about ready to vomit. Beside him, Ching-Ching maybe already has.

BRAVO BURNING

"Are you men all right?"

"In the pink, sir," Ching-Ching says with a happy chirp.

"Glad you made it through. You all did a fine job."

"Thanks awfully. Guess we were too late to join the dead," Roland mumbles from his stump. "Guess there were just too many in line ahead of us, sir."

"I see you haven't lost your grip on unreality, kid. Look, you men made a hell of a fight up here. Nothing to be so down about."

"What exactly do you want me to say, sir? How *up* I feel because we slew some little communist boys?"

"Why don't you *try* saying that?" says Sheridan, bending over, trying to catch Roland's down-staring eyes. "Better than saying little communist boys slew *you*, kid. 'What happened on this hill was no small feat of arms and will be remembered' is what I'd say."

"Remembered?" Roland still won't look up. "By whom exactly, sir? The wives and children of the dead?"

"I'm sorry for them. But there was something very special displayed up here last night called American valor. And it had damn well better be remembered."

"It's all right with me, sir. You sure don't have to sell the bright side of death to me, sir. I'm a captive here. Sell it to the media, sir. We might even be on TV if we keep up the old image, sir."

Roland's head droops lower—he's gagging.

Sheridan frowns, starts to say something, cuts it off, and jabs a finger at Roland. "Get this man a medic if he's sick," he instructs Ching-Ching.

Roland lifts his head a little. "That's all right, sir. What's our next goal? Another hill, sir? All the hills? There's no doubt we can take them all, sir. We can improve our image and show everybody how good we really are at killing communists, sir. And how good we are yet to become. I really look forward to it, sir."

156

"Get this man a medic," Sheridan says softly and walks off, his day spoiled a little.

"Yes, get this man a medic," Roland half gags, half laughs. "I sit here watching seas of maggots eating the brains out of human beings, and that officer says, 'Get this man a medic.' That's what this hill needs, all right, a medic. Well, I don't need any medic. I'm burying *them*, aren't I? *I'm* the man with the shovel, aren't I? See how the living go strutting around feeling so big and brave and superior to the dead, telling each other how big their balls are."

"Dead is dead, man," says Ching-Ching, watching a couple of grunts drag away the NVA machine-gunner by the heels, his coffeepot skull going *bumpety-bumpety* past ol' New's body being wrapped in a poncho. "That's all I see."

Now comes our colonel, ordering Rodeliano to recon this western slope and beyond during the night and try and drum up a little more NVA business.

Only a few days before, he had dressed down his lieutenant as one of those who often lacks "*agggressiveness*, who does not always give me a-hundred-ten-percent effort, who gives me excuses instead of results, who wears his asshole wrong side out when it comes to soldiering, who is in need of counseling, who gives me a large case of the ass. Now pull your head out of your ass, Lieutenant, or it will be my thorny duty to ask you to turn in your bars. Be advised: If you can't perform, you are replaceable."

That was then, this is now. Now the colonel congratulates his lieutenant on a job well done. Now he is behind his lieutenant one hundred twenty-five percent. Now all is forgiven.

"Good man, Lieutenant, good man. If you need any help, just holler. Forage in the forest, Lieutenant. Find me some more of the bastards, and I'll bring down the world on them. Find 'em, fix 'em, and I'll fuck 'em. We'll draw a little blood, won't we? Hell, blood makes the grass grow out here. Now where is your Private Ripp? I understand he wiped out half the fucking—"

The colonel's attention is suddenly diverted by bigger business. The general is arriving. The colonel scurries to the nearby LZ, where Lightning Blue's leader is already emerging from his chopper. There are salutes, smiles, handshakes, and the colonel shows the general the victory. They troop our way.

"This is one damn fine effort, Colonel," General Edgar Whitehouse is telling our colonel. "Too bad they won't stand and fight a little more often."

"Us seventy, them zip, sir," says Gurgles. "Just tell me what hill you want me to take next. I'll do anything you want me to, sir."

Frederick the Great, who had not set foot on the hill during the fighting, totes out the numbers: a better than sixteen-to-one kill ratio; this many weapons captured; that many prisoners taken. All in all, one of the great statistical triumphs of the war. The figures are preliminary, of course.

Whitehouse, a tall gray man with eyes like winking blue stars, ebulliently announces he will say a few words to the men. Trumpets seem to sound. A few yards away, a television team, the first of the media to arrive, cranks up.

"Men . . . soldiers . . . or should I say *heroes?* First, I want you to know that I am proud of you. . . ."

The general is sweating. It is wiltingly hot, and the stench of rotting humanity makes speechifying difficult.

"And don't think the folks at home aren't just as proud. Years from now, when you are members of veterans' organizations and telling your friends how you took Hill 711, you will look back on your experience here as your finest hour. . . ."

The general carefully places the forefinger of his right hand under the rolled-up section of his left sleeve, lifts it and brushes it across his steamy forehead. The razor creases of his fatigues are beginning to droop.

"What we have done is taught the enemy he cannot even conquer the rain forests without terrible consequences. On top of that, I think the Hanoi war geniuses will think twice before

they ever tackle Lightning Blue again. The enemy may win the
headlines, but on the battlefield, where it counts, we win, and
we are winning big. We will win the last battle because Americans have never learned the meaning of the words *quit* or
lose...."

Some of the troops yell and break into applause. The general
is making his talk in the middle of Bad Company's sector. He
tells us he is recommending The Bad Ones for a Meritorious Unit
Commendation. An aide hands the general a washrag for his
face. Another aide whispers in his ear.

"American soldiers," says the general, beginning to move
away, "I am sorry to leave, but there is a war out there that
must be attended to. Just let me say, 'Keep it up, men. Let the
enemy know there is no place he can call his own.' The enemy
is steadily weakening, increasingly hurting, all the indices of
progress are on our side. We have pursued him into his redoubt
and kicked his ass. This enables us to get on with WHAM—
Winning Hearts And Minds—which enables us to get on with
Nation Building. This enables us—but I have talked enough.
I leave you with your battalion commander, the man who led
you to this great victory, whom I'm sure you would like to hear
from—"

"*Noooooo,*" comes a moan.

Our general departs with his party. Our colonel, looking proud
and inspired, prepares to impart a few more words:

"Now, men, the general said some fine things. At this point
in time, I want to add something very important to that. Now,
what am I trying to say?"

We don't know, so our colonel swings his jaw out like an iron
gate to tell us.

"Now, men. You have a golden opportunity to add to your
victory laurels out here. Intelligence tells me that that forest out
there is still seething with enemy assholes, and that is music to
my ears. Once we've had our little party—I promised you beer,
and it is on the way—I want to see you actuate your full poten-

tial as a fighting battalion. Our lethality must grow and grow. Men, I know you won't let me down. The general has great faith in us. So let's be big. Bigger than we have ever been. Let's dream a dream out here. Let's kill the sonofabitches! We can't just sit up here relaxing. Do you get the picture? Ever Forward, Never Backward. Kill the enemy! Kill the enemy! As a great old coach used to say, 'I want you to play every down like it's the last down of your life.' "

Chow time, eat-a-little-death time. You gagged just breathing that hill, much less trying to digest it. I sit against a scorched log, pull out a can of beans and franks from the big pocket of my fatigues, open it up with a P-38, and try to swallow without inhaling.

My hand had brushed against Char's crushed letter in my pocket and jumped away from it. Electric shock. Can't read it. Won't even touch it. The guy they say killed thirty or forty or a hundred NVA can't look at a little piece of paper. The boy who once fished drowning bugs from swimming pools has just terminated thirty or a hundred gook human beings . . . Jesus . . . I remember one. . . .

Out front of the log, some grunts have shoveled up another army: eight smooth, gleaming, white skulls. A column of black ants comes marching over the crowns and through the holes . . . the eye sockets of Indochina upon me. . . .

Overhead, a Phantom circles and dippity-doo-das around. At the other end of the log, Willie the Moose takes off his boots— "Ahhhh"—and puts his feet up on a couple of skulls. A look of near ecstasy floats across his face as he airs his feet. "Brains is fine, but feets is beyond compare. . . ."

Humming pleasantly *Nobody Knows the Trouble I've Seen*, he heats up some spaghetti, which is "terrible" when eaten cold, but "devastatingly fine" when hot, much to be preferred over common "grenades and rocks" (meatballs and beans), which are for "peasants."

"Well," says Canny, shaking his head, "I got to say, like when you're really, really hongry, there ain't no better than ol' grenades and rocks. They just keep bein' there and bein' there, spoonful after spoonful."

"Great news," comes Red Dog's strangled voice. "I think these fuckin' C-rats is contaminated." He plops a can down on one of the skulls. "Let 'at fucker try it. He looks like he could use a bite."

"Damn!" gasps Canny, spitting. "Jailhouse coffee is better'n this shit."

"Whyn't we gettin' no hot meal after all we done?" grouses Skinny Lenny. "Only time we get a hot meal anymore is soup. The hot meal is cold soup."

"New C-rats for us was boxed in '52," says Canny.

"That's 'cause we're rompin', stompin', ass-kickin' infantry," says Harry. "Hard-core."

"Well, this old hard-core wants a beer," says Canny. "Ol' coach promised us beer. Where's 'at fuckin' beer?"

"I'll go down and check it out," says Harry. "There's a bird coming in now."

"Say 'C-rats' back home," says Canny, "and they don't know what you're fuckin' talkin' about."

"Except my old man," says Harry, standing up, laughing. " 'C-rations? Yeah, I remember C-rations,' my old man used to say. 'They still got those C-rations?' 'Sure, dad,' I told him. 'They still got 'em. Probably the *same* ones.' "

Circling around the skulls, Harry heads down the slope toward where The Smoker is hollering commands out of the side of a mouth stuffed with food, chewing and hollering. Tossing away one can and grabbing another, he dips in three fingers, scoops out a dripping glob of something, and pokes it in his maw. The Smoker is consolidating our victory. He's directing the building of a new LZ to get more choppers in, and the choppers are hauling in supplies and hauling out casualties as fast as they can. Already, the POWs and the used-up American

BRAVO BURNING

and South Vietnamese airborne who helped us take the hill have
been carried to the rear. The word is that Hill 711 is our baby
to have and to hold.

Sitting there, I remember the letter I found near ol' New's
bunker. Chewing beans and franks, I read:

"Dear Sally,
Well Sally it's hardly anytime to Thanksgiving and Christ-
mas but you cant guess it in this place. I have started to
write you about five times Sally. This is the fith. And
everytime here come the dang incoming or the NVA
themselfes. So Sally we sure have been having it pretty
ruff and taken a lot of KIA but I guess you heard about
it in the news.

Well Sally hows life treating you? Real fine I do hope.
As for me I'm still humping but I don't know how much
longer. Because this place is driving me crazy. One reason
is weve had contact day or night for weeks and when you
see your buddies buying the farm it really gets to you bad
and I dont know how much longer I can take it. I can't
sleep for its like sleeping on pins and needles. I jump
everytime I hear a blade of grass bend. Well Sal if it
wasn't for God I sure wouldn't be here today. So Sal
please do me one favor and when you say your prayers
say a word for me. Sal the way its going us men on this
hill needs people to pray for us. For in the past week weve
had 50 killed and 200 wounded. Right now I dont even
know how I'm going to get this letter off this hill. The
NVA are all around us in fact.

Well Sal I'll close for now saying be good and behave.
And I know it's a little late but I'll say it anyhow. Happy
Birthday and many more to come. Sal on the money no
need to send it to me. I sure cant use it where I am. Go
out and buy yourselfe something and think of it as my
Christmas present to you. Is that a deal? Sal I sure hope
that by this time next year we can be together."

It stops there, unsigned. I keep on eating beans and franks with a white plastic spoon and gaze up at a sky as sweet-blue as a baby's dream. I gaze out over the smoking hills and hear more shit going on out there, and the can shakes in my hand. There is the strong urge to get up and do a little fast roadwork like that time back in the chow hall. I keep on eating. Into pound cake now. Pass the peaches. And say a word for me, Sal.

"Ho, ho," Red Dog is teasing Kelly, who's writing a letter to his girl on the back of C-ration boxes. "I got a stamp in my wallet if you want to mail it."

"She just likes to know what's going on," stammers Little Boy Blue, starting to blush.

"Nothing wrong with that, man," reassures Ching-Ching.

"Writes her even while he's eatin'," teases Red Dog. "Writes her even while he's slappin' his dong."

"Nothing wrong with that, man."

"At least he can write," says Roland, who sits staring at the skulls, rubbing his temples. "At least he's washed his mouth out with the human language."

"Well, wash your mouth out with this, buddyfucker," says Red Dog, unflapping his *Playboy* girl. "Look at 'at, men. Now 'at's a real woman. She can break her pussy off on my ol' two-by-four anytime. She can have a load of my heavy lumber any ol' day. You gotta picture your gal, Kelly?"

"Nothing like that," Kelly says. "But she's a real Mississippi magnolia. And that's what she is, too."

Now he smiles, lowering his voice. "Soon as this is over," he says softly, glancing around, "we're getting married. She wears a gold dog tag. It says, 'I belong to a soldier.' What we want is a real wedding, you know. Whole dang thing. Something we'll never forget. It'll be great having our parents and all our friends. And all you guys. If yawl can get there. Because we're ready. I'm ready, and she's ready. It's going to be great."

"Yeow! Damn fuckin'-A, I'm ready!" shouts Red Dog. "I met me a little Doughnut Dolly down at Cu Chi 'fore we left. Just kept dancin' with me. Couldn't keep her hands off of me. I knowed she wanted it bad."

"Women there were gettin' *paid* to dance with you, dummy," says Canny.

"Boo sheet. Gals know what I got. Want some of my good ol' Southern root oil is what they want. Bring an ol' dead pussy back to life, what I got. Yow! Next time, I'm gone lay the lumber on her. Bigger'n life. Use 'em and lose 'em, 'at's what I say. Ain't 'at right, Roland?"

Roland closes his eyes.

Canny sniggers. "Only pussy Dog can get is 'at car-wash stuff outside Cu Chi gate. This little Veet gal said she'd be happy as a pig on slop to do us all for three bucks. Right there in the road. Dog was ready to get down on it, too. Get a hundred bucks worth of clap, too."

"Six guys in Weapons Platoon humped her ass for a case of C's, and she couldn't even get up and walk away," says Red Dog.

"Six brave boys humped your butt, you wouldn't get up and walk away either," says Roland.

Now Harry comes back up, a blaze of hair and freckles in shimmering heat that makes the corpses bloat and sing and dance and snarl and not care about women. The rest of the media better come on and record this event, this victory, I'm thinking, because my own thinking is getting a little bleary, deary. The trouble is, now that we have won this victory, we should just fly our butts out of here. Why must we hang around here staring at victory? It should have ended at sunrise. On that high, hard note at sunrise is when the fucking victory should have ended.

"What's the matter up there?" I hear The Smoker yelling. "*Yeww* big guns think it's limp-dick time just cause you got lucky last night? Then you don't know gooks."

· · ·

We don't know gooks. Because late in the afternoon of our victory, the first 122-mm rocket comes sailing into Bravo's position on the western slope. Red Dog, his cup of Kool-Aid blown all over him, is aghast at this kind of sneakiness.

"You see 'at?" he yells, gawking. "Come right down out of the blue. When ever'thang was nice. You see 'at sneaky dink shit, Canny?"

"Ain't you learned a litle bit?" grunts Canny. "When ever'-thang's nice, that's when they *do* it to you, dipstick."

They are arguing about when the NVA do it to you when the NVA start doing it again.

"Hit it! Mortars!"

We go back down in a scramble, saying more fast words to heaven, faces mashed into the dirt, mashed into boots, mashed into crotches—*The dignity of man*, I'm thinking, *the towering dignity of man*—as some big-ass farts in my face.

"Where's our air? Where's our gunships?" somebody is shouting.

"Heard those poppin' out of the tube," gasps Willie the Moose. "Hopes they's firin' blind. Hopes they don't have a spotter. Hopes they don't move that tube an inch to the right."

Now something rushes in just below us and hits the new LZ, where a lot of fresh ammo is stacked. I'm really learning the music now. Pissing on myself learning it. The hill moves. Shrapnel is playing all sorts of wild sick songs close to my head.

They've got Hill 711 plotted like a cemetery. It seems like a whole damn regiment is firing at us from down there in the same bitch jungle I thought we conquered last night. I jerk a flak jacket over me and wriggle under it like a worm under a leaf. *Whoooom!* My head jams against a rusty shell canister, and one eye peaks through the hole in my helmet at the sky falling. A big chunk of it falls precisely on the sandbag where coach made his speech about victory and Big Mo being on our side. But where is victory? Where is Big Mo? Where is beer? Where is coach?

17

Something's Burning

*"If there wadn't no God,
I think I would shit."*

—Red Dog

The artillery repeatedly works up and down the hill. It's been going on all night for thirteen nights.

We are at the top, entrenched under a maze of giant stands of bamboo. The incessant shock waves crack and bend them over us like great curving bows. Chunks of steel whack like burning baseballs through the battered trees, and chips of wood and hot metal tumble down around us.

The good news is that this is friendly shelling that might kill us. The American bombardment is to keep the heavily reinforced NVA, dug in all around us, from massing for another attack. Bravo Company marched up this hill with one hundred twenty-one living souls, and we are down to eighty who can shoot. Battalion casualties are running about the same level, and we are unable to evacuate our dead and wounded. NVA gunners, their .51-caliber machine guns and other antiaircraft weapons equipped with flash suppressors, are positioned along the lower sections of the hill and on nearby ridge lines, and they shoot down or drive off every chopper trying to land.

Finally, the artillery stops. With moonlight jumping over our backs, we stare down the slope through a chill yellow mist drifting over ferocious tangles of burnt brush, skeletal trees, and an unburied chaos of bodies. Between shellings, we hear the whisper-babble of NVA, the bolts of their AKs snicking, the sounds of shovels clinking against dirt and rock. Then a listening post seventy-five meters down our western slope again reports heavy enemy movement, twigs cracking, figures darting.

"They're all over the place," whispers Skinny Lenny over the radio. The string bean, a changed man, had volunteered to go out there. We crouch as Billy Wilson speaks softly, surely into his radio, "Okay, so we're gonna work the big stuff in closer, real close. Just get way down in that hole. Way, way down—"

Then the shells come crunching in from fire bases Americans have set up on other, less-contested, hilltops. The explosions jar your spine. They unravel your core. They convince you the human race is mad. Shells crisscross over us. I close my eyes and follow the trajectories. The ones from the left are bigger, but fewer. Those from the right come in volleys of four, six, eight. *Firepower.* The sheer murderous noise of it makes men cringe and curl up like dead leaves.

There's a pause, and Skinny croaks, "No more, no more, that was *perfect!*"

Willie the Moose lets out a subdued cheer, "Rat on, baby, rat on. Teach them mothafucks to play with us."

"Shhh," says Wilson. Already, movement is reported by another listening post. Again Wilson calls in artillery, and again the earth rolls and shimmies beneath us.

Later in the night, Ching-Ching whispers to me, "Man, I been scared so long now, so damned long, it just stays dug in my belly like a claw."

We're five and six to a bunker, wrapped in poncho liners. "Who'd a thought you could freeze in Nam," says Willie the Moose with a hacking cough in the chill Highlands night. Roland, trying to sleep, makes sad little noises in the dark.

Each time they've hit us with a serious ground attack, it's been in the dark, usually between midnight and three, and each time we've driven them back, dead piling on dead, until what's out there smells like a smoking mountain of flesh, the infernal meat market. Only I think my nose is merifully dying a little. My ears feel all blown out. My mouth tastes like gun barrels. My right eye, trying to aim down-slope through drifting mist in the dark, sags to the sidelines . . . wanders off by itself . . . sees headless hill monsters . . . an old man in a derby hat . . . things. . . .

From time to time, we hear them down there dragging their dead away, and we shoot into those who are dragging the dead, and some of them also become dead. But the little men in pith helmets keep coming. I don't know why they want this particular hill so bad, any more than I know why we want it. It must be because they want it. Maybe this is the hill that "cuts the country in half."

So many things happen. In one attack, a grunt named Joe Bob Tucker sits shoulder to shoulder with me when a hunk of shrapnel comes spinning off the side of our hole and catches him —*thunk*—like a hatchet down the center of his face. It splits his forehead, nose, lips, and chin wide open, and suddenly he's Joe Bob Frankenstein.

The docs could save that face if only Joe Bob could be medevacced to a hospital, says Kelly. But nothing is moving off this hill. Our wounded jam up in bunkers or sprawl outside on air mattresses under ponchos lashed to bamboo stakes. Some of the wounded already smell like the dead, and the sounds they make —the gasps and rattles of their breathing, the cries all day and night, explosions of curses, babbling prayers—are more frightening than incoming, sometimes.

"Man alive," says Kelly, leg-wounded himself and hobbling from man to man, "I'm glad the people back in the world can't see this. I'm glad Aunt Sissy can't see this."

His fabulous Aunt Sissy, the school teacher who raised him, who lived on Apple Street in String, Mississippi, and taught "Expression," who is dead, but whom Kelly never refers to in the past tense. (And I'm thinking, *If Kelly could only see Kelly in the present tense*. Nobody ever got old-looking faster than Little Boy Blue—except Roland.)

At Harry's insistence, Roland rouses himself from near catatonia to squeeze off a round or two. Harry urges Roland to keep himself gainfully occupied, that there are people below dedicated to ending our lives forever, and we don't want that to happen, do we? Roland blinks, shoots blindly, and withdraws to his corner of the bunker, which is just a little earthen room with firing holes, a few dusty air mattresses for laying our bods down to sleep, burned-down candles, boxes of food and ammo scattered around, and a hammock Harry strings up. On top, outside, Red Dog has raised the battle flag of the Confederacy, which he claims he won in a poker game, maybe the only thing he has ever won in a poker game.

Day by day, we are boiling down to basic gristle up here. Harry goes out and takes big chances, volunteering for everything. I am volunteering for little. I look in a cracked mirror and see a cracked face. The great gook-killer does not want to grease any more gooks. Heroic chemistry: What's it made of? Harry slays red dragons. Roland and Ching-Ching are often not entirely here. They just shake their heads and stay as far out of it as possible, as Harry will let them, until they run out of stuff.

Ching-Ching, full of jitters and confessions, reveals to me that he had a little habit, a little *heroin* habit, before he climbed this hill. Just a sometime thing, of course. No big needle thing at all, oh, no. He didn't use the needle at all. "Hypodermically speaking, I'm cool." And he was in full control of his senses the whole time, oh, yes. He never tripped out before a mission, oh, no. So feel secure, man. It was just a little recreational smoking and snorting which could help a dude's morale, help him maintain his monklike calm in the face of danger, man. And how he wishes he had packed a little more of that in his pack, man, and a little less pound cake.

"I mean it's something I didn't feel all that good about when

I had it, but I certainly do feel bad about when I don't have it. See, Mike, this grunt he and me were just rapping, and he wondered if I would like to sniff a little cocaine once maybe, and so he got it, and like we tried it. Only it wasn't coke, man. So when I didn't wake up feeling too crazy the next morning, I thought, hey, that's not such a bad trip, why not try a little more of that? Why, man, if I could blow a little scag right now, this heinous hill would just practically disappear from my view. But this definitely does not mean I do not still love the high I get on grass, Mike. It's a nice kind of up high, and scag is kind of downways. So you see, everything is chemically cool. But the fact is, Mike, scag makes me not need the little chicks so much. Did you know that? Now when this United States Army takes away a man's sex life and sends him into these gruesome jungle regions, they had just better look the other way, man. Yes, you cannot lock a young man like me away from the little chicks, oh, no. Because something is going to happen, oh, yes. The Smoker keeps watching me all the time, waiting for me to screw up or something. He can't figure out whether I'm shaking from fear or what, ha, ha. What he doesn't know is, getting stoned doesn't hardly hurt my job performance at all. You can dig that, Mike. You've seen me in action. Why sometimes I think I can do it better, don't you? Chrize, yes. So don't worry, Mike, if you see me shaking a little bit, because I am in complete chemical command and am fast regaining my awesome cool." There's a pause while his hands shake a little. "Though I do really miss the little chicks, don't you? My goodness, yes."

By the fifteenth day, something is happening to us all. Death, wounds, crotch rot, *think* rot. The longer we stay, the more bats, spiders, and worms emerge from our inner places. We are also thirsty. We are into the dry season, but one day it rains, and the bunkers and trenches run rivers of sludge and we rejoice. Our bodies and bearded faces are dyed the color of earth and sun. Standing naked in the rain, we stick out our helmets,

tongues, and every container around to catch water. Choppers
are airdropping supplies daily—or trying to—but many water
cans burst open slamming the ground or spin on down the hill
into NVA-land. The Smoker catches a grunt about to use water
for shaving and looks close to using him for toilet paper, which
we don't have much of either.

One member of the Always First who is not thirsty, who managed to get off the hill in fine fettle, is Frederick G. Gurgles.
Coach is now headquartering on a hilltop fire base about eight
miles and a million trees away, but he often buzzes around high
overhead in his command ship, letting us know of his concern,
firing down messages lamenting that he had to be away consulting with the general when the NVA closed down the hill,
fretting that his ass is not down in the grass with us, vowing
that he shall return. But as the days pass, he grows increasingly
impatient, ordering Watson to "secure that goddamned hill once
and for all," to be "more positive" in the enemy body count
department, and threatening to "march in there with a few hundred good men and wrap that battle up." This is according to
Bad News, who is Harry's best news source. Through Bad News,
he can keep in touch with the thinking of the higher superiors.

The trouble is, we are completely cut off on the ground by the
NVA. No relief column has been able to fight its way through
that jungle, and we lack the strength to break out of the en-
circlement. Banzai Sheridan chews on cigars and remains staunch.
That's also according to Bad News, who no longer leers at us
with his old hot-shit superiority, who almost desperately seeks
to share the bad news with us, and looks more and more like the
terrified rat that runs back and forth across my boots during
shellings.

This little rat, whose tail is missing, seems different from the
others. It is called Lucky Rat by me and Fearless Freddie, after
our coach, by Harry. We won't let anybody shoot it, even though
after sundown we'll shoot about anything that moves. Somebody

even unlooses a midnight blast into one of our own grunts, Corporal Krzysiak, as he bends over beside the bomb hole serving as the company latrine, and now half his tail is missing.

So many things happen. Old Turnip Greens Turner, now top cook in the battalion, gets shot down trying to defy the NVA and chopper us in a hot meal in powder canisters. The hot meal splatters all over the hill, but Turnip Greens is not hurt much. He keeps insisting he doesn't mind this at all, that he's damn tired of supervising pastry-baking in the rear anyway. Taking up a rifle, he says, "Listen, you greenseeds, didn't you know I helped invent jungle war? Hell, I been wanting one more crack at this anyway, just one more crack." Turnip Greens is our only reinforcement.

Then early one morning, Skinny Lenny, crawling in from his listening post, gets caught in a clearing about thirty meters down and out from our lines. NVA snipers start popping him, rolling him over and over with well-placed rounds. But they don't finish him. It's like they're trying to sucker somebody out there to fetch him. Each time the string bean gets hit, he seems to jump six inches off the ground. He's crying like a strangled cat, and Red Dog can't stand it.

"You ain't goin' out there?" says Canny.

"Fuckin'-A."

And suddenly, Red Dog is scooting over our berm of dirt and sandbags and going down for Skinny. He's firing the M-60 he calls Georgia Snatch. It's obvious he can't make it back up that slope with both Skinny and Georgia Snatch. Canny goes scrambling up and over and down after him. And then Harry, grabbing a poncho, goes. And then I feel my legs going up and over and down before my brain entirely registers what it is I am doing. Bullets go tracing by, smacking into the berm, and I'm moving close, close to the ground, sideways like a crab, and behind us the whole platoon has opened up in heavy covering fire. Hastily, we lift crying, busted, long-legged Skinny onto the poncho, a bucket of blood sloshing in the poncho, and come plunging back up, finally just pushing Skinny up and rolling him over the berm top like a battered log.

Poor Skinny. He's been hit seven or eight times, in his arms, legs, and back. Red Dog, who never bothered to duck, got a heel shot off his boot. Harry got a leg pocket shot off with three cans of peaches he had been hoarding in it. I got another chip knocked out of my helmet. Canny got nothing. Kelly jams compresses down on Skinny's wounds, gives him mouth-to-mouth, and then hammers on his chest when his heart stops.

But after a while, Red Dog comes giggling back to the bunker. "You know what? He ain't gone die. Naw, he ain't. They couldn't grease ol' Skin. He's gone get well, dang it. We're callin' a dust-off in here and get ol' Skin to a hospital, by damn—got to, got to."

Here comes the Huey. It is the first helicopter to challenge the hill in three days, and it barrels in bravely, following the contour of the hill like a wasp over a hedge. It slows into a hover, hangs there on the hilltop in the full view of God and the NVA, and soldiers thrust Skinny up hand-over-hand toward hands reaching out from inside, and then with Skinny mostly inside, the bird rocks and turns and lifts and gains speed and gains speed and goes *thud-thud-thud*ing toward the next ridge. We are all cheering when the explosion occurs. And that makes twenty-seven birds down since we've been up here and one poor Skinny.

Red Dog instantly charges over and starts whacking away at a prisoner with a bamboo stick, nearly wiping away the man's mouth before we can pull him off. An hour later, he strings up an NVA corpse by the neck, dangles and swings the corpse from a tree curving out over the berm for all below to view.

"Hey, gook assholes, shoot this fucker!"

When nothing happens, Red Dog jumps atop the berm and starts practicing with Georgia Snatch, bapping the dead soldier back and forth, spinning him around and around, flesh hunks flying. When still nothing happens, he leans out and gives all of Gook-land the big finger. "Bite on 'at!"

We finally get Red Dog calmed down and, at Rodeliano's insistence, the corpse hauled down, whereupon Red Dog starts slapping strips of tape all over the riddled figure.

"Sorry about 'at," he apologizes. "'At'll fix you up. If you wanna make a complaint, it's invenereal to me."

Red Dog is reprimanded, mildly, by Rodeliano. The Smoker commends our raging Dog on a job well done. "Lets the gooks know what they're walking into up here. Oughta turn the whole miserable country into a free-fire zone and have done with it. Quit fucking around wondering whether we shot the wrong gooks today or bombed the wrong fucking whorehouse in Hanoi. Ain't no way to win a war."

"What about the prisoner?" someone asks Rodeliano.

"We could kill the sumbitch," The Smoker suggests. "Let Red Dog gnaw on him for a while."

Red Dog is not the worst. On the seventeenth day, a kid named Collins sits behind a log, eyes like smoke, uniform in rags, slowly jerking the legs off a long millipede, one by one. He's got it pinned on the log with a medical needle. Under another needle, he's pinned a spider that looks like a meatball with eyes.

For a while, he had done just fine on the hill. For a while, he had acted more gung ho than anybody, standing up, shaking his fists, leading the cheers when American big guns sent shells, timed for airbursts, hissing over a hump of the hill to scatter the enemy massing below for an attack.

But the longer it goes, the quieter Collins gets. He sits behind the log, moving his head slowly back and forth and humming something with no discernible melody over and over and over. Roland tries to talk to him, but the kid just keeps jerking legs off the millipede. When Roland dawdles, Collins reaches down and suddenly shoves his knife up under Roland's nose.

"Want some?"

Roland jumps back.

Collins is trying to present Roland with a bamboo krait, a foot of poison. When Roland doesn't acept, the kid cleans it off the blade with his fingers, slices its head off, seems ready to eat it.

Roland looks imploringly at The Smoker. "This man needs help, Sergeant."

"From what I've seen, bub, you're the one who needs help. All this man needs is a shave, a couple of beers, a piece of ass, and he'll be feeling hunky-fucking-dory."

"I doubt that, Sergeant. I really doubt that."

"Oh, yew doubt that, do *yeww*?" says The Smoker, standing there all hairy-stinking-grinning without his shirt, scratching belly scars. "Well, maybe he's got a little something more than what you got, bub."

Just then, Collins jerks something else out from under the log, and again Roland retreats.

"Ears," chortles The Smoker, taking the jar crammed with them. "Hey, we got us a knife fighter."

"Left uns," mumbles the kid.

The Smoker unscrews the jar lid and makes as if to empty the contents on Roland, who dances backward and keeps going until he is back in his corner of the bunker. Collins is the only ear connoisseur I've seen up here. He's the same kid who takes to squashing frogs in his hands, who now blandly sits out on his log during shellings, but who shoots up a bunker fighting off a rat trying to "encircle" him. He is caught the next day eating a bar of C-4 explosive for breakfast, but is not caught that night after dinner cutting his throat with his knife. There's something we didn't know about Collins. He had once been captured and held in a bamboo cage by the other side for weeks. They had beaten and spat and urinated on him and poked sticks into his anus a lot before he escaped.

On the nineteenth day, we are told that the NVA are preparing for their greatest attack. Major Sheridan orders us to burrow even deeper into our holes. He vows the NVA will not retake Hill 711, that he will call in the B-52s first to dump right on our heads. The big bombers have been hitting the jungle all around us, but not so close as to break up forces hugging the hill and pressuring us from trenches that zigzag almost up to our lines now.

One evening, Sheridan summons me to his command bunker. He's drinking gin by candlelight. He's sweating in his undershirt and half-laced boots. His eyes go one way and his hair the other. A dead cigar grows out of his mouth. He looks grayed-out. He looks supremely fucked, like this hill has sat on his face for a while. I had heard that he had been rebuked again by our colonel for not displaying the necessary offensive posture. For allowing the Always First to be surrounded. The Always First should never be surrounded, insists Gurgles, who is trying as hard as humanly possible to return to the hill and assume hands-on command, he says, so that he can wrap this battle up.

"Clerks and warriors, kid," Sheridan says, winking.

He holds up the nearly empty bottle and gazes blearily at its dull yellow gleam. "There's the last. Well, it's been a bash. We hung a good one on, huh, soldier? How you like it up here?"

"When's the colonel coming in with that relief force, Major?" I ask, eyeing the battle map behind him.

"It will be a noble effort, I'm sure. Or maybe he's just jacking off with his mouth again. And so what? Hell, I love it here. May never leave. It's the battle that counts. After the battle comes the shit. Comes the clerks. Clerks and warriors, kid. . . . Smell that out there? The lovely aroma grows stronger. . . ."

He's slump-shouldered across the little makeshift table from me, gaunt, his collarbones protruding, looking thirty pounds thinner than the plump-cheeked fellow of long ago. He wipes at his weeping willow mustache, stares at the bottle with the last gin, which has not moved. Suddenly something big bangs down on the hill. The bunker shakes. The major laughs.

"Just pissing on us. Shit, I love it here. Gothic simplicity and all that. . . . Listen, Roland, reason I called you over . . . whether we make it out or not . . . I've put you up for the big one, kid, for what you did getting up on top this bastard. Or maybe I ought to shoot you."

"It's Ripp, Major. What big one?"

"Read my lips, kid. *The* Big One."

"I didn't even know what I was doing, Major. I wouldn't do it again."

"Don't say it, kid. Don't wanna hear it. Who knows what they'll do? Thing is, *you fucking did it*."

He lifts the bottle. "Toast, kid. We been down the old road. Here's to the road, kid."

Sheridan removes his cigar and drinks, passes the bottle, and I drink. It hits my belly like a rocket getting started.

"Hell with all this blubbering," says the major. "So how's things, kid? How's the little lady, the little wife back on the old homefront doing?"

"Doing fine, last I heard."

"Damn fine. That's one for our side. Knew it'd work out. Those things usually work out. Damn fine, damn fine. Well, we've given it the old shot, kid, and we'll keep on giving it the old shot. What the hell, what the hell."

I watch one of those little green sideways-walking bugs sail down from his nose into a wet spot on the table, watch it walking sideways on booze. I fish it out with my forefinger and blow on it, blow it gently away.

"Listen, Roland," he's saying, "everything's been said here is deadwood, affirmative, kid? Top secret. Fate o' the Republic and all that. That a roger, kid?"

"That's a roger, Major."

On the twentieth day, Bad News visits our bunker to tell us we have reached the end of the line. He says we are going to be inundated in rivers of NVA or assassinated by our own bombers. He says this will happen tonight or tomorrow night or soon. By now, Bad News and Lucky Rat could almost be twins, only Rat is more cheerful. Bad News leaves practically weeping. Even Willie the Moose looks shaken. The big fellow from Kentucky, who now humps Rodeliano's radio around, says to me, "I'm holdin' hopes and prayin' that we make it, Mike."

But my facial muscles no longer respond to the gravity of this situation.

Some of us have reached a certain point. What worried me sick weeks ago, fails to trigger much of a sweat today. We're being shelled ten to fifteen times a day, and much of our time is spent in our bunkers just waiting for the roof to fall in. I feel all sweated out. Other times, I just sit and scratch. I have a case of the galloping scabies, and the mites are having their way with me. When the shelling grows heavy, I scratch faster.

One day, a chopper sails down a batch of mail along with water and ammo. Uncle Ned writes that he no longer believes the Vietnam deal is advancing my underwear career. Too much bad press, too much bad television. He wonders if I have seen any real action. He reminds me that he never believed in the Vietnam business worth a damn, just throwing good money after bad.

The thing to do now, or as soon as I could shake loose from whatever it was I was doing, was to concentrate on my future life in the company. He would be sending me some materials soon that would help me keep in touch with current trends. He had me slated for a "slot" that would prove "profitable" in the years ahead.

"But as you know, Mike, I run a tight ship, every man carrying his own weight, and I can't be seen playing favorites. While you've been off seeing the world, your buddies have been stuck right here with their noses to the grindstone. As you know, I demand performance, total commitment. I cannot abide anything less. I need high flyers to fill the ranks of this organization, hard chargers, and I want you to be thinking on these things before you come back. So hurry and get that mess behind you. Shuck that uniform. People here are turning against it over there. It has a bad smell, and the smart fella knows which way the wind is blowing. We're just peeing our money away in the wind, it seems to me, and we ought to get out and quit wasting our time on unproductive jungle endeavors in these no-account countries."

For some reason, Vietnam has ticked Uncle Ned off. I remembered how he had disciplined out-of-favor subordinates by not sending them Christmas cards, and that same tone of Scroogean rectitude had seized his letter. Aunt Tettie is more forthcoming. Though she was under sedation again to stop the cavalry charges of her bladder and the sudden troop movements of her heart, though she said her equilibrium was shot and her mind was going, she wished me well. She said that I had always been her "Angel in Heaven," that "God is seeing all," and that "time will tell."

Besides the mites and being overrun and killed and not advancing my underwear career, I also occasionally think about my wife. For a long time, I had literally ached for her presence, got physically ill longing for her. Now she merely marches into my groin at night, tap dances on my balls, and marches off. I don't blame her. Heck, no. We couldn't just spend the rest of our lives copulating. Heck, no.

I think about my wife while gazing at the captured Playmate nailed by Red Dog on the bunker wall over the flame of our candle, at the smoke curling up past her great pink rear and mammoth cream-colored mammaries, which flow down nearly to her navel. I imagine Char in that kind of picture, but Red Dog calls her Doreen, his Desirable Doreen. During a lull in the shelling, he giddily confides that he named her after a member of womankind who once had the big, big hots for him back in

Lickskillet, where there wasn't much to do except come to town and sit against a wall and whittle, or go find somebody who liked to diddle.

"Oink," goes Canny.

"Yes, I would like to take out a young lady or something like that one more time," sighs Ching-Ching, staring through his cracked dusty glasses at Desirable Doreen.

"Sheet," pooh-poohs Canny, "her left booby is bigger'n your whole head. Be like a li'l gnat tryna swallow a bale of hay."

"If given the chance," says Ching-Ching, "I feel confident I could meet her needs. Man and woman. What a neat arrangement, practically. Chrize, yes. I would donate half my remaining blood to be given that one last chance."

"Boo sheet, takes a man like me to meet her needs," says Red Dog, slobbering a little tobacco juice. "But I ain't donatin' *my* blood for no cunt or nobody. I'm Aryan. My blood is precious. Us Aryans can fuck twenty-four times a day."

Harry turns drowsily in his hammock, grinning. "Love at first sight, huh, Dog?"

"Well, it's sure *sumpin'* at first sight," says Red Dog. "I sure know what I wanna do to um at first sight. I'm Aryan."

"We bad," says Harry, who is very red-eyed, his arms bumped-up and purplish, his undershirt riddled with rips and tears, one dirt-caked sleeve hanging to his elbow. Like the rest of us, he's so nicked, cut, scraped you can't tell where the red earth stops and the blood begins. But he's still full of it. "Hey, Mike, who's winning?"

"We are," I answer. "We are winning *big*."

"She's my boocoo woman," Red Dog is going on. "I get a tooth-ache down in my root for gals like 'at. I sure know I want to whang-whang um at first sight, heh, heh."

"How gratifying for them," whispers Roland, pale in the shadow of his corner.

"Right now," says Canny, "I'd whang-whang a rat. Where is

'at little rat anyway? 'At sweet little rat is lookin' better and better. I'm gone ring 'at rat's chimes."

"Hell, it's got tits, ain't it? It can hump, can't it?" giggles Red Dog. "Man, when we climb down off this hill, I'm gone whang-whang um all. Just line up, here I come, little babies. Your asses is sweet grass and I'm your mighty lawn mower."

"You can stop dreaming," rasps Roland from his corner. "You heard what Bad News said. We're not getting off this hill, and we all know it."

"Don't know doodly squat," snaps Red Dog. "Ain't no dinks gone take us over. Ain't 'at right, Harry?"

"Never happen," says Harry, yawning. "Remember to wake me up if that happens."

"'At's right, by damn. You know, Harry, when I get out, after what I been through, after what we did, I'm gone retar, light me up a stogie, get me a Cadillac, and just cruise around town and let the gals just gaze upon me, and drool upon me, and stuff like 'at. Like those good ol' World War Two heroes used to do."

"When you get out?" rasps Roland. "Talk about dreamers. Man, don't you know you're talking about the *future*. Do you think you've got a *future*? Do any of you really think you've got a *future*?

"Well, up yours right now, peckernose. Ol' God knows we're up here. He won't let us down."

"God?" rasps Roland. "Look around. Do you see any *God* up here? If God was on this hill, He's dead and rotting by now like everything else. Like we're going to be in a few hours."

"Why 'at's jus' a rotten lousy lie," growls Red Dog. "Ain't no gook can ding God. Why if there wadn't no God, I think I would shit."

"It doesn't matter, because we're all going to be dead soon, finally and forever dead. Dead. Dead. And there's nothing we can do about it. We can't even blame those poor people down there shooting at us. They're just doing what they have to do, and they'll just keep coming and keep coming, and there's nothing we can do about it."

"Aw, 'at's real tough titty." Red Dog spits about half a jaw of tobacco juice onto a sandbag beside Roland. "Hell, they ain't no way those shitlickers can beat us, ain't 'at right, Harry?"

"Whatever they've got down there or anywhere," Harry replies sleepily, "is not good enough. We can't lose."

Red Dog, staring at Roland, starts to sing softly: *"Roland's goin' home in a body bag, doo-dah, doo-dah. . . . The poor sumbitch is daid, he got it right in the haid. . . ."*

Canny picks it up: *"Ol' Roland's daid, othey say . . . he bought the farm today . . . the fucker's gone underground . . . he's sort of spread around. . . ."*

"Crazy—" Roland shudders in his corner. "Crazy . . . crazy."

"Well, 'at's what they pay us sixty-five cents an hour for," mutters Canny, picking at a big boil on his sun-fried nose.

"The way I figure it," says Red Dog, "Charlie ain't got no real chance with us. Far as I can see, we're not havin' any trouble doin' a good job killin' him. Hell, he's already tried to ding me, and he's missed ten or thirty times. If he can come that close and miss, I know I flat got it made, heh, heh. All the rest is un-irrelevable."

"Too bad that poor dude Collins didn't feel like that," says Ching-Ching. "It seems weird to take the trouble to waste yourself in a place like this."

"Maybe he just saw too many dead things," murmurs Roland. "Maybe we all have."

"Boo sheet, all I ever seen is your chicken butt crawlin' under a sandbag ever time a skeeter flies by," mocks Red Dog. "Man, if I'd a knowed you was in the army, I'd a joined the navy."

Roland sinks deeper into his corner, leans back on sandbags, closes his eyes. "There's nothing less humorous than unhumorous humor."

"Up your humorous. I'll tell y'all like I tol' Canny," Red Dog goes on, nodding his head sagely, "the trouble of it is, some folks will just lay down on you when you need 'em. Some folks wouldn't piss in your ear if your brain was on fire."

"It doesn't matter what you say anymore," Roland replies, eyes closed, "because none of us will be here tomorrow to remember this discussion. We'll all be dead, dead, d—"

"Hey!" Harry lets loose a groan. "Just let that cheerful crap sink, huh. So this hill is bad, and the last hill was bad, and the next hill will be bad, fucking bad. Now some of us may differ on God and foreign policy, but try a little humor on yourself, Rol. Try prayer. If that doesn't work, beat your meat or something."

"Don't know 'bout no fern policy," Red Dog goes on. "All I know is, they ain't no little Ho Chi Minh Japs knockin' my butt off this hill."

"Japs?" Roland sounds like he's choking. "*Japs?*"

With a flourish, Canny unlaces and flops off one of his cruddy boots, an act he considers daring, unwise, because he swears every time he takes off a boot, the bad stuff starts happening.

"But once in a while, you got to get these dang boots off," he bitches, lifting his leg and letting the other boot drop. "My ol' feet done tooken all they damn can. Only it's bad luck."

Ching-Ching shakes his head. "Chrize, yes. All we've got left is luck, and ninety-nine percent of that is bad."

"Naw, it ain't so bad up here," says Red Dog. "Hell, y'all couldn't give me no desk job. I don't like wearin' no starched fatigues. It's like when I was makin' big money hangin' Sheetrock back in the city once, and quit because I didn't like them cities. Yeah, I want to stay out in this field. I had a buddy 'at got hit out here. Remember ol' New from Valdosta? I had two buddies 'at got hit, really. Poor ol' Skin. They's both dead right now. They were some really great good guys. Look, when slopes ding my buddies, I'm gone stay out in this field till I find 'em and stomp their head against a tree or sumpin. 'At's all she wrote. 'At's the funnest part of combat. Ain't 'at right, Harry?"

"Couldn't be righter, Dog."

"I'll mess on 'em bad, just like those great good-old guys, those World War Two Americans messed on the Japs. Ain't 'at right, Harry?"

"Mess on 'em, Dog."

"Ain't 'at right, Mike?"

"All she wrote, Dog."

I am staring again at the increasingly desirable airbrushed Doreen over the flickering flame, whose only blemish is where she's been fragged by a chip of B-40 rocket low in her right buttock. Doreen's creamy breasts and milky thighs, her butter-milk belly and ice-cream ass are enough to fill one with a regular dairy of desire. Looking at Doreen gets me to thinking of Char again. My swollen member, all gorged with blood and no sex and mites, bumps against my belly, alternately swings upward, swings downward, does a little jig. Let that free-lance artiste do what he wants. Just leave me out of it.

I'm sitting there all filled up with this, when this little loach, this little lost observation helicopter actually touches down on our piece of hill, making history by mistake.

The pilot doesn't know where the hell he is. He thinks he's supposed to pick up some colonel, some Gurgles. No, that's another hill. We need all kinds of supplies, and all this bird is carrying is batches of newspapers and magazines for some rear outfit. We jerk that shit out and start loading a couple of the worst wounded, even as the first incoming crunches down.

"Come back here, mothafuck," howls Willie the Moose, wav-ing his hands underneath, "and take me with you!"

The NVA antiaircraft teams have opened up. And the little helicopter is fluttering up gamely, crippled bird in a storm, starting to sputter and trail flame, and then it falls in a slow, eerie tumble down into one of those misty valleys out there.

"Din wanna go anyway," whispers Willie.

"When we go, we'll fuckin' walk out!" swears Red Dog. "Cause we're the fuckin' hard-core."

Tap, tap. As the chopper sinks, I tap my lucky hard-hit helmet. I'm into a good bit of tapping up here. I tap my helmet often, tap the stock of my beautiful, nearly burned out piece, tap the same lucky trees going out on early morning patrol. Then crouch there on patrol, staring into the fog, tapping and watching, tapping and sniffing somebody's coffee smell that drifts up and mixes in with that of up-churned, refried earth, the night's hangover gunpowder, old and new death. I unfailingly tap the same battered but unbowed wood on the way back. I sometimes mumble stuff during these walks in the park. Incantations to the good forest spirits. Little prayers. Some days it's God, other days it's Luck. Days like today it's screw it all and let it happen—it will anyway. Only say a word for me, Sal.

It still doesn't happen. We're back in our bunker reading about ourselves. The Always First is in the headlines, cofeatured with a massive "antiwar rock-and-love feast-for-peace" happening back in America.

We have been labeled the Lost Battalion. In some of the stories, we are perceived as sort of gallant defenders of a Vietnam Alamo. Other stories concentrate on the "agony of Hill 711," and the "American Dien Bien Phu," and how the foe with "inexorable Dien Bien Phu–like tenacity" closes the ring around the new clearly doomed hill in what bodes to become the most tragic setback of this ill-fated war."

"Boo sheet," sneers Red Dog. "Them fuckers don't know shit from Shinola. I ain't seen them up here nowheres."

One American senator charges us with "arrogantly misusing American firepower to devastate innocent mountain folk." Another calls the battle an "unmitigated disaster" and the foe "well nigh invincible." He calls for American forces to "lay down their arms with honor" in order to "save lives." A student leader offers to "personally go to Hill 711 to negotiate the American surrender."

Running alongside the agony and the arrogance are stories

and pictures of thousands of love-and-peace-feast young men and women frolicking in a stream, climbing trees, cavorting along a muddy hillside, some in states of undress and seeming stress, looking a bit stoned, a bit out of their gourds, looking about as filthy as we do.

Ching-Ching starts reading aloud to us: "The unseasonable heat made nudity almost essential . . . so that some of the demonstrators were virtually forced to dispense with their clothes. . . ."

"Wow"—he removes his glasses and wipes off some of the dust —"why can't I be in a place like that? Where it's so hot all the young ladies are just *forced* to *dispense* with their clothes. Here is a beautiful young lady running gaily through an alfalfa field or something who has been *forced* to *dispense* with all of her clothes except two or three little leaves she is wearing."

"Well, jus' looka this guy here," Red Dog says. "Looks like he's pissin' on the flag. And looka here this big fat fruitcake standin' in the rain with a towel wrapped around his three bellies, heh, heh. Shakin' his fist and butt and hollerin' at the sky, 'You can't beat us! This is a struggle for survival!' Heh, heh. You can tell he ain't no man by the way he stands. All we need is more like him and they's not agonna be no more American Army. They's not agonna be no more American mankind. They'll jus' be American fruitkind. Like ol' Roland there. Ol' Rolandkind, heh, heh. And looka here this sissy sumbitch's eyes. You can tell he's all doped up, jus' like Roland. Dope and air conditionin' has near ruint the American people, like it's ruint ol' Roland there. Hey, Roland, don't you wanna see some pitchers of your peckernose friends?"

"You may call them that," Roland replies softly. "But I think what they are doing is pretty beautiful. Just because they take off their clothes and play a little music doesn't mean it's not a spiritual happening. And why shouldn't they be a little stoned? When they're stoned, there's no war and no bomb. At least they're trying to reach down into their deepest feelings, which is more than we're doing."

"Boo sheet," jeers Red Dog. "Pissin' on the flag. Jerkin' off in public. 'At don't thrill my spirit none."

"These are our kids," Ching-Ching reads slowly aloud, "the cream of our youth, the finest in our history, the new heroes. . . . They are our conscience, pointing the way. I am proud to march with them, to follow them, fighting the brave fight. . . ."

"Well, which yuts 'at silly fucker talkin' about?" asks Red Dog. "'At guy pissin' on the flag or us? Listen, I'll tell y'all like I told Canny here, any guy what won't fight for his country is lower than a snake's balls. Ain't 'at right, Harry?"

But Harry has sunk like a sandbag into sleep. This is supposed to be our main rest time, before sundown. I'm flopped on an air mattress, scratching. I'm sleepy but can't sleep. Canny has ducked outside to talk with Kelly about boils. Ching-Ching is still reading, but finally he shrugs and says, " I wish they'd sent one of those books where on every page a lovely young lady is dispensing with her bra and baring her bosom for Lance or Rance or some heavy dude like that. Page after page of bosom baring is what I need. Good deep inspiring junk like that."

"Yow!" Red Dog suddenly yelps. "Looka the bumps on this uns log. She done got her tail end stuck out so far this way and her headlights poked out so far that way, it looks like she's goin' two ways at once. Now 'at's my kind of race car. Yowww! Gets my engine runnin'. Yowww!"

He starts pinning the new one up next to Desirable Doreen. "Gone whang-whang um all," he talks busily to himself. "Cause I got the whang-whang blues. Cause I was born to whang-whang. Cause I'm a dang whang-whang machine. Hell, I'd whang-whang a duck right now. Why not? Heh, heh. It's got tits, ain't it? It can hump, can't it? Heh, heh."

Roland sort of winces and crawls out of the shadow of his corner, shaking his head. He goes out to urinate, then comes back in and puts both his arms around me like a child. "Mike," he whispers, they're all over the place."

"What're you talking about?"

"They're *all over the place*. We'll probably be dead tomorrow. They'll just keep coming and coming, and there's nothing we can do about it. I just want you to know . . . thanks for everything, man. . . . You've been a good friend . . . just want you to know. . . ."

He looks as if he's lost about two pounds of his face.

Something's burning in the forest. Great teak and mahogany trees have been burning like trash, and there is this other smell floating up like something out of Auschwitz. There are bodies down there, many, many burning bodies. For three days and nights, B-52s lay so many strings of bombs so close around us, we seem to be going deaf and dumb.

At first, the NVA keep coming up the hill in their big push— and keep coming and keep coming—and then on the twenty-fifth day, they begin to crumble. The B-52s, bombing tactically with one rolling wave of thunder and lightning after another, break up the charge, the siege, the trees, the people, everything. I don't think they've bombed that close to friendly troops before in the war.

We call these raids *archlighters*, lighting up the world. I never do learn the NVA word for them. Whole squads of NVA are found sitting side by side in caves untouched by shrapnel, their faces shoved sideways into Silly Putty, their nose and ear places caked with blood, their chests crushed by the pressure of blasts thirty meters away. Others seem to have gone mad, concussed out of their minds. We find them running around on all fours, mouths agape, gibbering, hopping up the hill without their weapons as though begging to be shot. Whole units caught near the center of the blasts have virtually disintegrated. We see them hanging from and stuck to trees in odd little bits and pieces like paper dolls run through an electric fan. And it's all burning now in a terrible forest fire, burning, burning. . . .

. . .

And yet, here they come diddybopping upward in another, surely the last, pitiful charge, and I do not want to kill them anymore. The great gook-killer has taken over the operation of a .50-caliber machine gun. I do not want to fire it. Sometimes things work out, and this seems to be one of those times. The great bombing and artillery mauling has been going on since dawn against an enemy that really has nowhere to go. They are hanging all over our wire. Some come tottering up, waving their dirty flags. Some come screaming.

I do not have to fire, because before the enemy's latest assault can get very far, and with the sky turning pleasantly bright, here come a few more air strikes, the reliable F-4 Phantoms. Beejesus, they catch our foe mucking along right out in the open, messing on them with a few napalm pies, scattering them every which way. So I don't need to shoot anybody. All I have to do is watch them dropping their packs and weapons in the boiling, bubbling effervescence of this wonderful hill, slow dancing toward obliteration—and yet some of them, to their short-lived credit, are still trying to fire, still trying to take this hill. It is pitiful. This hill belongs to us.

"Come on," Red Dog is yelling. "Right this way, babies. Yeow! It don't get no better than this!"

I do not fire. The good soldier knows that once he shoots, the enemy begins to know where he is, and the more he shoots, the better the enemy's chances are of finding him. Also, I had been led to believe that someone was going to assist me in firing this big piece, but everyone seems to be otherwise employed. For the good soldier, of course, the first principle is to know his weapon and how to use it. I'm not too familiar with the nifty-fifty, but because of battlefield depletions, they have thrown me behind it, which requires me to proceed methodically and carefully. No need to rush. The previous operator of this piece has recently been greased in the enemy's last futile charge, as has the previous, previous operator. I myself have little fear of being greased, or even threatened, in this rabbit shoot. Though bullets ping and rip into the sandbags around me from time to time, it is just one of those days. Well, not entirely. Actually, I am feeling not quite right.

I do not fire. A finer field of fire you could not ask for. Our whole line seems to be just pulling triggers without thinking. What is there to think about? You aren't going to miss any target on a day like this. Not with the nifty-fifty anyway.

But someone keeps demanding that I fire. I know that voice. So with the sure knowledge that the only good battlefield is an empty battlefield, I prepare to fire. Short, deliberate bursts of nine to fifteen rounds produce the most efficacious results, as I recall. Although there is much to be said for the timely long burst.

This battle, by all textbook precepts, should be over by now, but they keep coming like a plague of rabbits, even seeming to multiply at times. But it is pitiful. They are hippity-hopping upward with incredible difficulty, living the great life, dying the glorious death—you have to admire their grit, their manic tenacity. Some of them are squatting dazedly in holes, trying to squeeze off a round or two; some are falling, flopping down heavily and not getting up. Yet some who fall continue to crawl passionately upward. What for? What is Uncle Ho feeding them? It may be a psychological victory for them, but it is a truly prodigious body count for us.

They are getting closer, but I still cannot clearly see their interesting faces. Of course, properly identifying the target is of the utmost importance to the good soldier if he is to use his piece in the most efficacious manner and thus improve his fitness rating. . . .

But there's that voice again, commanding me to bong the Cong. Obediently, I jerk back on the cocking lever once, twice, then, hunching over, sight through the smoke over the long barrel, tracking the rabbits, feel my hands tighten on the handles of this truly impressive piece, prepare to unleash. . . .

But I still cannot discern the features of their faces in all this smoke. It is a cardinal rule. The good soldier should know whom he is killing. I am feeling not quite right, and all this is on my mind when I become aware of that voice off to the left urging me, really urging me, to "squeeze that goddamn trigger *yeww* fucking dirtbag!"

There is no mistaking the voice of my old top sergeant. He just has no manners. The Smoker has always had this peculiarity of shouting at a soldier, no matter how close to that soldier's ear he was. And getting kissed earlier in the day by a mean piece of shit to go with his face has not only lessened this peculiarity but made it worse. We have come a hell of a long way together, but I have never quite gotten used to the way my old top sergeant addresses his fellow human beings. Really hurts my feelings. Some people really have the knack of turning things to shit.

My trouble is, I'm just not quite up to the old snuff today. Sometimes, being a good soldier isn't easy, and that little hopper-like creature on my cruddy left boot seems to sense it. Gazing up at me earnestly pop-eyed, antennae twitching, with what seems to be not only curiosity but also genuine hopperly concern, it appraises me, I appraise it. I hope he realizes all this is not my doing. Mankind, little fella. Just keep fucking each other in the nose. It is greenish-yellowish in color—or is that yellowish-greenish? A creature with sizable, really sizable, the most sizable hind legs I have ever seen on that type creature. But what is it doing in this place? What does it want of me? Is it the reincarnation of some Frenchman who once manned a big gun on this hill? I sit there wondering. And then the hopper creature makes a sizable leap off my boot up onto a forward sandbag. I hope it hasn't felt rejected by me as an individual, or even as an American conqueror of his hill. Maybe it just wants a better view of the proceedings. Maybe it wants to be my forward observer and help me out. I hope so, because I am feeling not quite up to snuff. Still, I know all I need is a shave, a couple of beers, a piece of ass, and I'll be feeling hunky-fucking-dory again. . . .

"FIRE YOU FUCKING CLOWN! FIRE! FIRE! FIRE!"

My hand jerks on the thumb trigger and the old reliable with the big bang really starts jumping, jarring the setting right out of my class ring. All in all, an easy shoot. I am doing my duty, and we are winning big. They tell you what to do, and you do it. Whoever set this one up for our side deserves to be commended. Whoever set this one up for their side deserves to be hanged— or at least slapped on the wrist.

I have stopped firing. I can't see too well. Maybe Kelly can give me an aspirin. My right eye seems to have come down with something. What is there to fire at anyway? You just need a garbage truck to sweep through there now. But there's that yammering at me to keep on shooting. Shoot the smoke. Shoot the fire. Shoot the dead. . . . Where did my little buddy, the hopper, go?

I am feeling not too terribly terrific, but I am blowing them away. People really do treat each other sadly. But all in all, I find the fifty to be a really utilizable instrument of doom, one that can impress itself upon a battlefield situation with considerable authority. Once you get it grooved in, why you can fire it with a mere thumb. You have to give Mr. Browning all the credit; he made one damn fine piece. Taking nothing away from the handy M-16 as an instrument of doom, you just can't go wrong with the nifty-fifty. All in all, I think I fire pretty efficaciously, once I get my rhythm going. . . .

REWIND

Kelly. Been a busy little bee. Swimming in other people's blood and last words. He can't hardly walk himself. No problem, says Little Boy Blue. In a couple of days, it's his birthday. Big 19. No cake. Back home in String, population 400 (about half dogs and chickens), he could stuff himself on cake and cream.

"I'm the town soldier, actually. Everyone looked up to me the last time I was home. Everyone had me over. Folks even wanted me to talk their kids into joining up and doing something useful with their lives, instead of just running around. Aunt Sissy wants me to be someone of strong character someday, and I guess I'll be a doctor."

He told me that he had been saving his pay religiously for that day of days: when he and his Mississippi Magnolia did their deed and tied the golden knot. He really wanted Mr. and Mrs. Ripp to be guests of honor at the wedding, dagnabbit, and I told him we sure would come if we could. Being that I was an old married man, he asked my advice on being married and all. Was it keen? He showed me a bunch of letters he hadn't been able to mail, written on all kinds of paper, just piling up in an empty grenade box, getting rat-chewed and dirty. He hoped his girl understood. "Could she?" he asked me. Can girls understand? If I got off this hill, and for some reason he didn't, would I promise to go see her and explain it?

I told him not to worry about it, because we were all coming down off this wonderful hill. And Harry told him the same thing. No problem.

"But just in case, Mike," he said, feeling around in his pockets for his lucky tooth, "you know, like maybe just in case. . . ."

18

There Go the Bad Ones

They are suddenly inside the wire, dancing on our behinds. I don't know how this happens. Has something escaped me? There came Gurgles with a sky full of helicopters that is the relief force that is supposed to end this battle. Before he can officially end the battle, the battle starts ending us. A bunch of us Bad Ones, about half of what is left of Bravo, are cut off from the rest of the company and the battalion by kamikaze enemy who finally drive us off our piece of this Whang-fucking-Bang real estate— black-magic enemy who don't accept the science of victory by body count, who seem to be trying to tell us something. We try not to listen, we try to bump their butts back down into that burning bush once and for all and forever.

But NVA are hanging all over the wire and all over our bunkers. Desirable Doreen is captured, the battle flag of the Confederacy flutters and falls. They come in a great clattering of automatic weapons, we're getting shot to shit, hand to hand, eyeball to eyeball. I am finally seeing their fine faces.

They've taken over the nifty-fifty. I hadn't felt anything and I don't feel anything, but there is a large patch of blood spread-

ing on the left shoulder of my fatigues, and then I reach down
to the left of my groin and feel a lot of wet. Maybe I'm urinating
on myself again. There's Canny, one boot off, one trouser leg
hanging in shreds, a mudpack of a bandage stuck on his knee,
being dragged along by Red Dog through the mangled trees
behind and below our recent position.

"Bigfoot, this is Playboy. Tally ho, yellow—"

"Roger," Harry is shouting into a radio. "Bring it on in!"

"Am rolling inbound," answers the radio. "Get your heads
down!"

The gunbird swoops over us, burping fire, sighing *shuu shuu
shuu*, machine guns and rockets pounding the tangled, burnt
brush and twisted bamboo to our rear as we retreat through
waves of smoke down the backside of the hill.

"Outstanding run!" Harry cheers at the radio. "Do it again,
Playboy! Again!"

"Heads down! We're rolling in, right in your back pocket!"

For a moment after the gunship goes over, there is silence.
Nothing moves except smoke, and then there they are: green
helmets, the whites of their bayonets floating through the
bamboo mist. . . .

We are trying to lay down a base of fire, trying to organize
something, but Bravo seems gone as an organized fighting unit,
and the survivors are going.

Willie the Moose, still strapped to his radio, big, sad eyes
looking like dimming lightbulbs, tries to belly forward to somewhere, though he's nearly chopped in half.

Harry, flattened out beside the dying Moose, yells into the
Kentuckian's radio to a hilltop fire base, "Foxhead, Foxhead!
Where the fuck are you? Bring that stuff in NOW! We're being
crawled over by beaucoup bad guys! Bring that shit down on
top of us! Now! RIGHT NOW!"

I'm crawling toward Harry and Moose when one of them
shouts and pops out of the bamboo—he's all dirt-smeared, wear-

ing a loincloth—and aims a grenade like it's a cherry pie he wants me to bite on, and I squeeze off *bam, bam* with my M-16, finger clutching the trigger the way your mind clutches the last second of breathing.

But such a fine, nice, girl-boned face he has as he steps closer —did I miss?—ever curiously closer, eyes darkly inquisitive, lips beginning to curl back in some surprise as he steps closer, too close. Perhaps I look like something he's never seen before, an evil spirit or hill demon or American imperialist fucknose, because all this pretty-boy NVA in the loincloth does is look rather surprised at first, and then very frightened, suddenly slack-jawed—he must know how badly this hill has screwed him even as his own grenade cooks off in his hand and blows him up.

Blows me down. After the flash, a bulldog-looking soldier with his jaw poked out like Gurgles comes in firing, and I fire full automatic, the rifle nearly jumping out of my hand, the burst bumping him sideways, but then he comes on in a furious dreamlike float that carries him banging headfirst into the log that has received his bullets. I hunch there on one knee, staring at his one-eyed stare.

Then all the evil music I have ever heard in Vietnam clangs down on us, great cymbals crashing in my ears, one roaring black percussion note after another. It is no longer clear who is killing us. . . .

When I open my eyes, Rodeliano lies twitching across Moose, all his animation, his calculations, ruminations, hesitations, all his weighty management responsibilities pouring out of him through the unequivocal shrapnel holes in his chest. Little Boy Blue, who has lost his lucky tooth, leans over the lieutenant, trying to administer meaningless morphine, before he takes the hit that wastes the back of his head and the rest of his life. Didn't quite make it to nineteen.

Ching-Ching, knocked backward against a tree trunk, his sorry glasses dangling from his nose, his thin body sliding slowly down the trunk, half smiles—all smacked out one last time, man, on that good NVA stuff—until the hard chemistry tripping through his neck brings him all the way down forever.

Something is running down my leg, and I am running crooked-legged, straining, stumbling over Moose . . . they keep killing him . . . the way you try to break out of a dream . . . Harry has what's left of us up and moving . . . run, grunt, run . . . the backward charge of the fearsome bad-asses, bailing out, galloping pell-mell through the upchucking earth . . . going down, getting up, plunging on bleeding through the thickets, a rosy spattering of someone to my left, a choking cry to my right . . . I am wiping someone else's blood from my eyes . . . no time for sympathy, no time for nothing except wild-animal fire-in-the-forest running. . . .

Dazzling sunbursts of firepower. Everything smashed. Gaping red shell holes everywhere, not a tree that has not been snapped or crunched into smoking splinters, even the hill's informal graveyards blown up. And then another barrage comes hammering down like a drunken carpenter bashing everything in sight. Hammer of Thor. Good old U.S. steel annihilating us to keep us from being annihilated. . . .

One whistles down and scores a direct hit on a stack of NVA dead directly to the front. Another knocks me down and rolls me over. I am moving again when something blows through me like your hot breath blows through a busted paper sack and blows one boot off and my fatigues into rags. I am trying to get up. This last blast has me babbling to myself. I want out of this place. *Say a word for me, Sal.* I am on my knees, and it is like everything has been pushed out my ears, and every time I try to breathe, I am sucking in clouds of hot dust. I stagger up again and am jolted forward, and then the back of my neck is exploding into the explosion on the side of my jaw. I want out of this place. *Say a word for me, Sal.* And then down again, but still

197

there in my mind between the bumps and flashes, still scrambling, pulling and bulling on through the thorny, ripping brush, looking for something to crawl under, something to stabilize gravity. Then just lying there in the wounded earth. . . .

Consciousness keeps arriving and departing on little trains in my head. . . . I wake and savagely claw at insect life feeding on raw meat . . . blood-caked, slime-caked . . . making peace with the fundamental ooze . . . think and move like a lizard . . . babbling to the shadow surrounding the shadow, seeing the white inside the whiteness. Dry-mouthed. Pissing once and it comes out brown.

This time, walking down a dark street with big whispering trees, with long porches and summer-night voices murmuring, a swing creaking somewhere . . . and then moving slowly toward me from the shadows of a yard full of shrubbery and dark, weeping trees comes an old wrinkly-faced man wearing a dark derby and carrying a black walking stick . . . I've seen him on this hill before . . . he taps, taps slowly through the smoke past the clumps of dead, past the individual dead, pausing here and there, prodding meat with his stick. . . .

Help me, please, Jesus, because I have never done anything deliberately evil to deserve this it is just that bad today is good tomorrow I didn't want to kill anybody you understand but the timing the circumstances the crazy way of things, perplexing, a daemonic flummoxing perplexing concatenation of events in any event I hold no grudges the ants crawling on me are good the grinning rats are good the wriggly life in the fluid trickling out of my leg into battlefield slime is good the maggots are good it is only nature's way the shells howling down my ass are good the highly idealistic NVA are good they smile I smile only just please get me out of here and I will never even think of dinging anybody ever again. . . .

And they will bury me formally in Larchmont if they can find the missing links the proper parts. Statistical sorrow, official regrets, shock, dismay, lugubrious handwringing, it didn't have to be. He got it in the Nam trying to take some highly important hill or swamp or something he greased fifty godless gooks he deserved better. Posthumous congratulations. Bestowing the medal of something on my grateful remains in the name of bearing any burden and opposing any foe in the defense of what was that again and nobody remembering. . . . Laid out for viewing before the great floor-to-ceiling windows with the view of the huge sycamore, the magnolias and crape myrtle stirring outside, old windows with red satin valances and long white lace curtains flowing out into the room with the two-foot-thick walls, the seventeen-foot-high ceiling, the one-hundred-forty-year-old mirror, the framed Confederate war bonds bought in 1862 (payable in 1872), the pictures of those who had trod the floors back even before it was a Yankee bastion, long-dead faces gazing primly down upon the new corpse, and everyone will murmur and gravely nod and *tsk* and remark how well he looks to be so blown up no midlife burnout for him. . . .

And a most respectable number of concerned Larchmontians gazing down on the high school football flash who made the Vietnam varsity who established his running game in his not-cheap coffin and Aunt Tettie going round squirting the flowers with her water pistol and Uncle Neddie, leading citizen, will be leading the mourning and the mutterings—"Told the young fool not to go, just throwing good money after bad, I missed my war"—however He Gave The Last Full Measure Of His Devotion To God And Country In Death There Is Dignity And Glory In Death Little Mike Was A Winner A Hard Charger A High Flyer A Credit To The Underwear Game His Life Was Not X-Rated He Trod The Respectable Path Until This Unfortunate Weird Conflict Resulted In His Untimely Demise He Was Twenty-Four. . . .

As they lower the body into the hallowed earth way up there by the crumbling-to-ruin but highly revered Confederate Cemetery virtually under the corroded-green, pigeon-dappled, raised saber of The General himself, almost in the shadow of the Unknown Confederate Soldier, who stands there brooding over broken gravestones, rifle barrel pointed down *This Monument Embodies Hero Worship and Devotion to the Memory of the Lost Cause and Honor to the Soldiers Known and Unknown Who Rest in Its Shadow.* You can smell the honeysuckle, see the river gleaming in the distance from the hill where I'm being buried. . . .

And the pallbearer in red socks—(Who's he? Why, it's that sly rascal Winkie Green, caught peeping in Miss Amy Bottoms's bathroom window when he was twelve, shame, shame, as was her custom she bathed with the windows wide open)—shaking his head sadly while staring at Char's free-swinging ass which next to the corpse is the center of pallbearer attention on the slow hump to the grave . . . and our saintly, bejeweled old preacher going on and on about knowing me in better times when I wasn't so dead by the hand of those dastardly atheists across the sea and as it starts to rain sprinkling his immutable dust intoning this poor dumb malodorous beer-swilling baby-killing Vietnam motherhugger didn't bring all that much into this world and there sure ain't much left worth taking out but you got to accept death like a dog accepts fleas, scratch at it but it don't do much good . . . raining harder now, water dripping faster from the trees into the grave, feet shuffling impatiently, let's get this over, get it done, people are getting wet here, the rain really starting to blow and umbrellas flapping and feet scurrying and. . . .

Char stays . . . leaning over sweetly, flashing the V-for-peace sign as I go downward, her golden hair parted in the middle and flowing out like angel's wings, like that time under the spring campus sky and she was leaning over me holding my face in her breasts, no, that was me leaning over her holding her breasts in my face, and she was so sweet and beautiful and love-trembling I could hardly speak and can't speak now as she slips down her panties over the long curving slide of her hips and legs, jerks them off, raises them high, a black flag, and with a little scream throws them down through the last light onto the coffin . . . oh just please get me out of here Jesus no more backsliding I've learned my lesson just please please please get me out of here just please please please get me out of here. . . .

19

Fear of Flying

A sound squeezes through my brain like a raindrop through a crack in the ceiling. I lay there looking into the bloody eye of the dragon, blinking stupidly at the sun, sizzling in the sun, but now the sound is coming on louder and louder. . . .

I'm jacking up again, gonna get my shit together, gonna stand up, gonna. . . . Squinting, I see a helicopter blowing out of the sun blur, low-levelling over the hill with everything going at once, hammering and hissing and smoking. Then another gunship appears out of the same sunspot, hanging its butt down even lower.

There's a terrific racket of shooting back and forth as the second chopper goes over. The ship bellies upward and a machine-gunner inside, harness stiffening, hangs half out the door like a punch-drunk aerialist. He's firing back and down into the trees, the sixty jumping all over his shoulder, hot brass flying out of the bird like afternoon sun speckles.

And then a third ship, which has hung back making little circles in the sun, swings down and comes rolling around the hillside, lower and lower until it seems about to crack into shattered remains of trees in front of me. At the last moment, the pilot zooms it upward, hovers, aims it toward the tiny clearing where I'm on my knees babbling, comes *whap-whap-whap-*ing down in swirling dust and leaves, just mising a sliver of tree trunk stabbing upward like a fifteen-foot bayonet, missing a jagged chunk of rock.

Up there a soldier out on the skids yelling, looking even wilder and weirder than the terrain, waving a forty-five, a laughing mouthful of broken teeth. I feel myself laughing, I feel myself crying. It's the same apeshit asshole I rode into these hills with. I want to embrace him. I want to kiss him. I want a drink of water.

He pulls me up by the armpits and deposits me into a collection like I've never seen, like they've swept the hill scooping up forest junk, the bits and pieces of what's left of us. Crazyhouse wounded swamping the ship, a tangle of arms and legs and blood slinging all over. One man down to his shorts and about eighteen bandages. There's even a terrified Vietnamese in there, so bloodied you can't tell whether he's North or South. I'm just holding onto a leg, any leg, as we start to lift.

I see Roland in there, half-buried under bodies, not moving. The chopper lifts slowly. But we are almost up and safely away when I hear the ship taking hits. *Knock. Knock. Pop. Pop.* Hear metal tearing and rotors clanging.

When you're low and slow, that's when they get you, and they are getting us. The engine hisses and starts spewing fuel. Beginning to smoke. The pilot steers hard-right away from the hill with the engine dying, and then it dies and there's only an eerie whistling as we half glide, half tumble smoking down the sky toward the bottom of the hill.

NVA are running out of caves, popping out of trenches along the slope as we go down. There are muzzle flashes everywhere. The engine suddenly sputters on again, but the pilot can't pick the ship up. NVA are running in the broken trees just below, firing AKs, firing everything. I can see their fine faces, see one laughing, see him raising his machine gun. Rounds rip up through the floor like popcorn popping, and the bird is bucking and shaking, so punched up I don't know how it hangs together.

Then this big-bear sergeant wakes up and rolls over, flailing and kicking and cursing. There's a lumpy bandage over his jaw, but there is Old Smoke. Jamming his boot in my crotch as something human blows by my face. I see the copilot slump over. The Vietnamese screams and tumbles around, clawing for something to hold onto. He tries to hold onto Old Smoke—bedlam as the ship goes bouncing down into a bombed-out clearing at the bottom of Hill 711.

The Huey bounces back up, and we are undulating about five feet off the ground, rotors whapping and whining, the bird shivering all over, spinning round and round in clouds of dust like a no-headed chicken. Then it goes skipping and bouncing across the clearing toward the trees. The pilot struggles to pick it up, tearing hell out of the machine, about to pop its rivets. And now incredibly we are getting up . . . staggering up . . . angling up toward the trees.

We are higher, rocking to the right, engine pitch changing moment to moment, blades chopping treetops. We're rattling all over, rattling and smoking and stinking. All this time I'm holding onto The Smoker's leg, and The Smoker is trying to assassinate the Viet. Our sergeant has gone berserk. Raging and bellowing, trying to throw out the Viet.

"Get the gooks out! Get the gooks out!"

Trying to kick him out. Now he's got a wrench, trying to bash him out. Trying to hammer him out right over me. Three or four times I'm nearly out the open door myself. But the Viet grabs the pilot's neck and flight helmet with one arm, locks this other arm around the pilot's arm that is fighting to control the stick. The Smoker keeps slugging with the wrench. The Viet has the pilot in a death grip. Tries to crawl into his lap. Bleeding all over him as the ship careens along side-to-side almost in burning trees.

Finally, cracked in the skull repeatedly, the Viet is clubbed over me and out of the ship by the bear with the wrench. I look down and see this bloody filthy little guy hanging from the skids, dragging along, bumping along through the trees. He won't let go. He just sticks. He's looking up at me, eyes red, hair blowing, holding on, holding on.

The ship is groaning and shuddering, but we're still climbing, climbing . . . and he's still dangling, rocking in the wind over that murderous bitch jungle. I just look at him. We must be five hundred feet up now. The next time I look, he's gone. Missing in action. . . .

20

Don't I Know You?

Somewhere, they pulled me out of the chopper and carried me inside a tent. I saw hands ripping off my rags, hands entwining me with bandages, hands stringing on a plasma bottle. My right leg was hurting terribly. There was blood and mess all over.

A radio was playing, *"All around the islands we must go, taking it sweet and slow. Show me how to do the hula. . . ."* And then a voice burbling in, *"Remember, troops, no matter where you are, if you lose your toothbrush, you're in trouble. . . ."*

Then they had me on a stretcher, stumbling and sliding down a ditch behind a line of sandbags, and we were out in the open again, very bright, and a fifty was clearing its throat someplace. I heard a helicopter winding up, and they placed me where the world was red. No, that wasn't the world, that was a face. From time to time, it would raise up and vomit a little.

I heard boots tromping, numbers shouted, places shouted, then a boom-cracking sound, and things swelling, things getting heavy, something heavy and gray sitting on my head, breaking little things in there.

Awake. Clammy all over. Hot little sweat-popping waves going up and down my spine. The old flinch to concussion making me laugh queerly now, only I wasn't feeling concussion in here, or was I?

"Water, damnit!" a voice shouted.

Now the red face raised up on the next stretcher, his used-up, blood-stinking bandage coming all apart.

"Well . . . so what's your name, Jocko?" he asked, fluid clotting at the corners of his mouth, his eyes full of graveyard glory. "Don't I know you?" And then his head thumped down.

"Water! Water!" shouted the other voice, which I'm almost sure was mine.

Then holding on. We are going up in the air again—"What's going down, down?"—Climbing over hills and trees, rising above all that down there, the cold air hitting us as we get higher, the sun rolling off the world straight ahead, leaving behind that smoking earth-cancer, the meanest mother there ever was.

And the face beside me lifting slowly again, bandages all undone now, eyes blinking, bloodied lips moving, the bone of one cheek showing through the freckles of that grinning face. And now he was saying something, face shoved up close to mine, and I could just hear him over the wind and the whistling and the clattering.

And he was holding onto himself tight, still full of it, not ready to give it up. My best buddy, Harry the Hammer, dying hard, hard. Our eyes connected. "Man, this is really . . . this is really . . . Ain't this a bitch?"

FAST FORWARD

You had to look past the little things at the overall scheme, the bigger picture, the larger purpose. Viewed in that perspective, the difficulties encountered by Bravo Company and the Always First Battalion might seem a less-than-terrible price to pay.

Indeed, General Edgar Whitehouse would proclaim a big, big

victory. As he would put it to the media, "We were in the right place at the right time. We pursued the enemy into his redoubt and smashed him against the anvil of American firepower."

The bad fortune of Bravo, the victim of last-gasp, go-for-broke, desperation tactics by the enemy, won big headlines but was not militarily insignificant, the general would note. "The following day, enemy forces were driven off the hill for good. That's the way war works. . . ."

General Whitehouse would state that he could not overstate the scope of the victory in the hills around Dak Toy, the centerpiece of which was the saga of Hill 711. He would stress that South Vietnam had not been cut in half, which would have happened had the enemy been allowed to waltz through the Highlands unopposed. He would point out that the enemy had been thwarted at every turn, had suffered huge losses and been forced to withdraw his badly battered big units back into Laos and Cambodia from whence they came, that the enemy's logistics, his offensive timetable, and his overall strategy for the coming year, 1968, the Year of the Monkey, had been badly crippled.

This was somewhat in contrast to the prevailing media version of the reality of Hill 711, which held that the wily enemy, after inflicting heavy casualties and withstanding everything American might could throw at him, had simply faded back into that awesome jungle where he was so clearly the master, his point made, his purpose accomplished.

The "lost battalion" (60 percent KIA) was given a great deal of media attention. Lieutenant Colonel Gurgles—soon to be full Colonel Gurgles—would travel to Saigon and tell a press conference:

"Now some of the early accounts of the battle for Hill 711 could have come from the emotionally strained. I am not referring to our sometimes hysterical friends of the media, ha, ha, but to young soldiers who were wounded, mentally shocked—

young soldiers for which the sights and sounds of battle were not familiar. But ladies and gentlemen, we came through.

"Now ladies and gentlemen. It may seem that we were *lost*, but ladies and gentlemen I can assure you we knew where we were at all times. We were on top of Hill 711 in the Central Highlands of South Vietnam opposing communist aggression. And we were imposing our will on the enemy at all times. We had that hill, and the enemy didn't.

"Morale? Yes, ladies and gentlemen, I'll be very honest with you, I will speak to that. I will address myself to that. As one of my best sergeants was telling me not so long ago, 'Colonel, all these men need is a shave, a shine, a few beers, and they'll be ready to roll back into that field tomorrow.' Now that sergeant knew what he was talking about. You give my straightlegs an order and they'll go out there and do the finest job in the world for me, by gosh.

"Now ladies and gentlemen. Do I look lost? Do I look whipped? Do I look like a broken man standing here before you? Sure, we were attrited fairly hard up there. But you can compare what we did up there to a tough football game. Now, the fullback may come back to the huddle and tell the quarterback, 'Hey, I can't hit that hole again, they're creaming me.' But give that fullback that ball again, and you won't see him running off to the sideline crying to the crowd.

"What he does is rare up and hit that hole again, and like as not, he'll win that game for you, by gosh. Now you people. That's what I asked of my men up there on that hill, and they came through for me. Because the truth is, ladies and gentlemen, we love to hit the enemy. We enjoy. Our fighting image is not sullied. You ask about morale. To be very honest with you, ladies and gentlemen, a morally healthy atmosphere exists at all levels of my command. Morale? Yes, it's amazing, fantastic, and so on and so forth. Why I pity the next poor enemy that mixes it up with the Always First, the Ever Forward, Never

Backward Battalion. Just pity them, ladies and gentlemen. Do you begin to get the picture, ladies and gentlemen?"

In a few weeks, Hill 711 wouldn't seem to matter all that much. One day while recuperating from my wounds, I would read in a newspaper that the meanest mother was being voluntarily abandoned. Our general would be quoted as saying, "It is no longer considered tactically viable. It no longer serves a useful purpose in our new mobile posture."

Of Third Squad, only Canny, Red Dog, Roland, and I survived. Canny took rounds in an arm and leg but would soon recover. Red Dog never got touched, not a nick. Roland's physical wounds were minor, but he would take on the guilt and coloring of every war crime committed, dreamed, or imagined. He would read about it and confess to it, becoming a kind of media attraction for a while there. He would get better.

As for some of the others, the end of Wilson was most curious: After it was all over on Hill 711, there came this one, last, wild-ass, 122mm rocket fluttering in through the twilight, just a little postscript from the green machine of the other side that they were still in business, and suddenly Billy Wilson, finally drinking that victory beer, wasn't anymore. Major Sheridan, disgusted with Frederick the Great, would leave the battalion and go elsewhere to die. The old banzai kid would find perfection while serving as advisor to an element of the ARVN 25th Division—called the saddest, most inept regulars on any side during the war—trying to teach the poor little bastards how to shoot straight during the Tet Offensive. The Smoker, his face stepped on by a rocket-propelled grenade, would return to duty in Vietnam after extensive cosmetic surgery that took off about a yard of his scowl but didn't touch his mind. Bad News Benson would pull some time in a psychiatric ward, for which he was grateful, it got him out of the war. As for me, I would heal nicely and be summoned to Washington.

21

Why We Can't Lose

"It is you and men such as you who go forth willingly and neither complain during crisis nor doubt in the darkness, who fight fearlessly, with the clear and certain knowledge of the rightness of our cause, which keeps America great and undefeatable. . . ."

The Medal of Honor was being presented to me by the President of the United States.

A bit earlier, I had been chitchatting in the Oval Office with the Secretary of Defense, the Secretary of the Army, and the Joint Chiefs when the President had hurried in.

"Hi, folks. Sorry I'm late, but I had a little problem with the Supreme Court."

When the President sat down and crossed his legs, I noticed he had lint on his purplish socks. How amazing, I thought, all that power can't keep lint off his socks. Maybe it was VC lint.

While we sat around getting acquainted, me staring at the lint, I had the urge. Before it was too late, I wanted to make this shining confession about how it was with me being a hero. Tell him something true about Bad Company and Hill 711, impart a few realities. But how could a corporal, a one-legged corporal, speak to the President of the United States of lowly ass-in-the-grass realities? He was the President of the United States. I had been declared a hero. We chitchatted. We exchanged jokes.

Then we had gone out onto the south lawn of the White House, me on crutches, stump below the right knee swinging. (They had promised they wouldn't have to take any more of it off. Of course they had said they could have it in the first place, but it wasn't exactly there, was it?)

They had the Old Guard out there, the fife and drums, the whole nine yards. The south lawn was beautiful that time of year, everything in bloom, about as far from the Meanest Mother as you could get. The morning news had said that Saigon had been rocketed for the thirteenth consecutive day, but that the outgoing COMUSMACV was not alarmed by the enemy's desperation tactics and attempts to win psychological victories and big headlines without achieving significant military gains. On the ground, where it counted, we won the battles, stressed COMUSMACV. The enemy would fail again, as he had failed before, and would keep on failing to the end. Because Americans don't quit. Americans don't lose.

The ceremony was splendid. To see the powers assembled in full plumage. To hear the words spoken. Old Harry should have been the one. Or Banzai Sheridan. I saw Uncle Ned and Aunt Tettie out there fairly glowing, proud as punch, Uncle Ned having renounced his renouncement of the war for the occasion.

". . . the Medal of Honor for conspicuous gallantry and intrepidity at the risk of life above and beyond the call of duty is awarded to Corporal Michael Andrew Ripp, Infantry, United States Army. . . ."

The reading of the citation went on, describing my exploits in the capture of Hill 711. It was all about going up the hill, nothing about coming down the hill.

". . . without hesitation, he left his sheltered position and moved from position to position through hails of enemy fire. . . . With great coolness and courage, he. . . ."

And on and on . . . words, lovely words . . . words that should sleep with better grunts than me.

". . . and with utter disregard for his personal safety, hurled back the enemy's own hand grenades, inspiring the men around him to superhuman efforts. . . ."

And on and on . . . stop that sentence, there's a runaway sentence loose here.

". . . personally slaying forty eight of the foe . . . until the long awaited daylight brought defeat to the enemy forces and their surrender and retreat back into the jungle . . ."

Words, lovely words, a whole lot of word-fucking going on here . . . perhaps a few of them were even true.

"To you, Corporal Ripp, may I personally express the gratitude and respect of all your fellow countrymen. We shall always be grateful for the inspiration you have given us in these times. . . ."

When it was over, the five-pointed star held by the blue sash around my neck, the American eagle perched over "Valor" around my neck, the President raised his big hand, pawed at my shoulder, and whispered, "You gonna be all right with that leg? I know it's hard—"

"Feeling no pain, sir."

"Best kind to feel, son."

Then he said he was sorry my wife couldn't have witnessed this occasion, shared in the honor and the glory.

"Yes, sir."

"I don't know what we fellows would do without the support of our womenfolk," drawled the President softly.

"Yes, sir." *Unless you had a thing, Mr. President, that wasn't the real thing, that was another kind of thing. A thing that got burned with the rest of it back on that hill, burned and buried.*

"I owe this honor to her, sir, that's for sure. She was my inspiration."

"With young men like you," the President went on softly, "how can we lose?"

"We can't, sir."

BRAVO BURNING

He smiled at that. The President was dreaming with his eyes
open. Everyone was dreaming. Those were the days of dreaming, the days of Vietnam. It was that kind of time.

They say I looked a little bent, a bit chewed-on at the edges
for a while after that. I lost weight, looked jaundiced; my cheekbones could cut you up. I hobbled around rather hunched over,
eyes twisted back into somewhere else; puffy, glinty slits of
mean light, lizard eyes. I kept waiting for something to explode,
the evil music to play one more time. But the old run-rabbit-run
feeling has fled from my body pretty much, and I'm not bitter.
Heck, no. I know bitter men, of course.

Occasionally, I see Harry. He comes humping up the hill
toward the house through the shadowy trees, and sure enough,
he's got that look about him, still full of it. Good old Harry.
Damn, I always hope it's him. Gee, I wish it could be him. And
then I shake my head and he's gone, like smoke into twilight.
Tree lines can do that to you.

Actually, those days are beginning to come into focus. It took
a while, but I am getting the picture. Sometimes, when I'm out
sitting on the porch or by one of the big windows, gazing toward
the river . . . dreaming back on the old Bad Ones, I can even
believe I'm a hero.

Now.